DEMON CHASER III

David Berardelli

DEMON CHASER III

"It's Hell with the Wrong Shoes"

GRAVESTONE PRESS

A GRAVESTONE PRESS PAPERBACK

ISBN: 978 1 78695 655 2

Gravestone Press
is an imprint of Fiction4All
www.fiction4all.com

This Edition
Published 2021

Cover Art: Linda York

PART ONE

The Messenger

DAY ONE

Orlando, Florida

Chapter 1

Daniel Grove sat stiffly at his desk, his eyes glued to the intercom on the blotter in front of him. The rich blue Orlando sky filling the large office window facing him promised another clear, sunny afternoon, and the soft light-blue walls of his office encouraged a calm state of mind. But right now, he didn't notice the perfect sky or the soft-colored walls. At the moment, he wouldn't care if a dozen of the world's hottest babes were gathered in front of his desk, squirming out of their clothes.

It had been twenty-four hours since Mr. Waite's latest rampage and Daniel was still smarting over the tongue-lashing. The incident had happened shortly after Daniel had come in, shrugged off his Armani jacket and eased his slim frame into his comfortable leather office chair.

Then, precisely at 9:00, the light connecting to Mr. Waite's office line came on, and Daniel, as usual, felt the chills scurrying up his back like an army of frightened rats.

“Any progress, kid?” The booming, low-pitched voice sounded as surly as always.

“No, sir.”

A pause. “Nothing? Nada? Zilch? A big, fucking zero?”

“No--yes, sir.”

“Kid, this whole thing is really pissing me off. You know what I do when I’m pissed off, don’tcha? To refresh your memory, I turn assholes who’ve pissed me off into shiny brown shit-smears on the carpet. Now…you don’t *want* me to turn you into a shiny brown shit-smear, do you, kid?”

“No, sir.”

“I can’t imagine you *wanting* to become a shit-smear. That wouldn’t be *my* primary career choice, if I were in your shoes. Besides, none of the others I’ve done that to have cared for it. Know why?”

“Why, sir?”

A deep sigh. “Kid, if you really need to ask, maybe I should turn you into one. You haven’t exactly been dazzling me with your brain activity, kid. At least, not lately.”

“No, sir...”

“Then *do* something, goddammit. Get something done. Find those three!”

Click!

Hopefully, this morning would turn out better. So far, there were no voicemails. There were only two emails, both sent by Mr. Waite in the last twenty minutes, about a couple of new escorts who’d been referred to him. Daniel went into one of the confidential files to check the status of the directory. He added the girls' names, went back to his mail program, and replied to Mr. Waite. He got up, poured coffee, went back to the desk, sat back down and raised the cup to his lips.

Mr. Waite's light came on at 9:30. Daniel cringed in his seat. *Here we go again…* With a trembling hand, he touched the button.

"About damned time you came in."

"Good morning to you too, sir."

"Don't give me that cheery Mr. Rogers shit. You know what I want to hear."

"Y-Yes, sir."

"Well?"

Daniel knew Mr. Waite only cared about finding the missing threesome. This had been bugging both of them the last two weeks, ever since Ashley Parker, Tiffany, and Chip had vanished right from under their noses.

"Well, sir, I had a hunch--"

"What happened with it?"

"It didn't quite pan out."

"Are you telling me you *still* haven't made any progress with this?"

"Yes, sir, I didn't."

A deep sigh. "The clock is ticking, kid. And in case you're wondering, yes, I'm still thinking about doing the shit-smear number on you."

Click!

Daniel sighed and had a sip of coffee. He couldn't blame Mr. Waite for being so angry. It was Daniel's fault the threesome had snuck out of town. Daniel had been in the hotel when they'd disappeared. To make matters worse, he hadn't even realized what was going on until it was too late.

This was not very good business for a career-minded young man who considered himself on the ball and several rungs up the ladder to success.

Daniel had been on his own since he'd graduated from Rollins College ten years earlier and moved out of his parents' comfortable ranch home. He'd supported himself quite well with his own web designing business and hadn't relied on his rich father for help. He'd been around the block a few times and seen all sorts of things. The people he'd dealt with weren't always nice, honest or respectable. But that was no shock; he knew how cruel people could be. He also knew that when you dealt with people, you should be prepared for all sorts of surprises.

Mortal people, that is.

Mr. Waite wasn't mortal. He was a super demon and had come to the mortal world straight from Hell to rule for the next hundred years. He'd been up here just a few months, and in that brief period of time, had made some interesting changes. Since his arrival, the prostitution and drug industries here in Central Florida--as well as neighboring states and those connected to the pipeline running from Mexico and South America--had seen a substantial jump in weekly revenues. Profits from illegal immigration had skyrocketed. Sales from firearms and explosives had gone through the roof. Most significantly, mass murder, serial killings and every other conceivable type of violent crime had come back into the limelight.

Mr. Waite had been busy and was an expert at his game.

Daniel couldn't complain. Mr. Waite had set him up in the escort industry, and Daniel had been earning more than ten thousand dollars a day ever since. This was great money, especially considering how little work he actually did. He came in at nine in the morning, joined in on two or three conference calls, and kept an eye on laptop activity. His main function was monitoring the girls' schedules to make sure the appropriate escort was available at the appropriate time. He enjoyed an expensive two-hour lunch, came back in for about an hour and then drove home. He was on-call the rest of the evening, but whenever there was a problem, he merely referred it to one of three other people in charge of the escorts.

Not bad at all.

Except, of course, when Mr. Waite had a major problem.

In this case, Daniel couldn't blame the big man for being upset. Ashley, Tiffany, and Chip had slipped right out from under Daniel's nose, destroying Mr. Waite's major land deal and embarrassing him in front of his associates.

Daniel faced a bright future with Mr. Waite and didn't want to face it dead. Or as a shit-smear. He knew he could fix this problem. He also knew the solution was probably a simple one. No one could just disappear.

But somehow, they had. They had slipped out of the hotel and vanished. And Mr. Waite had been angrier and ten times more frightening than Daniel had ever seen him before.

Daniel had personally seen the demon in action. Mr. Waite loved explosions and lived to blow up things. Just hours after they'd first met, Mr. Waite had blown up a shiny new BMW in downtown Orlando. While having a quiet lunch with Daniel and his father, Mr. Waite glanced at the restaurant window facing the street. In the next instant, a loud, dazzling explosion turned the block into a smoldering battlefield.

Only days later, Mr. Waite forced a law-biding, God-fearing businessman to rush to a hardware store, purchase chemicals and insecticides and then drive to the nearest church and burn it down.

Not long after that, Mr. Waite turned two guys he'd been looking for into steaming turds before sending them straight to Hell.

For the last two weeks, Daniel had been struggling for a solution to their present problem. He'd even considered using a detective agency to hunt down the threesome, but quickly realized the folly of that decision. He'd be required to furnish names, addresses, occupations and detailed descriptions. Social Security numbers, if possible. Credit card information. Next of kin. Car tags. Registrations.

First names and vague descriptions just wouldn't cut it. He didn't even know if the redheaded Chip was male or female. And it wouldn't help one bit to mention that two of the three people they were looking for were already dead.

But they must be found. They soured a deal worth billions to Mr. Waite. The Arabs purchasing the land had planned to stay the weekend, look over the land, sign the papers and take their private plane back home on the third day. During their stay, they were promised entertainment. Because of scheduling conflicts, the assigned escorts hadn't been available, and Daniel was ordered by Mr. Waite to drive Tiffany, Ashley and Chip to the Village Resort Hotel, where they would then be taken to the dignitaries' rooms.

But something happened to sour the deal, bringing about an abrupt end to the visit. The four billionaires left their luxurious suite without notice and flew back home immediately.

Daniel blamed himself for the fiasco. He was determined to fix this, one way or the other. When he left the office that afternoon, he finally let his logical reasoning take over and, in no time, knew what had to be done.

Ashley Parker was the key to this puzzle.

Daniel had met Ashley several weeks earlier, at the O-Town Café, where Daniel, his father, and Mr. Waite had gone for lunch. Ashley had worked there as a waitress and was assigned to their table. Daniel liked her long black hair, her pleasant air and the way she smiled, and was deeply embarrassed by the abrupt manner in which Mr. Waite had treated her during their meal. Daniel obtained her home phone number later that same day from her boss. He called her that evening, took her out to dinner soon after, and discovered how much he liked her and enjoyed her company.

He hadn't known at the time that getting involved with a girl like Ashley would not be wise. Ashley wasn't from Daniel's neighborhood and would not fit in with his new life. His parents wouldn't accept her. Ashley's alcoholic mother would be a horrible embarrassment to the Grove family.

Daniel hadn't been aware of all this until Mr. Waite had brought it to his attention during dinner one evening. Mr. Waite, an expert at manipulation, knew how to persuade someone to come around to his way of thinking.

It had taken only a few seconds for Mr. Waite to adjust Daniel's attitude using a simple mind-scan technique. Daniel had no memory of what had actually happened, just that he suddenly felt totally different and no longer had any desire to date Ashley.

Daniel felt foolish and angry about his former way of thinking. He knew right then that with this new positive outlook, he would soon become a successful, savvy businessman. And no one could stop him.

Since that night, Daniel had no further trouble analyzing things and no longer clung to the same foolish values that had previously held him back.

From that moment on, his analytical mind would automatically step in to handle every given situation. He found that he no longer experienced confusion, and instinctively knew what he wanted. When he entered a restaurant, he routinely rattled off his order as if he'd studied it for hours. When he awoke in the morning, he knew what he wanted for breakfast and what he would wear. When he plopped down on the couch in front of the widescreen in the evening, he no longer had to waste time channel-surfing. He knew what he wanted to watch.

And in this particular case, Daniel knew exactly where to start looking.

After work, he drove to his comfortable Winter Park condo. He shrugged out of his custom-tailored clothes, fixed supper, stepped into the shower and took a short nap on the living room sofa.

At half past midnight, he got up and put on something casual. He got into the Vette and headed to Orlando, to the area just a few blocks down from Huey Avenue, where the Parker home sat in disheveled misery on a small lot fronted by overgrown grass and surrounded by neglected hedges.

Ashley's mother worked at the Fly Trappe on Michigan, but Daniel didn't want to go there. For one thing, he didn't want to leave his prized Vette unattended in that neighborhood. For another, he'd dealt with Lynn Parker on two previous occasions and knew what to expect. He suspected she'd have him thrown out of the bar if he tried approaching her there.

He relaxed in the Vette, which he'd parked two spaces down from her driveway. Then let his favorite R&B CDs relax him and soften his mood.

At around two-thirty, he drifted off.

He was awakened when Lynn Parker's Toyota pulled up the drive, followed by a Dodge Ram pickup. Parker had brought home another drunken companion. She was obviously drunk herself, her mousey-brown hair unkempt, the two top buttons of her sleeveless black crepe blouse undone, showing off her laced bra. She carried her handbag over her shoulder and her black spikes in her left hand, padding barefooted on the cracked pavement, toward the house.

Just as she was about to unlock the front door, she turned and saw Daniel coming up the walk. She groaned, her face wrinkling. Her date simply squinted at him. In a loud, shrilly voice, she yelled, "Get lost!" Then spun around and scrambled to get the key in the lock. She dropped her shoes in the process but pushed the door open. She snatched up her shoes, grabbed her date by his necktie, dragged him inside and slammed the door.

With an exasperated sigh, Daniel cast the anger aside. No need for anger in this case. All he had to do was take a breath and calmly let his logical reasoning serve as his guide. This task was simple, and shouldn't take more than thirty seconds, tops.

His pulse hastened as he moved closer to the door. Taking another deep breath, he pressed his index finger to the doorbell and held it there, until the door finally yanked open. Parker stood there, glaring, her wide-open blouse showing off her bra, protruding clavicle and soft paunch. She held a drink in her hand. The fierce expression in her glazed eyes made him flinch.

"All I need to know is--"

She tossed her drink at him. "Fuck yourself and never come back!" The shrillness in her voice made his ears ring.

The door slammed in his face.

Daniel stood there nearly ten minutes, looking down at his wet clothes and shoes, and the scattered dark stains on the concrete stoop at his feet. His silk shirt had cost him a hundred bucks, his jacket five hundred. Luckily, the suede slip-ons only went for eighty-five.

But none of that mattered. He was Daniel Grove. Just thirty years old, he was earning ten thousand bucks a day. He made more money in one hour than this worthless bitch earned in a month.

And she'd slammed the door in his face. *Again*!

He wanted to kick it down, stomp inside and strangle her.

After taking a few more deep breaths, the rage subsided. His fists remained clenched as he turned on his heel and trudged back to the Vette.

His one and only lead had failed. He knew where Ashley's mother lived but was still unable to locate Ashley or her friends.

He was going to have to think of something else. Mr. Waite would not remain patient much longer.

DAY TWO

The Visitor from Chicago

Chapter 2

Braithwaite, known in the mortal world as Brett Waite, CEO and founder of Waite Business Diversities & Consultations, sat at his desk, waiting for Adele to buzz him and tell him his visitor had arrived.

The desk clock digital said 10:05. Tired of waiting for results from the Grove kid concerning the missing threesome, Braithwaite had called the Chicago Diocese yesterday afternoon and was informed that one of their key representatives was presently available and would fly to Orlando early the next day.

Braithwaite had wanted to use someone local for this matter, but his usual contacts weren't available. Dortmunder, his main subordinate, was busy running drugs through their new pipeline. Braithwaite presently employed several prospects supervising the distribution of assault weapons to the Taliban in Syria and Afghanistan, but none knew the right type of person for this sort of venture. Braithwaite didn't want to take time out of his hectic schedule to ask the League of Demons to get together in the Castle down below to select someone. The League always took forever to gather everyone together. Besides, demons all tended to suffer from ADD and were cooperative only when it suited their own purposes.

According to Chicago, the man named Andras was made to order for this type of job. Formerly one of Al Capone's busiest triggermen, Andras had been responsible for more than sixty contract hits, most of them politically sanctioned. Due to a quirk of fate, Andras had died at the hands of an overzealous cop just days after the St. Valentine's Day massacre but returned in the early sixties at Balberith's request to fulfill several high-profile jobs sanctioned by organized crime.

Braithwaite had seen Andras briefly outside the Castle of Demons a couple of centuries earlier. Andras' spiritual form was that of a winged angel with the head of a raven, suggesting superior hunting instincts. Andras possessed the remarkable ability to infect humans with uncontrollable rage, thus inciting the massacre, as well as many brawls, and much of the street fighting resulting from the Peace Movement during the mid-sixties. Braithwaite felt Andras more than qualified to complete this job. The fact that Andras had remained in Chicago all these years at Balberith's insistence spoke volumes.

According to what Braithwaite was recently told, Andras had been extremely busy in the political arena. Due to his influence, modern corruption and graft had plagued Chicago just as it had during the Capone years, spreading like wildfire to many parts of the country, especially Capitol Hill.

Braithwaite didn't want the Grove kid agonizing unnecessarily over this present dilemma. He wanted the kid to concentrate on his job as Manager for their thriving escort industry. Though Braithwaite was steamed over the fiasco, he realized the kid was only partially responsible. The Arabs had demanded the kid keep his distance once the escorts had been delivered. He couldn't keep a tight handle on the situation if he wasn't allowed to stay close.

It was time to push the blame to the side. The threesome had to be found. Braithwaite's reputation was at stake. He couldn't let any inferior slip away and get away with it. Because of their actions, his plans had to be shelved. Possibly for weeks. The threesome had also embarrassed his foreign friends. Braithwaite still couldn't get them on the phone to discuss what happened. Several international calls to Aghali, his associate in Saudi, had accomplished nothing. According to Aghali, the Arabs did not wish to discuss the matter.

Braithwaite glanced once again at the desk clock. 10:11. He sighed. A watched pot never boiled. Andras would show. He just had to be patient.

His rage suddenly flared. *Patient, my ass. Some colorful fireworks might relieve some of this stress.*

Braithwaite raised his three hundred and fifty pounds from his comfortable chair and lumbered over to the window. The sidewalks, as always, were crowded. Local idiots as well as the usual clueless tourists crossed leisurely at the intersection. It would be amusing if one or two vehicles suddenly developed brake trouble.

He closed his eyes. Just as he was about to focus, he suddenly felt another presence in the room. He opened his eyes and turned.

A man stood in front of the door in a dark suit, light-gray tie and tan loafers. His arms were crossed in front of him. A look of mild curiosity covered his dark features.

Braithwaite felt a little uncomfortable about the silent intrusion. It was no easy accomplishment to surprise a demon as powerful as Braithwaite. This stranger had not only slipped into the room undetected, he looked like he'd been standing there quite a while. Braithwaite was impressed, but at the same time mildly agitated.

"Andras?"

A nod.

"How'd you get past my secretary?"

"If you don't mind, I'd rather not give away my trade secrets."

Braithwaite watched him for a few moments. Good thing he needed this man's help. Otherwise, Braithwaite would have already pureed the man's brains onto the carpet. "I'll let you off the hook for that, since I obviously need someone of your skills."

"I wouldn't have done it otherwise. Your powers are well-known. I'm not ready to be sent back down to the Valley."

Braithwaite held back a grin. Andras had savvy. They were off to a flying start. "Have a seat."

Andras sat in one of the two chairs facing the desk. Braithwaite figured him at around six feet and a trim one-sixty-five. He looked like someone you'd expect to see managing a bank or selling insurance. Average features--certainly no one you'd remember. Simply put, Andras blended in. Another plus.

Braithwaite rested his elbows on the desk blotter. "I might have seen you before, down below. The spirit form of the raven, correct?"

"Yes. I'm a hunter."

"No wonder you're good at being invisible."

"You can't be a good hunter unless you're invisible when you have to be."

Braithwaite had been told a few things about Andras' hunting background that sounded damned impressive. "Chicago told me about one of your accomplishments."

"Such as?"

Braithwaite grinned. "1963, to be precise."

Andras nodded. "Thanksgiving weekend."

"A very bleak one, as I recall."

"For the mortals, it was pretty bad."

"Balberith selected you personally?"

"He told me that an additional shooter was needed that weekend in Dallas. Someone who could achieve total anonymity would be most suitable. In other words, someone nobody would ever notice."

"I was down below at the time, but we all heard about it. As brilliant a plan as any I'd ever heard of."

"It was merely a matter of finding the right place to hide at the right time."

"How long have you been in Chicago?"

"Since I left Dallas."

"You were in Chicago when the Diocese took in Capone and his staff. This was, I believe, in the early twenties."

"Balberith ordered me back there. He understood how well I manipulate politicians. Capone proved to be a powerful political magnet."

Braithwaite pulled a cigar from his gold case. He offered one to Andras, who declined. "Scents leave trails. People remember scents."

Braithwaite nodded. Andras really *was* a pro. "I take it that you're at least partially responsible for the political mess in Chicago that's been rampant in the last couple of decades?"

"Chicago has been a hotbed of corruption and graft the last hundred years or so. Balberith wanted me to stick around to make sure things stay that way. It's not much of a challenge anymore. Mortals have become infinitely more corruptible since the computer age started."

Braithwaite sat back and pushed a thick gray plume toward the ceiling fan. "I take it you've done a lot of missing persons cases before, then?"

"Dozens. I'm a hunter, after all. But since I've been so busy in other areas during the last fifty years, I haven't chased down anyone in quite a while."

"What were you told about this job?"

"I was called in yesterday by a couple of associates in Cicero. They told me you needed someone for quick detective work."

Braithwaite told him what had happened at the Village Resort.

When Braithwaite finished, Andras said, "No wonder you want them found. Training camps are big business nowadays. The wave of the future in this country."

"As of this moment, there are thirty-five training camps in fifteen states and the numbers are increasing rapidly. When I came up just a few months ago, there were less than a dozen. I'd like to have more than a hundred in full operation by the end of the year. Two in each state would make me very happy."

"I've heard of the big one in the Catskills. Southeast of Binghamton, New York."

"That's their educational camp in Hancock. It sits on seventy acres in the mountains."

"From what I've heard, it's impressive. And what with the growing number of Survivalists, neo-Nazis, certified nutcases and street gangs, the Feds have their hands full. Unless I'm mistaken, there aren't many camps here in Florida. Not big ones, anyway. Is this why you're pushing so hard for one?"

"The one I was about to get started is sitting on a fifty-thousand-acre parcel in Central Florida, which would make the one in the Catskills look like a bubblegum operation."

Andras nodded. “Fifty thousand acres. That *is* big.”

“Its location would enable it to handle weekly shipments for drugs, arms, the slave trade, and other related supplies. We’re talking a multi-billion-dollar operation, and when you add in collateral costs—disaster relief, reconstruction, insurance payouts from lawsuits and loss of life—this is big-time. If we’re lucky, a war could come out of all this.”

“Are you still working on the deal?”

“I can’t seem to get any cooperation from those damned Arabs. The three idiots I’m looking for must have put a hex on them. I don’t know how, but something screwy’s going on. There’s only one sure way to find out.”

“I take it you’re offering a bounty.”

“I want them alive.”

“I’d like to discuss my fee before I get started.”

“I’ll begin this operation with an initial allocation of three hundred large, which you’ll be able to draw from, at any time. Anything left you may consider a finder’s fee.”

“That’s a good motivation. Is there also a reward?”

“How about another hundred K, as a bonus?”

“Very nice. Any idea where I might start looking?”

“None.”

“How quickly do you want them brought back?”

“I’d very much like to have them in this office within the next two or three days.”

"And you've got no idea where they are?"

"This single detail, my friend, is what makes this such a challenge."

Andras stroked his jaw.

"Well? I'd like to know as soon as possible if you can handle it."

"It'll be tough simply because we have no starting point. However, I specialize in tough jobs."

"Excellent."

"I will need the setup account handled quickly. Ten or twenty K should be enough to get me started. I'll let you know when I'll need more."

"My protégé, Daniel Grove, keeps an office three floors down. He's presently managing Waite Information Systems. He'll take care of the necessary funds, as well as provide you with any information you'll need."

Andras got up. "I'll be in touch."

Braithwaite tapped some cigar ash on his glass ashtray. He flicked on his intercom to get on the line with the Grove kid. When he turned back to the door, Andras had already disappeared.

Braithwaite chuckled softly.

Yep. That bastard's perfect for this.

***

Daniel's intercom buzzed at 10:35. The hair on the back of his neck stood up when he saw the display.

"Kid, you're about to have a visitor."

Daniel froze. The big man sounded different. Pleased, somehow, if that was at all possible. No, not really pleased... He just didn't sound quite as angry.

"Did you hear me, kid?"

"Y-Yes, sir..."

"You sound confused. More so than usual."

"I am, sir."

"What part of my statement has confused you? You know what a visitor is, don't you?"

"Yes, sir. Of course. I'm just wondering."

"What about? C'mon, now. Let it loose. I'm pretty busy at the moment, so if you don't mind..."

"What sort of visitor, sir? I mean, what's this all about?"

"Whaddya think it's all about? You know damned well what's been on my mind the last two weeks. To make it simple, I got tired of waiting for you to pull your thumb out of your ass, so I sent for someone better equipped to take over. Guess what? He's here."

"Here, sir?"

Mr. Waite groaned. "Don't start that again, kid. Here. It means, well, *here*, rather than *not* here. Get it now?"

"What I meant was--"

"I just had a little chat with the man. He's pretty damned sharp, so I think we'll be seeing some serious progress very shortly. He's on his way down to see you, so be prepared to give him anything he wants. He has to know who he's looking for. He'll need detailed descriptions..."

Daniel stopped listening. Something had caught his attention. Someone was standing in front of his door. A man around Daniel's height. He was dressed in a nice suit, around thirty-five or so, and kind of scary in the eyes. They were a smoky gray, with a tiny reddish glint in their centers.

"Kid? You still there?"

"I'm still here, sir."

"Why so quiet? Did you zone out? Or did I give you too much information for that little brain to absorb in one session?"

"He's here, sir. I mean right here..."

Mr. Waite chuckled. "Snuck in on you when you weren't looking, did he?"

Something didn't make sense. "I'm sitting at my desk, facing the door... But I didn't even notice it opening, or--"

"Don't let it spook you. He did the same damned thing to me a few minutes ago. Just give him what he needs." *Click.*

Daniel stared dumbly at his visitor. He had no idea what to say to someone who'd just come in as if he'd simply walked through the door.

"I'm Andras." His voice was soft and low-pitched. It sounded more like a moan.

"Daniel Grove." Daniel stood awkwardly as the man approached his desk. Andras moved silently, like a cat. As he drew closer, the tiny red glint in his eyes stood out more sharply. Daniel decided not to offer his hand. This was not a man at all, but a demon. Daniel figured it best and safest to avoid all physical contact. He gestured to the chair. "Please sit."

Andras sat. "I'd like to be on my way as soon as possible. Mr. Waite wants you to brief me on this job. It shouldn't take long. I've got a photographic memory."

Daniel smiled. *Of course you do. You're a demon. You can slip through doors without having to open them.* "Just tell me what I can do."

"I'll need an account set up that I can draw from directly. Ten K to start should be sufficient. I'll need more later on. It all depends on where I've got to go to find those three."

"I'll get with Mr. Waite's accountants and you'll have the money available to you within the hour."

"Perfect." Andras moved forward in his seat. "Now you can tell me everything you know about these folks your boss wants me to find."

Chapter 3

The Fly Trappe sat on the north side of West Michigan, not far from South Orange Blossom Trail. The small white stucco building covered nearly half of the tiny concrete lot sandwiched between a ten-minute oil-change garage and a Chinese takeout restaurant.

The cabby dropped Andras off in front of the bar shortly after ten that night.

The dimly lit, air-conditioned room reeked of cigarette smoke, sweat and a harsh mix of cheap aftershaves. Twenty or so small square tables filled the main area. Half a dozen men and three middle-aged women sat at the bar. The men were all around thirty and wore jeans and tee shirts. The women, form-fitting clothes and cheap wigs. A rap number thumped loudly from the corner juke.

Andras grinned. If anything had brought down modern culture to new lows, it was rap. It not only had done away with most popular music, it had put most musicians, dance studios and record companies out of work. It made people angry, frightened and miserable. They no longer dressed up and went out on the weekends to enjoy themselves on the dance floor. They went out only to drink. Then hurried home, hoping they wouldn't get mugged by street gangs or killed on the roads.

When Andras lived in Chicago during the Capone era, popular music kept the country active and happy. Louis Armstrong led the pack, along with Bix Beiderbecke, Jelly Roll Morton, Sidney

Bechet, and Earl Hines. By the time Andras was brought back a few decades after he was killed by a street cop that bitter wintry day in March '29, music had evolved even more. The Dorsey Brothers, Benny Goodman, Charlie Barnet, Les Brown, Harry James, Russ Morgan, Bunny Berigan, Woody Herman, Count Basie, and dozens of others had literally swept the country off its feet. Singers like Russ Columbo, Frank Sinatra, Bing Crosby, Jo Stafford, and Doris Day added class to the entertainment.

People were happier back then.

Thanks to Balberith's painstaking efforts, it had become a different world. In the mid-seventies, his subs took over the music industry in New York City. Within just a few short years, rap had become the hallmark of entertainment in modern society.

Violence and hatred through music. The ultimate dream of every demon.

Andras found a vacant table in the center of the room and unbuttoned his jacket. Two waitresses handled the place. One was young and slender, the other older and sloppy. The older of the two was obviously the Parker woman Daniel Grove had told him about. His description matched her perfectly.

The younger girl sashayed over to his table. She was around twenty-five, flirty and obviously available, judging by her walk and how she thrust out her large breasts in his direction. He hoped she wouldn't become a problem. He was on a tight schedule and didn't have time for distractions. A quick toss in the back room with her could cost him half an hour and sour his chances of questioning Parker.

She stopped at his table and smiled down at him. A thick long strand of blond hair dangled over one eye. He was reminded of the "peek-a-boo" look tiny Veronica Lake had popularized in films back in the day. This babe had a tiny black mole on one perky breast and the tatt of a red heart on the other. She was definitely trouble.

"I have to talk to the other waitress."

"Ya sure, baby?"

He forced himself to keep his cool. He could easily start a brawl, but that would throw him off schedule, too. "If I wasn't sure, I wouldn't have said it, so you can take your oversized melons away from this table like a good little whore, and maybe I won't give your right tit a swastika to match that stupid heart on your left one."

Her face turned red. She looked like she was about to get angry. She simply spun around and stomped back to the bar.

Andras sat there another ten minutes before Parker finally trudged over.

Close up, she looked pretty bad. Her hair was brushed and sprayed but still scraggly. Her makeup had been applied thickly, with a shaky hand. Deep cracks framed her eyes and mouth. She'd once been attractive, but life had obviously turned brutal long ago. According to Grove, her husband had left her and their daughter Ashley for a younger woman. Judging by her appearance and her expression of contempt, she hadn't taken the rejection very well.

Andras had known a lot of women in his day. He'd never known any who handled rejection well.

"Whaddya have?" She sounded bored.

"Vodka martini. Very dry, with an onion and two olives."

She moved unhurriedly back to the bar and leaned against the counter, yawning while the barman fixed his drink. She obviously hated her job.

Five minutes later she finally brought his drink, laid down a napkin, placed the glass on top and went back to the bar.

He frowned. The drink had one olive and no onion. He knew he shouldn't have expected her to handle such a simple request. Sighing, he raised the glass to his lips and drank it down. At least it was strong and dry.

Ten minutes went by, then twenty. Parker stayed at the bar, flirting shamelessly with two well-dressed fat men on barstools. Not once did she turn in his direction. She was beginning to rake on his nerves.

All right, bitch. We'll just have to speed things up a little.

He focused on the pitcher of water at her elbow. *Tilt.*

It suddenly tipped over, soaking the bar counter, her skirt and apron. Then splashed the barman and the floor at her feet.

"*Damn, damn, damn!*" She grabbed her towel and frantically mopped up the spill. Scowling, the barman snatched up his own towel to wipe his forearm. The two fat men picked up their drinks and moved to the other end of the bar.

Parker pulled out her soaked notepad and a couple of wet dollar bills. Then slapped everything on the counter. She tossed the towel and stomped toward the hall entrance, where the sign REST ROOMS lit up the archway.

***

Parker was grumbling and blotting her face frantically with paper towels in front of the mirror when he slipped into the brightly lit room. When she noticed his reflection behind her, she glared. "This is the ladies' room, brainiac. You might wanna try the other one. It's even got a urinal."

Andras wanted to smile. This woman had slammed her door in Daniel Grove's face more than once. Tormenting her was going to be fun.

"Didn't you hear me? I said--"

"I don't need a urinal. That martini was pretty dry."

"I'm not in the mood for any shit, so you'd better just--"

A gun appeared in his right fist. It was pointed at her face.

"I'm not in the mood for any shit, either."

Trembling, she dropped the paper towels on the floor and backed up. Her skin had turned a chalky white.

"I need to know where your daughter is."

She opened her mouth, but nothing came out.

His imaginary gun was a silver 1911 Model Colt .45. A formidable-looking weapon. It was

Andras' personal favorite. He enjoyed producing it whenever the need arose. But he knew to be careful. People tended to faint or freeze up when they saw it pointing their way.

Like right now. This bitch had slipped into panic mode. Whatever brain cell she'd used moments ago had already switched off.

Time to change his approach. She couldn't tell him anything if she was too terrified to form words. He lowered his hand. The gun disappeared. "Your daughter. Where is she?"

She gawked at his empty hand. "Wh-What…wh-where…a gun...I saw a fucking gun... "

"You've been watching too many movies. Now tell me where your daughter is."

Her gaze didn't stray from his hand. When she realized there was no gun, she raised her head and lowered her jaw.

Andras could sense a scream beginning to take shape.

Pointing his index finger to the floor, he pulled two crumpled paper towels from beneath the sink and hurled them into her gaping mouth.

Her scream instantly turned into a muffled, choked squeal. Her eyes filled the sockets as she frantically clawed at the wad in her mouth. He rushed over, spun her around and pushed her against the sink. Grabbing her by the hair, he shoved her face into the basin.

Still choking, she made a feeble effort to resist. He grabbed her wrist and pulled her arm behind her back, let go of her hair with his other hand, grabbed her other wrist and jerked that arm behind her. He shoved his feet between hers and pressed his pelvis against her, mashing her stomach into the sink counter.

"Don't worry, this isn't a sex thing. I don't go for sloppy, loud, foul-mouthed bitches like you."

She gasped and choked, struggling clumsily beneath him.

"I just want to know where your daughter is. Once you tell me, I'm gone."

She hawked the towels wetly into the basin, arching her back while gasping for air. "Let me up, dammit! What--who the fuck…do you think you are?"

"You wouldn't believe me if I told you."

"I'm not in the mood for this--this bullshit!"

"Just tell me where Ashley is and I'm gone. I'll even wave as I go out the door."

She stiffened at the name. "Why do you wanna--"

"Just tell me where she is and you can be back at the bar, coming on to those rich fat men like nothing ever happened."

"I don't *know* where my daughter is!"

"Friends?"

"She doesn't have any."

"All girls her age have friends."

"She used to know some street trash. Gang sluts. She got in with the wrong crowd a while back."

"I guess your high-class approach to life proved a little too much for her."

"You're a--"

"Temper, temper. When?"

"When what?"

"You said a while back."

"Three, maybe four years ago, after her bastard daddy left us. She got knocked up and came back home."

"She doesn't see these sluts anymore?"

She shook her head. "She'd never go back to that bunch. She's trying…she wants to be respectable." She spat out that last word.

"Respectable? So she came home to *you*? Wow..."

"Listen to me, you--"

"Any boyfriends?"

She groaned. "I don't *know*, Mister..."

"Any relatives she might hook up with?"

"Ashley doesn't have anyone she'd—wait. She's got this uncle she always liked. Her daddy's cousin Rob. Haven't seen him in years, either. But she wouldn't go to see him. He's too far away."

"Where is he?"

"Last I heard, Pittsburgh."

"Pennsylvania?"

"Yeah."

"What's this uncle's last name?"

"Why?"

He let go of her left wrist and made a switchblade appear magically in his fist. He held it close to her face. "My shiny little friend wants to know the man's last name, lady. I suggest you comply. Otherwise, he's liable to get angry. When he's angry, he tends to do some really disgusting things. In this case, he might decide to scrape off that nasty wattle dangling underneath your chin."

"B-Belasco." Her whole body stiffened. She couldn't take her eyes off the knife.

"Good girl. Now...where in Pittsburgh?"

She swallowed loudly. "D-Don't know. Really. I really don't. Honest. He's got something to do with the fashion industry. He travels a lot. It's all I know."

"What's his company's name?"

"No idea."

He let go of her and stepped back. She braced her hands on the rim of the sink and straightened. Her hair had fallen everywhere. Still leaning against the sink, she brought up her right hand and pushed some brown clumps out of her eyes. She stood there, shaking, gasping and staring at her reflection. Her eyes were wet, her lipstick and eye shadow smeared. Her cheeks and chin were streaked with tears and slobber. He couldn't risk her screaming before he left the room. As a precaution, he sent over the thought

(*sleep*)

and grabbed her just as she collapsed. He dragged her into the stall and set her on the toilet seat, letting her lean back, her head resting against the dirty tile wall. One of her high heels had fallen off. He slipped it back on her foot, straightened and placed his right hand on top of her head. He moved his face closer. "When you snap out of this, you won't remember much. When you think something's coming back and get the silly urge to tell someone about it, you'll throw up, crap your panties and bark like a dog at the same time. This will convince you to keep your big mouth shut."

Andras quietly left the room.

***

Out in the muggy night air, the streetlamps splashed an eerie orange halo at the corner. The blinking neon of the Fly Trappe winked sporadically at the row of vehicles parked out front, facing Michigan.

Andras stood on the front stoop, watching the steady traffic. He glanced at his watch. 11:08. Not bad. He'd found what could be important information about Ashley Parker in less than an hour.

He pulled out the cellphone Daniel Grove had provided him and pressed 3 for the cab service. They answered right away and told him a cab would be there in fifteen minutes. While he waited, he phoned Daniel Grove to give him status.

Grove came on the line immediately. "What's going on?"

"Parker's got an uncle living in Pittsburgh. The mother says he's in the fashion industry. Man's name is Belasco. Robert Belasco. From what the mother said, Ashley likes him. I'd say Pittsburgh would be a good place to start looking, since we have no idea if they're still in this state."

"Pittsburgh? I don't recall Ashley mentioning him."

Andras sensed something in Grove's voice. "How well do you know this girl?"

Grove didn't reply right off. "I dated her once. Briefly."

Andras didn't like being brought into something without knowing all the facts. This sort of crap made the job more difficult. Grove had said only that he'd hired the girl to work the desk at his escort service.

Andras wondered if Braithwaite knew anything about this. The demon certainly wouldn't want his top employees dating one of their hookers. Grove looked and acted like the boy next door. There was obviously more going on.

If so, he needed to be told everything else about this before he hopped on the plane.

"Anything else I need to know about this?"

"No."

"How close were you and Parker?"

A pause. "Like I said, we dated once."

"And that was it?"

"Yes."

"What about the other two?"

"I told you everything."

"Everything?"

"Everything you'll need to know."

Andras could sense some tension in Grove's voice. This was obviously a sensitive subject. But now was not the time to get into something that might delay his trip. If Grove was holding anything back, it would eventually surface on its own. And that would be between Grove and Braithwaite.

"All right, then. I think Pittsburgh would be a good place to start. Unless, of course, you think they're sticking around the Orlando area, for whatever reason. Personally, if I'd soured a billion-dollar land deal for Braithwaite, I'd want to be at least a thousand miles away."

"As would I," Grove said.

"Parker might think that being with her uncle might keep her safe."

"If Ashley decided to make the trip to Pittsburgh, it makes your job simple. And if her uncle is involved in the fashion industry, that makes him a high profiler. Just a couple of phone calls to the right people might be all we need to track them down."

"I guess I'm off to Pittsburgh, then."

"I'll get with Mr. Waite and tell him what's going on. We can have a charter flight fueled and ready for you within the hour."

"That sounds good. It's a fairly short flight, so I should be in Pittsburgh long before breakfast. I'll need you to work from this end to let them know what's going on and also arrange for someone to meet me when I get there."

"I'll get in touch with one of our affiliates immediately."

Chapter 4

Pittsburgh, Pennsylvania

Marc Cassman, President and founder of Cassman Talent Agency, Inc, elbowed his way through the thick, noisy crowd. A *RESERVED* card sat in the center of the corner front-row table just ten feet from Stage Left, awaiting him. The phone call to Doug Moreland just a few hours earlier had gotten him the table, no questions asked. Cassman wanted to believe the co-owner of the Bel-Mor was giving him the same common courtesy all members of the entertainment industry gave one another. However, he knew better. He'd known Doug Moreland and Rod Bellman much too long to think along those lines. Those two had given him the front-row table just so they could watch him salivate over their new discovery.

Cassman had been a fairly successful talent agent for many years and constantly kept his eyes wide open concerning new talent. Even so, he realized Moreland and Bellman could be exaggerating about their latest find. If so, Cassman would have a giant belly laugh or two before going home, satisfied that he wasn't the only one in the business who could make a giant blunder about a new find.

However, a quick scan of the chaotic room told him something interesting was going on.

Cassman nudged the cuff of his tan suede jacket sleeve up a couple of inches and glanced at the luminous dial of his Rolex knockoff. Not even 10:00 and the room was packed. According to Freddie Bender, this Russo kid was pulling them in like cattle and had been packing the place since he'd started at the Bel-Mor last month.

Something about all this made no sense. You just didn't pick up an unknown magician, set him up as a headliner and watch him draw nightly capacity crowds. There had to be some sort of a weird angle going on.

Cassman had never trusted Bellman or Moreland. Those two knew nothing about show business. Bellman's old man had left him a carload of money made through real estate. Moreland had married the right lady. Moreland's better half was related to the Hunt family, who had received a rather large settlement several years ago, when a PAT bus T-boned the family vehicle, sending the mother and father into the hospital and putting the mother in a wheelchair for the rest of her life. Bellman and Moreland were distant cousins, joining forces when Bellman lucked into buying the old building on Penn Avenue. The three of them pooled their money. In just a year, they'd turned the abandoned hotel into one of the most popular nightclubs in the city of Pittsburgh.

In addition to their outrageous luck, they had the knack of snapping up talent at a bargain. Russo had apparently signed a contract with them for six hundred a week, performing one forty-minute show each night for three consecutive nights. Judging by the capacity crowds, Russo was obviously incredibly popular. Bender said the boy was pulling in twenty times what Bellman and Moreland were paying him.

Bender owned a dive on Liberty Avenue and had been a drinking buddy of Moreland's the last twenty years. Cassman had known Bender since high school. Cassman respected Bender as a business associate but didn't care much for the man's raging male hormones. Bender would nail a snake it he could hold it still.

But in spite of Bender's overactive gonads, he possessed a substantial amount of business savvy. Bender's club had been around for more than fifteen years. The man had a keen nose and knew how to find talent. He paid well, and when he latched onto a class act, he held on for dear life and didn't let go until the profits dipped.

Cassman learned about Russo two weeks ago, when he and Bender had lunch at the Garden on Smithfield. The moment Bender came into the restaurant, he began raving about a new magician he'd just seen at the Bel-Mor. Cassman was surprised as well as confused. Bender had been in the business way too long to rave about an act--especially a magic act. Bender specialized in musicians. And he'd never before gone on and on about someone else's talent.

Cassman set aside his personal bias. He knew that after being in the business so many years, he'd seen just about everything. He'd reached that point five years ago, when he'd turned away a young little Haitian, who sounded like a young Michael Jackson with a heavy accent, breathlessly whispering foreign songs into the mike. This same eighteen-year-old went on *American Idol* two years later, when the troop hit town. The kid didn't win, but he'd made it to the last five finalists and earned a big contract with a major studio in Los Angeles.

That was the day Cassman promised himself he'd never again be such a stupid, conceited chump. He hadn't scored with anyone potentially good since the Haitian boy. When Bender told him about this young magician who could do things no one had never seen done before, illusions not even Copperfield, David Blaine or Criss Angel could manage, Cassman knew he'd better take this seriously.

"You're really hooked on this guy?" Cassman had asked. "If he's as good as you say--"

"He's better." Bender bit into his bacon cheeseburger. He hadn't even noticed the three young skirts sashaying past the big bay window facing the street. Cassman spotted this right off. Bender had never ignored a skirt before in his life and always acted like a teenager with his first hard-on whenever a luscious babe came within sniffing distance. "He's as good as any I've ever seen." Bender held his gaze as he reached for his beer.

"Why hasn't Vegas snatched him up?"

"Bellman and Moreland won't let him go. I can't blame 'em. Not a bit."

Cassman had a slug of beer. Something about this just didn't make sense. Bender hadn't said where Russo had come from or who'd trained him.

Cassman knew how performers were, where their loyalties lay. If this boy was so damned good, why wasn't he in New York or Vegas?

"Why haven't *you* snatched him up?"

"Already tried. I took him aside after one of his shows and made sure Moreland wasn't anywhere close. Bellman's never around at night. He only comes in during the afternoons to do the books and share a shot or two with the hookers who come in during their lunch buffet. I offered Russo double what he's getting at the Bel-Mor. Twelve hundred for three nights, plus fifteen percent of the door. I offered him a guaranteed forty weeks, and I've been charging ten bucks cover at my place for the last five years. My place holds two hundred. The way this boy packs them in? That's another possible three hundred per night in his pocket. That's the best fucking deal I ever offered anyone."

"And he didn't *take* it?"

"He didn't even wanna talk to me."

"Maybe…well, maybe the boy just didn't--"

"Russo's a gold mine, Marco."

Cassman could tell the man was dead serious. Bender was a walking deposit box. He'd rather die than spend a dime if he didn't have to. But one thing Bender didn't take lightly was talent. Both he and Cassman recognized it, appreciated it and saw it for what it meant--security, as well as that retirement house in Malibu that Cassman had been dreaming about since he was a snot-nosed kid in high school.

And now, as he sat at the front corner table at the Bel-Mor, waiting for the waitress to bring his Manhattan, Cassman promised himself that he would forget about his contempt and jealousy for Bellman and Moreland and look at this boy Russo objectively.

He sincerely hoped everyone was wrong about Russo. It would tear Cassman up inside if he knew such an incredible talent existed in his town and he wasn't able to snatch it up.

***

At precisely 10:00, the excited male voice boomed through the p.a. system, making the walls of the big room vibrate. "Ladies and gentlemen, the one and only Jimmy-y-y-y… *Russo-o-o-o*!"

Applause. Yells. Screams. Loud, shrill whistling. Dozens of feet slammed to the tile floor.

Well-dressed and dapper, his thick black hair styled and combed to perfection, Jimmy Russo appeared from behind the maroon curtains and marched over to the center of the stage. As was his custom, he walked around in a little circle with his arms held out, his brilliant smile dazzling beneath the lights. The more he smiled, the more they applauded and cheered him on.

Jimmy considered himself lucky. The Bel-Mor was a prestigious club. The crowd reeked of comfort and affluence. Jewelry, styled hair, and expensive clothes embellished the large, revamped ballroom. His employers weren't exactly the nicest people in the world, but this was a cutthroat business, and he'd been playing the game all his life. But as long as they kept paying him, he couldn't complain. He was doing what he loved and knew how few people could make that same claim nowadays.

Magic was his passion; he was good at it. The best, actually, judging by how the crowd responded each night. "*Let your audience be your one true guide*," a very wise man had told him many years ago, when Jimmy, as a child, began learning magic tricks. "*As long as they're watching you, as long as they make you feel like you're the only one who exists for them, you're doing it right. Once you see them turning away or glancing at the door, that's when you're in serious trouble.*"

Right now, they were all gazing at him. Some were standing, others sitting, everyone smiling and clapping. Many were probably drunk or well on their way. This was, after all, a nightclub. Glasses and bottles covered each table. The waitresses hadn't stopped hustling since they'd come in. But every single person in that audience wore the same expression, one that clearly said, *ENTHRALL ME, JIMMY RUSSO*. And when silence finally crept back into the room, everyone would expect him to start up the routine that would take them on another dazzling trip to his special world, where dreams came true and the fantastic became the norm for the next forty wonderful minutes.

The applause lasted longer this time. He didn't check his watch but could tell by experience that it was definitely taking them longer to stop the commotion and settle back in their seats. The applause was also louder and less controlled than the previous night. Their energy and enthusiasm flowed heavily, creating a milky haze floating above everyone's head.

They were eager to embark on another trip. They needed release from their daily mundane activities and demanded escape. Forty minutes of entertainment and wonder, when they could relax and enjoy themselves again. Forty minutes of forgetting about reality, the daily rut. Rules. Obligations. They wanted to visit Jimmy's unusual world again, where strange, wonderful things took them right back to their childhood. They wanted to be fascinated. Captivated. Shocked. They wanted their blood to chill, their nerves to twitch. They wanted to feel their jaws dropping, their hair standing on end. Most of all, they wanted to experience something they'd never experienced before.

After nearly five minutes, the commotion finally died down and was replaced with a strained silence. It came reluctantly. A few claps here, a whistle or two there, with a "*c'mon, Jimmy, let's do it!*" thrown in for good measure. It was time to start the tour. Time for Jimmy Russo's magic bus to ease away from the curb of dreary reality and take everyone to the portal that opened up to the world of the bizarre, the fantastic.

Jimmy lowered his arms to his sides--his personal sign that he was about to begin. The room instantly fell silent. His gaze went to everyone in the room. He stood there, watching their anticipation, their torment. *C'mon, Jimmy*, their expressions said. *Do it again. Thrill me. Surprise me. Enchant me. Take me to your magical world, where wondrous things happen. Take us back to how it was when we were kids, when everything was magical and mysterious, where dreams stayed with us all the time, and everything good and exciting and wonderful sat off in the future, just beyond our grasp. Take us there again, Jimmy. Show us the Land of Oz, where we once longed to live before adulthood, good sense and logic shattered everything we'd all held so dear in our young, impressionable hearts.*

When the moment felt right, Jimmy turned to the mike perched five feet away. Then, taking a deep breath, he let it happen:

"Wanna see some magic?"

The room instantly turned into a deafening frenzy. Members of the audience jumped up and down. Applause ricocheted off the walls. Yelling, screaming and whistling saturated every square inch of air space.

As before, he waited for the silence to return. This time, it took only about one minute. They were anxious and ready.

He slowly approached the mike. In a much softer voice, he said, "Are ya sure?"

A loud male voice from the crowd said, "That's why we came here tonight, Jimmy!"

Someone else yelled: "Do it to us!"

"*Now*! We want magic *now*!"

The audience roared. Applause and whistling rang throughout the room.

A male voice toward the back said, "You might as well! You're here anyway!"

Laughter.

"Ouch." Jimmy winced and massaged the back of his neck. "That almost hurt."

Laughter.

Jimmy scanned the crowd. Everyone in the room watched him, waiting eagerly to see his first trick of the evening. As usual, he decided to start off with something silly and unexpected.

"Wanna see me pull a rabbit out of my hat?"

A couple of chuckles.

"Don'tcha need a hat for that?" asked a large, well-dressed guy around sixty sitting at a front table beside a large-breasted redhead decked out in a silver evening gown.

"A hat." Jimmy gave them his pensive look. He reached up and patted the back of his head. "Yep, a hat sure would come in handy. Now…where did I leave that stupid thing?" He looked down at his feet, turned and checked the floor in front of the curtain. He turned back to the audience. For ten seconds he didn't say a word, just watched them with a clueless look on his face. He shrugged and shook his head. Then he reached up and scratched the back of his neck. A moment later, he grinned and clicked his fingers. "Of course. How silly of me!" He unbuttoned his jacket, reached inside and pulled out a dove. He held it a moment and let it go. It flew into the audience, drawing gasps and applause. Then disappeared, drawing more gasps.

Jimmy reached inside his jacket again. He pulled out a baseball, a catcher's mitt and a baseball bat, tossing them one by one to the floor. Like the dove, they immediately vanished. More gasps, laughter and applause erupted from the crowd. "I used to play baseball as a kid," Jimmy said sheepishly. "But only as a hobby. The Pirates never expressed an interest."

Laughter. Someone yelled, "The bums could use ya!"

"I like doing this better," he said. "It's safer."

A burst of applause bounced off the walls.

He reached under his jacket once again and suddenly stopped. "What's this?" He pulled his hand out, clutching something that slowly expanded as soon as it was released from the confined space. A few moments later, it became a shiny black top hat. He grinned. "How about that? It's always in the last place you look." He displayed it proudly.

The audience yelled. The room roared with a fresh explosion of applause.

When the commotion settled down, he placed the hat on his head, pulled the wireless mike from its stand and went down the steps to the main floor. He walked right over to the long-legged redhead sitting next to her prosperous-looking date. She stared blankly at Jimmy.

He tapped the side of his hat. "Wanna see a rabbit hop out of this?"

She continued staring.

Grinning, Jimmy gave the crowd a quick scan. "That's the same response I got when I asked my ex-girlfriend to marry me."

Laughter and several howls danced erratically down the aisle. A woman in the center section of the audience yelled, "Ask *me*, Jimmy! I promise I won't just sit there!"

"I'll just bet you won't," he said. Laughter drowned out her reply. To the redhead, he said, "What would you *like* to see come out of this hat?"

Her eyes grew; her glossy red lips parted. "A diamond?"

He turned to the crowd. "Didn't see *that* one coming, did we?"

Laughter.

"Let's see if we can accommodate this pretty lady. We don't want her escort to take her home angry, do we? Every guy in this room knows what *that* means!"

Laughter. Catcalls. Her escort reddened.

Jimmy held out the hat. "Go on. Reach in there and take out your diamond."

She didn't move.

"I promise you it won't disturb the rabbit. He's a heavy sleeper."

A couple of snickers. She glanced at her date, who just shrugged.

Jimmy sighed. "All right, then." He reached inside the hat, pulled out a large white rabbit and held it up.

The crowd screamed.

When silence returned, he turned to the rabbit. "Sorry, Cedric, you'll have to continue your nap back in the dressing room." He lowered his arm and set the rabbit on the floor beside him. It hopped a few times and disappeared.

More screams and applause.

When the commotion died down, Jimmy turned back to the redhead. "If you don't want it, I can always ask that beautiful blond lady four tables down. The one with the really nice, um, smile. I guarantee she'll probably jump at the chance to--"

The redhead's hand instantly disappeared into his hat.

Jimmy grinned. "Works every time, doesn't it?"

Snickers.

The redhead rummaged around. Her jaw dropped and her arm stopped moving. She glanced at her date. "I found something!" She raised her arm and pulled her hand out of the hat. A large, bright diamond ring glittered between her thumb and forefinger.

She gasped.

The audience went wild.

Chapter 5

Tiffany couldn't stop smiling at the guy on the stage. Even though he was twenty feet away and the spotlight blurred his features, she could see that he was really good-looking and had the nicest smile. Very boyish. The kind of guy a girl could take home to meet her parents. The kind of guy the girl's parents would like.

Jimmy Russo reminded her of Lou Gates in some ways.

She knew she'd never see Lou again, but she still couldn't help thinking of him. Those few lovely days they'd spent together in Raven, Ohio would always remain in a special place in her heart. She could never forget his smile, which lit up his beautiful dark brown eyes. Or how he'd touched her, kissed her, made love to her.

She had to stop this silly reminiscing. That chapter had come to a close. It was senseless to agonize over it. She was a spirit. She had a covering, but as Chip had explained, it was only to help them blend in so they could get things done. In the end, a covering didn't matter. Nor did it change anything. A spirit could never sustain a lasting relationship with a mortal. Her bond with Lou had ended. His life, his future, his destiny—everything was out of her hands. She'd even placed a spell on him, which erased all memories of her and the love they'd once shared. If they ever did meet again, he wouldn't know who she was.

She had to concentrate on the present. She'd come here tonight to enjoy herself, and that was what she was doing. The cute guy in the dark suit was truly amazing. His hat trick had brought down the house. Tiffany couldn't help wondering how he'd done it. She knew a little about illusions, but taking all of those things out of your pocket? Well, it seemed like genuine magic, and not just some elaborately calculated trick created by diagrams, angles and mathematical equations.

His diamond trick wasn't bad, either. Tiffany was no expert, but that rock sure looked real. She sat five tables down from the redhead and her rich escort--much too far away to guess its authenticity. Even if she'd been closer, she wouldn't have been able to tell. Even though she'd spent her last four years as a mortal in Hollywood, where everyone was obsessed with riches, glitter and precious gems, she'd never cared much for jewelry. She'd always considered such ornate trappings unnecessary embellishments worn by neurotic women possessed by the overwhelming desire to be noticed.

Tiffany chose never to wear anything that would detract from her looks. Even as a young starlet fighting to break into the business, she wore jewelry only if the job required it, and never once considered marking her body with tasteless tattoos, studs, or piercings.

Jimmy Russo's diamond was most likely not legit. It would be extremely foolish--and horribly expensive--to give away authentic diamonds to members of the audience. But it was still a dandy trick, and she couldn't wait to see what else he'd planned for his routine.

"You're slobbering, Tifferoo."

His voice made her stiffen in her seat. She suddenly remembered Chip was sitting beside her. He was grinning stupidly, his bushy red hair wild and unruly, like a palmetto bush. She could tell he was about to send over another zinger. Chip was the master of zingers.

Still, she couldn't help wondering why she'd totally forgotten about him. Had Jimmy Russo enthralled her that much?

"Please close your mouth, Princess," Chip said. "The drool's staining your shirt. Here. Wipe your chin before you wet your pants." He picked up a napkin. "I'd give you a tarp, but the folks here would stare, and you know how shy I am."

"Oh, stop." He was *so* embarrassing. "You have to admit he's good."

Chip shrugged. "He's got possibilities, but that doesn't make me want to suck his face down my throat."

She swatted him. "I wasn't thinking of that and you know it."

"Ouch. Tifferoosky, you've got that same blank expression you had in Ohio, whenever you were near that restaurant owner guy."

Tiffany sighed. She wished he'd stop bringing up Lou.

It was time to change the subject. "I really liked his diamond-in-the-hat trick."

"It's been done a million or so times before, but I have to admit it wasn't bad. I even liked his menagerie-in-the-side-pocket trick."

"How do you think he did that?"

"Wish I knew."

"Everything looked real until it vanished."

"Could've been the lighting."

"How?"

"Every magician has got his tricks. This boy's one of the best I've ever seen."

She was surprised at that remark. Chip was a trickster and an amateur magician. He was a master at making things appear differently. He also had a huge ego, and certainly wasn't the type to go on about someone else.

He slid his chair closer. The crowd had gotten louder, and it was harder to talk without shouting. "So then, when do we leave this great and wonderful city of rivers, bridges and potholes?"

"When I'm satisfied Ashley will be all right, then we can go."

"She'll be just fine, Tifferoo. Uncle Robby-Bobby has taken her eagerly into his nest. If you remember, their reunion was so nauseatingly sweet, I almost hurled chowder."

"Can't you be nice for just once?"

"Me? Nice?"

"Just for once?"

"Sorely you just."

"Just what?"

He wiggled his ears. "Funny, my perky but sometimes pesky pet. Very funny."

"Getting back to Ashley... Once I'm satisfied she'll be okay--"

"Like I just said, the Ashley babe is just fine and dandy. Ol' Robby's got her staying with him at that ritzy-ditzy place--"

"Chatham Center."

"Whatever. He even gave her a job, so she'll probably never have to worry about being laid off or fired."

Chip was right, of course. Ashley's uncle had welcomed her with open arms. He'd set her up in a spare bedroom in his penthouse apartment and opened a line of credit in her name so she could buy clothes, shoes and whatever else she needed. Her job was easy--taking calls and appointments--but he promised her a promotion once she started learning the business. He'd also promised that she'd accompany him to several shows a month to get more experience.

So why didn't this make Tiffany feel better?

The reason was simple. The demon Breath Mint, or whatever his name was. And because of what she, Chip and Ashley had done to anger this demon, who didn't tolerate insubordination or disobedience. Each time she thought of what had been done to poor Digger and his friend Cal when Tiffany, Chip and Ashley were in Florida, she found herself shaking with fear and anger.

It was really no wonder that Tiffany didn't want to leave Ashley alone in this city. At least, not until she was absolutely certain her friend would no longer have to worry about demons.

Tiffany knew that was impossible. No one in this mortal world could ever expect to be totally safe from demons. Even so, she couldn't live with herself, knowing she'd left her friend defenseless. They'd left Orlando and were now nearly a thousand miles away, but somehow, a thousand miles just didn't seem far enough.

She couldn't shake the nagging fear that Breath Mint would eventually find them, no matter where they went. In the meantime, she knew she couldn't leave Ashley. At least, not until she'd found some way to keep her safe.

"I take it you're still worried, right?" Chip asked.

"Can you honestly expect me to feel any different? This is Breath Mint we're talking about. Don't you remember what we did? It only happened two weeks ago."

Chip scratched his pointed ear. "No, Tifferoo, I haven't forgotten. I was there, too."

"And don't forget what he did to Digger and Cal."

"That's right up there in the old Memory Palace, too. Don't forget, I saw him down below, when I was forced to stand in Olivier's stupid rock garden outside the Castle for twenty centuries. And by the way, his name is Braithwaite. Don't *ever* let him hear you slip with that Breath Mint thingy, or he'll—"

"Get mad? Throw a tantrum? You've got to be joking. He's always mad. He's always throwing tantrums."

"He *is* a demon, you know. Demons don't normally have admirable qualities--especially supers. At least, I haven't seen any. But what do I know? I'm only a stupid rock garden ornament."

She shook her head. "He makes a water moccasin look like a fluffy little chew-toy."

"Don't sugar coat it, now..."

"And aside from that, he's repulsive. I want to throw up every time I think of him."

Chip sighed. "Well, I guess we can safely say you've decided not to become a long-standing, bona fide member of his fan club." He picked up his pitcher and had a healthy slug of ice water. Then he set it down and belched loudly. Three tables of people turned their way.

She glared. "Did you have to do that?"

"It felt really good."

"I'm so glad your grossness is therapeutic for you."

"I feel another one working its way out. Where would you prefer it comes out?"

"Don't you dare."

"Look." He pointed toward the stage. "Our boy's ready to dazzle us again."

***

Marc Cassman couldn't take his eyes off the charismatic young guy in the dark suit. Russo was a walking stick of dynamite. He had everything--thick black hair, puppy-dog eyes, and a gleaming smile. He wasn't tall, maybe five-eleven, and didn't weigh much more than one-fifty. But he carried himself like a champ. His talent surpassed everything

Cassman had seen in his nearly fifty years, including Copperfield, Doug Henning, David Blaine, even Criss Angel. But more than anything else, Cassman noticed that Russo's presence filled the room.

The diamond trick wasn't anything new, but the opener itself was brilliant. All you had to do was scan the crowd. Enthusiasm and excitement sprang from every seat in the house. Each member of the audience had accepted this man and his incredible talent. Amazement had taken over the souls of everyone the moment Jimmy Russo had emerged from behind the curtains. His presence and charm had literally nailed them. The way he looked at them, smiled at them, talked to them. As with all natural performers, he'd seduced his audience, captivated them the same way a man would handle a beautiful woman. Cassman realized from the moment Jimmy Russo had stepped onto the stage that he was in the presence of a new sensation. Someone who could fill auditoriums. Casinos. Theaters. Convention halls.

Cassman knew great talent when he saw it and could smell success a mile away. And tonight he knew long before he saw the diamond appear in the redhead's greedy hand that Russo was going places. Cassman had never felt such power before, such natural poise and control. He'd never actually seen such raw showmanship, especially in a lad so obviously on the right side of thirty. Never in all his years of professional wheeling and dealing had he stumbled across such a freak of nature.

A phenomenon stood just five tables down, and Cassman could actually feel the heat generating off the man. Russo had incredible magnetism. This boy could very well be the biggest entertainment sensation in the last twenty-five years. From the moment Russo had stepped onto the stage, no one could take his eyes off him.

Six hundred a week was ridiculous. Were Bellman and Moreland out of their freaking minds? This place seated two hundred, easy. Every table was taken, every chair filled, every barstool claimed. Patrons stood in a long line, three and four deep in spots, from one end of the room to the other. Cassman estimated at least three hundred bodies in this room. At ten bucks a head, with a two-drink minimum, you were talking six grand, easy. Triple this same scenario for one week's time, and these crooks were pulling in eighteen thousand, while forking over a paltry six hundred to their new sensation.

Cassman had never ripped off any of his clients in all his years of handling talent. And he'd never consider doing anything that could scare off a priceless gem like Russo.

Maybe this was why Cassman was a member of the paying audience and not sitting in his office, like Bellman and Moreland, counting the mountain of cash this brilliant new talent had dumped in their laps.

It was pure greed. Russo needed larger crowds, bigger cities. He deserved better opportunities. Cassman had connections in New York and L.A. He knew at least three major producers who would love seeing Russo's work. These same producers had been known to shell out a quarter of a million for a short-term contract based on someone's hunch. With a sure bet like Russo, they'd be lunging for their checkbooks like gunslingers slapping leather.

If only Cassman could get to him...

With that kind of money hanging in the balance, Cassman could shitcan his musty hole-in-the-wall Market Street office and put Russo on the next plane to New York City, or even Vegas.

Marc Cassman suddenly realized that his career path might not be so abysmal. For the very first time in many years, he guessed that he might actually be within reach of that cache of gold that had been eluding him all his life. And now that he'd found it and knew exactly where it was, he should grab it before it disappeared.

He also knew he would die poor and miserable if he didn't find some way to snatch up this incredible phenomenon.

Chapter 6

When the applause finally subsided, Jimmy went back up the steps to the stage and slid the mike into its slot on the stand.

In the first row, the redhead was fussing over her new diamond. She'd slipped it on the appropriate finger and held up her hand, turning it at different angles so she could study it better. When she realized the lighting over her table wasn't sufficient, she put her hand down closer to the flickering candle and lowered her head until her chin rested on the table surface.

Jimmy stepped closer to the mike. "Want me to have the crew turn up the lights?"

Snickering trickled down the aisles.

The redhead ignored him. She probably wasn't even aware he'd said anything. She cared only about the diamond.

"How about a handy-dandy magnifying glass?" Jimmy asked.

A few chuckles. Jimmy held up his hand. A magnifying glass appeared magically in his fist.

Instant applause.

Still ignoring him, the redhead picked up her glass, gulped down the rest of her drink and stood. She obviously wanted to rush home and spend the rest of the evening gawking at her new diamond. She barked an order over her shoulder at her date. The man scrambled out of his seat, picked up her wrap from the back of her chair and draped it carefully over her shoulders. She let him take her arm, but her focus stayed on the dazzling gem on her finger. She kept her arm held straight out in front of her so everyone could see the diamond as she and her date marched up the aisle, toward the front entrance.

Jimmy grinned. "Looks like somebody's going home lucky tonight..."

Laughter and loud howling.

"Hope she remembers me in the morning."

More laughter.

"I also hope he's got the local cardio unit on speed dial."

A rush of laughter and snickering.

He wanted to be a fly on the wall in their apartment when she woke the next morning and realized that the ring had mysteriously changed into a piece of cheap plastic costume jewelry sometime during the night.

Someone in the audience said, "Do another one!"

Jimmy blinked. "Another what?"

"Hat trick!"

Applause.

He motioned for everyone to calm down. When the room grew quiet again, he said, "What would you like to see?"

The brunette in the front row held out her left hand. "A ring on *my* finger, baby doll!"

Laughter and applause.

Jimmy waited once again for the commotion to die down. It took nearly a minute. He was going to have to outdo himself to get their minds off that last trick. "How about a juggling act?"

"Hat trick!"

"Wanna diamond!"

"I'll take an emerald!"

"Hat trick! Hat trick! Hat trick! Hat trick!"

Jimmy waved them down. If they kept this up, he'd lose control. That would be the kiss of death. *Woo the audience*, he'd been taught. *Treat the crowd like a beautiful woman. Have them eating out of your hand, but don't let them eat you, and make sure they always know who's in charge.*

"How about if I promise to show you a juggling act greater than any you've ever seen?"

Silence.

"If you don't love it, and I mean *love*, as in salivating, panting, heart-throbbing, eventually losing total control of many of your favorite bodily functions…*then* we'll do another hat trick."

Laughter. The females in the audience giggled. So did the blond beauty sitting next to a skinny, weird-looking guy with wild red hair. Jimmy had noticed her when he first came out on stage. She was probably in her mid-twenties and had the biggest blue eyes and the brightest smile he'd ever seen. Her hair was a thick honey-blonde, shining like woven gold in the dimly lit room. Babes made up at least half the audience, but this lady stood out just as brilliantly as the glittering stone he'd just produced for the redhead. Everything had just faded away as this blond beauty slinked into his sights. The room, the audience, the candles, and all the sounds in the room. Everything had turned into a thick blurry darkness around her.

Snap out of it.

He struggled to remember where he was. And why he was here.

You're on stage, you idiot. Stop ogling that golden fox and do your job.

Where was I? Magic trick? No. Juggling. Yes. You just made a deal with your audience. Don't screw it up.

Jimmy held out his hands. "Deal?"

"Deal!"

Applause. Cheers. The thumping of feet.

"Deal!"

"Deal! Deal! Deal! Deal! Deal!"

"All right, then. Watch. And be ready to be amazed and astounded--"

"And having an orgasm!" yelled one of the females in the center of the room.

Squealing.

Jimmy smiled sheepishly. "I'm not even gonna touch *that* one!"

Laughter and applause. Then silence.

He held out both hands in front of him, palms up, and began raising them alternately, in a slow juggling motion. First the right, then the left, up and down, increasing his rhythm until his hands were moving rapidly. "Pretty good, huh?"

Some laughter.

"Oops." Jimmy stopped moving his hands and stared at them. Then he grinned. "I guess I forgot something."

Chuckling.

Jimmy closed his eyes. A beer bottle magically appeared in his right hand. The applause started up again. He juggled the bottle a couple of times, adding a baseball that had also materialized out of thin air. The applause and cheers grew.

A tennis ball appeared. Then a coffee mug.

The room roared. Someone shrieked. Several people got up from their seats and crept closer to the stage.

Jimmy slowed down his rhythm, making his movements longer to force the juggled items higher in the air. A horseshoe suddenly appeared in the mix. Then a drumstick.

"How am I doing?" he asked.

The room exploded in applause. Many others jumped up from their seats and migrated toward the stage.

"Something else?" Jimmy asked, his hands pumping.

"A DVD player!" a woman shrieked from the seats.

"A crescent wrench!" a man said from the crowd in front of the stage. "A big one!"

Jimmy shook his head. "You guys sure are tough!"

"An elephant!" yelled someone from the back of the room.

Howling.

"An elephant?" Without interrupting his rhythm, Jimmy tilted his head. "Whaddya think I am? A magician?"

Laughter.

Jimmy closed his eyes and focused.

The small portable DVD player and crescent wrench appeared among the mix, and Jimmy was soon juggling eight different items. The crowd standing at the front of the stage gawked silently, their eyes and mouths wide-open.

The whispers came out in gasps: "My God... He *did* it!" "Can't *believe* this guy!" "How the hell is he *doing* that?" "Dude's better'n *any*body!"

Jimmy continued for another full minute, alternating his speed before gradually slowing down. The items disappeared, one by one, until he was juggling nothing but a pair of shiny black dress shoes.

His eyes grew when he noticed the shoes. He shook his head. "Now where did *they* come from?" Without pausing in his juggling, he glanced down at his feet. Only his black socks were visible. "Now would you look at that? I wondered why the floor suddenly felt so cold!"

Everyone in the place jumped up and began applauding and screaming.

Jimmy tossed the shoes one last time, and they disappeared in mid-air. He lowered his arms and looked down. His shoes were back on his feet. He held out his hands, flashed a gleaming smile and bowed.

The entire room vibrated in utter pandemonium.

***

Chip strongly suspected something about Jimmy Russo wasn't quite right.

The diamond-in-the-hat trick was nothing new, but all that stuff coming out of his pockets seemed, well, just too fantastic. Since Russo had been facing the audience at the time, it was impossible to tell if something was rigged to the back of his suit. If so, Russo wasn't at all the dazzler everyone thought he was.

However, that juggling routine defied logic. Chip had seen hundreds of jugglers and magicians in two thousand years. It didn't take a genius to figure out how impossible it was to pull things out of thin air in the middle of a juggling routine.

When the beer bottle appeared, followed by a baseball, Russo suddenly had Chip's attention. Then the tennis ball materialized, followed by all that other stuff that simply could not be concealed in the pockets of an ordinary mortal sport jacket. And what about the DVD player and crescent wrench, which were added at the request of audience members?

Most of all, how could Russo take off his shoes without interrupting his juggling, then put them back on without anyone seeing him do it?

Something fishy was going on. Russo was doing things that were both impossible and miraculous. And as any demon knew, the impossible and miracles simply did not happen in the mortal world. Not without help, anyway.

Chip wanted to look into this but didn't want to get Tifferoo upset. She tended to get all defensive and protective whenever she liked someone--particularly a guy. Right now, she was acting ridiculously smitten. Russo's boyish smile had apparently done a serious number on her hormones, and his jugging routine had her mesmerized. She was standing up, clapping, jumping up and down, and yelling. She wasn't acting at all like the subtle quiet babe Chip had grown to know and love.

Tifferoo was a hot, delicious-looking babe, and as laid-back as they came. But even so, she had a red-hot temper and could do serious damage if her buttons were pressed the wrong way. She wasn't a demon, just an unfortunate spirit who'd wandered into hostile territory--just as Chip had done centuries earlier. Even though he hadn't known a sweeter soul, he'd seen her turn scary when the situation called for it. In Orlando, she did some frightening things that baffled the imagination.

Chip had no idea why Tifferoo's powers had been growing so steadily since they'd left Hell. He only knew that she'd turned into a genuine ass-kicker and had already sent the demon Gutril down to Hell with one swift kick. And judging by how much she hated demons, he knew she wouldn't hesitate to do it again.

When the commotion finally died down, she sat back down. She was smiling brightly and her cheeks were flushed. He hadn't seen her that flustered since she'd hooked up with the restaurant owner guy in Ohio. When Tifferoo fell for someone, she plunged into it, head-first. She was definitely not the wishy-washy type about anything. And when she felt something, she felt it all the way to the very depths of her soul.

He strongly felt she was falling for Russo just like she'd fallen for the restaurant guy. So what was he to do?

Since they were buds, he had no choice but tell her his suspicions.

She had a sip of her strawberry daiquiri, reached up and pushed some thick golden tendrils away from her face. Her skin looked flushed. "That was some juggling act, wasn't it?" She turned back to the stage. "I've never seen anything like him--like *that*--before." When he didn't reply, she lowered her smile a few degrees. "What's wrong?"

He forced himself to focus on nothing in particular. He didn't want her in his head, sorting through it. Whenever she did that, he was as good as dead.

"There's something on your mind, isn't there?"

He needed to lighten the mood. Then she'd forget about him and go back to her salivating. "I've got a little gas building up."

"It doesn't look like gas to me. Not this time, anyway."

"How can you tell?"

"You look really silly when you have gas."

"How can you tell?"

"Good point. So what's wrong?"

He gazed into those big baby blues. Hopefully, she wasn't doing her head thing again. Like her other powers, this one came to her quite suddenly one day in Orlando. It had taken him completely by surprise and made him a little resentful. It sucked that she could do so many cool things that he couldn't, even though he'd been an inferior for centuries, while she'd been a spirit just a few short months.

Even so, he found that he wasn't as resentful as he should be. Tifferoosky never abused her powers. And only used the head thing in extreme situations.

"Tiffy-Poo, you aren't by any chance getting into my head again, are you?"

"Not this time."

"You're sure?"

"I'd know, wouldn't I?"

"You're not lying to me, are you?"

"I never lie to you."

He recalled that little secret she and the Ashley babe had shared in Orlando, when the two of them did the head thing with Chip right there. "Never?"

"Not unless it's totally necessary."

"And you're definitely not in my head right now?"

"I only do that in emergencies. This isn't one of those, is it?"

He gazed into those eyes once again. She was no longer smiling. Now she was worried about what was on his mind. He felt like a jerk. She'd been acting like a kid again for the first time since she'd messed up the sheets with that guy in Ohio. Now she was all bummed out, and it was his fault. He needed to change the mood so she could start having fun again. His suspicions could wait.

He shrugged. "I guess I'm just jealous. Take away that boy's good looks, charisma and charm, and what have you got?"

She blinked. "A terrific juggling and magic act?"

He smiled sheepishly. At least she was happy again.

"I wanna meet him," she said.

"What?"

"I'd like to tell him how much we liked his act."

"Tifferoosky, listen to the crowd. I'm sure he already knows--"

"I wanna tell him in person."

"Can't you just--"

"I know you'd be uncomfortable, so I wouldn't expect you to come backstage with me. Not if you don't want to."

He was growing nauseous. If she actually met Russo, she'd figure it out. And if she discovered Russo could actually be a demon, she'd be crushed.

"You okay?"

"Whaddya mean?" He was growing uneasy. She was giving him one of her looks again. He couldn't tell if she was reading his mood or actually inside his head. Whatever she was doing, he didn't like it.

"I mean just what I said. Are you okay?"

"I'm just fine and dandy. Why do you ask?"

She moved closer. "Do you think I'm stupid?"

"You? Stupid?"

"Me. Stupid."

"Just what are you getting at?"

"You obviously don't think I know, do you?"

Chip felt the blood draining from his face. In spite of what she'd told him, she'd obviously done her head thing. "Wh-What are you talking about, precious?"

"I'm pretty sure I know what's bothering you, because it's bothering me, too."

He was afraid to ask. "What's bothering you, Tifferoo?"

She moved closer and lowered her voice. "Jimmy's too good, isn't he?"

"Howzat?"

"He's too good to be just a really great magician."

"Tifferoo, what are you saying?"

She sighed. "I think Jimmy Russo's a demon."

Chapter 7

"Before I leave you good people for the evening," Jimmy Russo said, "I'd like to dedicate the last part of my act to magicians the world over who say that it's all done with mirrors!"

Applause.

"Personally, I don't use mirrors." Jimmy grinned proudly. "I do need a mirror once in a while to make myself presentable for the ladies. Know what I mean?"

Whistles and catcalls from the audience.

"But as far as my act goes? No mirrors. Not a one. Want to know why?"

Someone yelled, "Why, Jimmy?"

Laughter.

Jimmy chuckled. "I'm glad you asked. And since you brought it up, let me tell you why. I don't use mirrors because I don't need them."

Applause and cheering.

"Let me show you just how much I don't need them." He reached into his jacket pocket, pulled out a small hand mirror and held it up so everyone could see what it was. Then he tossed it directly at the audience.

A dozen people shrieked and jumped out of their chairs. Just as the hurled mirror approached the table, it disappeared. Laughter resonated down the aisles. The people who'd abandoned their seats stood in the aisles, looking around. When confusion set in, they turned to one another and laughed in embarrassment.

Jimmy held out his hands. "Are you folks trying to tell me you don't trust me? You thought I'd actually toss a solid piece of *glass* at you?"

Laughter. The people returned to their seats, several of them still looking around suspiciously.

"Honestly…" Jimmy shook his head. "You really know how to hurt a guy."

"Just reflex action, Jimmy," one of the males at the tables said.

"Nothing personal, right?" Jimmy asked.

Several people yelled, "Right!" simultaneously.

"All right, then, since I just got rid of my one and only--oops." Jimmy reached into his front pants pocket and removed another mirror, this one smaller and oval-shaped. "Forgot I had this one." He tossed it at another part of the audience and grinned when the panicked group reacted identically to the first group. Once again, the mirror vanished. The people who'd scattered stood amongst the tables, dazed.

Jimmy shrugged. "I honestly thought I'd already tossed that little sucker!"

Once again, the embarrassed patrons returned sheepishly to their seats.

"I hope everyone's all right now. That really was my very last mirror. I'm trying to remember when I used it last, but sometimes I just can't remember things. They told me at the hospital I've have days like these."

More howling and applause.

"But let me say this. I speak from the heart, and I can truthfully say that—uh-oh..." He tapped his jacket just above his left breast pocket. He smiled sheepishly. "I do believe I missed another one." He opened his jacket, slowly and laboriously removed a large mirror at least two feet long and a foot wide and held it out in front of him. "Would you believe I forgot I even had this bad boy in there?"

The crowd moaned. People at the front tables sat back and pushed out their chairs.

"A little gun-shy, pray tell?" he asked.

"Oh, yeah!" one of them said.

Jimmy laughed. "I promise this is the last one. Except for the really big one in my dressing room, which they don't seem to trust me with, for some strange reason."

A few snickers.

"But just so no one has a coronary, I promise I'll be really cool about this one." He dropped it to the polished floor a couple of feet in front of him, shattering it. Shrieks and gasps erupted in the room. An instant later, all the pieces but one vanished.

The audience roared in applause.

When the applause died, he bent and picked up the single piece of glass. He tilted his head as he gazed at it. "You lost?"

Some laughter. He tossed it at the audience. Like the others, it disappeared quickly.

Another roar. The room went berserk.

Jimmy stood proudly, smiling and bowing. They truly loved him. In the morning, he was going to have a long talk with Danielle. This time he'd hold his ground. He was a rising star and deserved to be treated as one. Not as some selfish bitch's lap dog.

When the room grew quiet again, someone yelled, “More, Jimmy!”

He grinned. “I really wish I could, but--”

“More!”

“More!”

“More! More! More! More!”

He motioned them to settle down. When they stopped yelling, he said, “Tomorrow night, folks, I promise you even greater magic!”

The audience broke into a standing ovation.

Jimmy waved, moved quickly toward the curtains and disappeared.

***

Strands of greasy dark hair dangling over his forehead, Doug Moreland stumbled out of his office at the end of the hall, in the rear of the Bel-Mor. He wore a white silk shirt and black dress slacks. He also wore a maroon tie. The knot was pulled down, the top two buttons of the shirt undone. He gripped a half-empty glass in his right hand. When he saw Cassman, his glazed, blood-shot eyes grew.

Cassman could tell he was in for a rough time, but he’d expected it. He and Moreland had never been friends. He just hoped he could talk some sense into the arrogant jerk.

“I figured I’d be seeing you sometime soon.” Moreland closed the door behind him and did his best to stand up straight. Moreland was nearly half a head shorter than Cassman, even with the two-inch lifts the weasel usually wore inside his two-inch heels. Cassman’s imported casuals had only an inch heel, but it still put him at an impressive six-four.

"We've got to talk."

"Sure looks like something important's weighing on the big man's mind." Moreland sipped his drink.

"By the way, thanks for the front-row seat."

"I figured you might not be so busy in the evenings lately."

"That was considerate." Cassman sighed. It was difficult keeping his composure. Moreland had never been one to let a good dig slide.

"No problem. I guess you stopped by for a little chat. Or did you wanna ask how Bellman and I have been doing lately?" He jabbed a thumb down the hall behind Cassman, toward the stage. "I'll bet you've already figured that out by now, huh?"

"Yeah. That I did."

"So why the visit? I'm sorta busy right now."

Cassman glanced at the half-empty glass and wondered how many of those Moreland had already sucked down. The little man's glazed bloodshot eyes suggested he'd been drinking quite a while.

"I want to talk to you about Russo."

Moreland raised his glass to his lips and sipped. "What about 'im?"

"Let's not be coy. You're taking advantage of him."

"So?"

"I think Russo needs a break, and you and Bellman--"

"Why's this bugging you? Jealousy?"

"Partly." There was no reason to lie.

"How's this for an educated guess? Bellman and I have got a terrific draw with Russo, and he's making us a ton of money. You're still all bent outa shape over that little Indian shit you let slip through your fat fingers a few years back, and you'd like another chance at the good life."

"That's not quite it. And by the way, the boy's Haitian."

"The point is, you haven't been able to find a decent draw anywhere in Allegheny County in the last five years and it's killing you. It's chafing your ass that two lucky amateurs, as you insist on referring to Bellman and me, have stumbled across this gold mine. Admit it."

The conceited little weasel was certainly right about that. But that wasn't the issue. Bellman and Moreland were mishandling Russo and could care less about the man's best interests. They saw a cash cow, snatched it up and were milking it dry. They either didn't know how to handle a talent like Russo or couldn't see past the pile of money the boy was raking in. Cassman had been in the business a long time and had learned a few things. He knew that if you wanted to thrive in the business, you treated a potential phenomenon like Jimmy Russo with kid gloves. Not as your personal slave.

"The kid's a great draw." Moreland finished his drink. "You can't get your dirty paws on him and it's killing you."

"It's killing me that you're not actually helping the boy."

"We're paying him."

"There's a lot more to this business than a paycheck."

"We're giving him a steady gig. Any idea how many other talents are out there, waiting tables? Or cleaning motel rooms?"

"Of course. I also know there's usually a legitimate reason why a great talent stays away from the stage. It could be a bipolar thing. It could be insecurity. He could be in the wrong town. Any number of--"

"Get to the point, Cassman. Like I said, I'm busy."

"My point is this: You could be paying him double what you're paying him and you'd still make a ton of money."

Moreland grunted. "Bender's been flapping his gums again. I should know better than tell that pompous gasbag anything. Cassman, this is a business. Both you and I know that. Hell, you more than most should know it. You've been playing this stupid game since the dinosaurs roamed the earth."

Cassman knew it was a game. He just didn't like hearing it coming from Moreland. When this little bastard said it, it sounded much dirtier than it was. But that wasn't the issue.

"You and Bellman are greedy, and you've been lucky enough to find a phenomenon. The thing that irks me is that neither of you has any goddamned idea what the hell you're--"

"He's that good, isn't he?"

Cassman wanted to use his knuckles to wipe the stupid grin off the other man's face. "You know he is."

"And you'd like to have him for yourself, right?"

"You know I would."

"What makes you think you'd be any better for him than we are?"

"I'd take much better care of him."

"Then why not make a phone call and talk to the boy's agent?" Moreland suddenly dropped his jaw and covered his mouth. When he lowered his hand, he added, "That's right. I forgot. Bellman and I *are* the kid's agents. How silly of me!"

"Yeah. Silly." Once again, Cassman thought about using his knuckles on the idiot's face.

"Okay, hotshot. Let's hear your proposal. I'll tell you right away what you can do with it and then you can go home and get ready for another slow day at your office tomorrow morning. Is that simple enough?"

"Since you obviously have no intention of listening to me, I'd say it's *too* simple."

"It would be a waste of time. Cassman, we've got an iron-clad contract with Russo. The kid signed it, and that's that. Now, if you don't mind." He jabbed a thumb at the door.

Cassman took a deep breath and tried one last time to appeal to Moreland's sense of fair play. "You're taking advantage of him. It's not fair."

Moreland sighed tiredly. "Russo's got a steady gig. He's a keeper. We both know it. The audience knows it, too. That's why they keep coming."

"A steady gig? That's all he deserves?"

"New flash, Cassman. Russo's a performer. Know what that means? Oops, that's right. You haven't handled one of those in a while. Well, here it is in a nutshell. A performer performs. On a stage. In front of an audience. For money."

"The boy's young. He's got dozens of productive years ahead of him. A better cut of the pie would--"

"It would spoil the kid. You know damn well what happens. You find a good act and give him a chance. He proves himself, then what? He hears all that applause, thinks he's a star and decides he wants more. You say no. He throws a tantrum and threatens to fuck up his act. Then you panic and decide to give in. You tell him you're gonna give him a fresh contract and rip up the old one. Well, guess what? He skips out on you and ends up in Vegas, making fifty grand a week, and you're back on Liberty Avenue, trying to figure out how you're gonna make next month's rent. Tell me I'm wrong."

Cassman hated it when a dirtbag like Moreland said something that was pretty much right-on. But that just didn't apply here. Moreland and Bellman were merely cashing in on a phenomenon. Cassman had no doubt whatsoever that the two would dump Russo the moment the boy's earnings dipped.

The door marked DRESSING ROOMS opened. Russo appeared in faded jeans, black tee shirt, a black windbreaker and gray athletic shoes.

Moreland's eyes lit up. "Cassman, if you really wanna have a little chat about the status quo, let's get it from the horse's mouth himself."

Cassman knew damned well that Russo wouldn't be able to speak with Moreland standing there. "This isn't really fair, you know. If you--"

"Russo! C'mon over here!" Moreland waved at him. To Cassman, he whispered, "Let's ask Golden Boy himself about his plans for his career."

***

At the far end of the bar, a neon sign marked RESTROOMS lit up the archway. Beyond it, a long, brightly lit hall went past the restrooms, payphones, a room marked CLOSET, and two unmarked doors.

At the end of the hall, nearly a dozen females had gathered in front of a door marked OFFICES/DRESSING ROOMS. Most of the women held drinks. All were smiling and acting giddy. One of them, a tall, bosomy redhead, tried the door. It held fast. She knocked and waited. It remained shut. The skinny, middle-aged blonde beside her pounded on it. When nothing happened, they both pounded and yelled. The others immediately joined in.

"Tifferoo?" Chip stood behind Tiffany, trembling. They were both about twenty feet from the unruly group. "You really wanna go through with this?"

Tiffany was also a little frightened. She knew how dangerous women were when they'd been drinking and grouped together. "Well, we do need to talk to him..."

"Can't you just email him or something?"

She patted the front of her tight jeans. "I guess I forgot to bring a computer along with me."

"You realize we'll have to get past this bunch if you wanna see this cute juggler guy of yours."

"His name is Jimmy Russo, and he's not exactly mine. And yes, I already got that."

He peered around her shoulder. The women were still pounding. One of them began kicking the door with her black leather boot and cursed when some of her drink spilled on the floor. "This could be dangerous. They're kind of crazy."

"That doesn't matter. We have to find out about him."

"I thought you'd already figured that out. Back there, you said--"

"We need to find out for sure."

"Is this all because you think he's cute?"

"He could be in trouble, just like we are."

He scowled. "Yeah, we wouldn't want to just leave things as they are, would we?"

"What fun would that be?"

"What if he's a bad boy? What if he's evil? What if he pulls the wings off butterflies and kicks little dogs, or superglues people's butts to barstools when they're not looking?"

"What?"

He shrugged. "I was on a roll."

"I don't think he's bad."

"How can you be sure? Lots of guys like him are bad. I should know. I can be a bad boy, too." He smiled sheepishly and wiggled his ears.

"I have this feeling about him."

"It's called lust, shady lady. You're still in mourning over your restaurant owner guy, and Russo reminds you of him."

"That's not it at all. You know we've got to find out what's going on before we can leave Ashley. If Jimmy's bad, and if there are others here just as bad, Breath Mint won't have any trouble finding her or us. I don't want him finding her--especially if we're not here to protect her."

"Who's gonna protect *us*, honey bunny?"

"At least we know how to blend in and disappear. Ashley doesn't. And don't forget, her uncle lives here. They're both vulnerable and mortal. They don't stand a chance against demons."

"Uncle Robby-boy flies all over the world. Ashley said he's only in town four months of the year."

"But he still lives here. And now, so does Ashley. We need to do something to make sure--"

"I know, I know." He stared at the drunken women. They were still yelling at the door. "Tifferoo, is this gonna be another Digger thing?"

"Whaddya mean?"

"I mean, if your cute juggler guy's in trouble--"

"You mean Jimmy Russo?"

"Yeah. Him."

She could tell he was being obstinate because he was frightened. But she knew he wouldn't purposely turn his back on someone in trouble. "You'd want help if you were in trouble, wouldn't you?"

"Before we take this any further, how are we gonna know if Russo's actually in trouble?"

"We ask him."

"What if he lies to us? If he really is a demon, he's not gonna be honest or trustworthy. Demons don't do honest or trustworthy."

"Would you lie if you were in trouble?"

"He doesn't know who we are, precious. When you don't know who you're talking to, you're not inclined to trust them. For all he knows, we might be working for Braithwaite. If you'll remember, that's exactly what we were doing in Florida."

"I'll know."

"Sorry. I forgot. Your head thingy, right?"

She smiled.

The door finally opened. A huge, mean-looking man in an ill-fitting suit appeared. He had dark hair cut close to the skull, tiny black eyes and a low forehead. He looked irritated. The women began arguing with him, demanding to see Jimmy Russo. He told them to go away. One of them tried slipping past him. He grabbed her arm and pulled her back from the doorway.

About twenty feet behind the bouncer, two men were standing out in the hall. One was large and broad, the other small and wiry. The bigger man had short curly brown hair, the small man glossy black hair. The little guy was grinning and looked drunk.

A moment later, Jimmy Russo appeared in the hall. The smaller man gestured, and Jimmy shuffled down the hall, toward them.

Tiffany turned to Chip. "Can you possibly cause some sort of distraction?"

"Anything in particular?"

"What do you think would scatter this crowd really fast?"

He went silent. A moment later, his face lit up. "Methinks now would be a nifty time for Elvis to return from the dead."

She blinked. "*You've* heard of Elvis?"

"Tifferoo, Bedouins know about Elvis. Now stand back. And be prepared to witness true greatness!"

Chapter 8

Moreland the weasel and a tall, broad guy in a nice-fitting suit stood outside the office. As usual, the little jerk had a glass in his hand. Judging by his jerky movements, he was as shitfaced as ever.

"Hey, kid." Moreland waved him over. "Someone wants to have a little chat with you."

Jimmy could tell Moreland was up to something. He'd never seen the other man before but could tell he had money. His suit was custom-tailored, his shoes imported. He also wore glittering cufflinks and a pricey-looking wristwatch. The man's hair was professionally styled, his green tie knotted impeccably.

As soon as Jimmy came closer, the man held out his hand. "Marc Cassman. It was a real pleasure to watch you work."

"Thank you." The man's handshake was firm and warm. "Glad you enjoyed it."

Sincerity and amazement showed clearly in Cassman's tiny blue eyes. "It's been a long time since I've seen such mastery, such showmanship. I commend you. As I watched you work--"

"Hey, kid." Moreland slapped Jimmy on the arm, instantly destroying the moment. "We need to settle something, right here and now. Cassman, here, thinks--"

"Elvis!"

A shriek shot down the hall. Then another. Then several gasps.

"It's Elvis!"

"My God! It's really him!"

Another shriek.

"What the fuck?" Moreland twisted around. "Hey! Ross!" He glared at the bouncer standing in front of the open doorway, grappling with a female. Behind her, a group of females were running after a dark-haired figure in a white outfit moving in the other direction, toward the front entrance. "What's going on down there? Do we need to get the damned cops in on this?"

"Elvis!"

"I *knew* you weren't dead!"

"It *can't* be him, silly! That's only an impersonator!"

"He looks too good to be an--"

A scream.

Ross pulled away as the female wrenched free and chased after the others. He was careful to block the doorway. "I got it, Boss. Looks like there's an Elvis impersonator wanderin' around out there."

"What the fuck is this? Vegas? Close that fucking door! We can't hear ourselves think!"

Just before Ross could close the door, Jimmy caught a glimpse of the blond beauty he'd seen in the audience during his act. She was standing off by herself, smiling at him. She wore a red tee shirt, faded jeans and red open-toed pumps sprinkled with silver sequins. Her honey-blond hair hung in ringlets over her shoulders. She had a perfect figure, and looked fabulous.

"Hi..."

The soft, alluring voice flowed inside his head, filling him with warmth. Without thinking, he started down the hall toward her.

Someone tapped his arm.

It was Moreland. "Where the hell you going? We're trying to have a little chat here."

The door slammed shut, snapping him back to harsh reality.

"Sorry." He couldn't get that gorgeous face--or that soft, sexy voice--out of his head.

Was it her voice? Or was it his imagination?

"I really enjoyed your act."

Damn. He heard it again.

He began rubbing his temples. He needed rest. He hadn't been getting much sleep lately. Aside from working here, staying close to the Bel-Mor so he wouldn't anger the Dark Lady, his days had been pretty damned--

"You okay, kid?"

Snap out of it. "I'm fine."

"Listen here, kid. Cassman wants to know if you're happy working with us."

Jimmy could hear the arrogance in his boss's voice. Moreland knew how Jimmy felt about their stupid contract. Both Moreland and Bellman knew Jimmy would be long gone if there had been any way to break the damned thing. But there wasn't--at least for now. Like it or not, Jimmy had to stay here.

Now he knew what was going on and what these two talking about. Cassman was obviously an agent. Jimmy should have been able to tell by the suit, the jewelry, and the rah-rah tone.

"Cassman thinks he can cut you a better deal. You know. More money, prestige, maybe even some travel. All that fancy crap that turns out to be, well, crap."

Cassman said, "Mister Russo--"

"Call me Jimmy."

"Jimmy, let me tell you a little about myself. I've been in this business--"

"Since the dinosaurs roamed the earth, kid." Moreland chuckled. "C'mon, Cassman. The kid doesn't wanna be bored to death."

"I'm just trying to tell him why I've--"

"Okay, kid." Moreland winked devilishly. "Ask him who he's representing right now. Go 'head."

Cassman's heavy features flushed.

Jimmy sighed. The little bastard had done it again. He truly loved embarrassing people. When Jimmy first met Moreland and Bellman, he could tell Moreland had a complex about his small stature. It didn't take Jimmy long to realize the little guy was more messed up than that. Jimmy had learned that ever since Moreland had married into the Hunt family, he'd more or less discarded his old self and expected everyone else to agree with this new mindset. Marrying into the right family had, in Moreland's own personal view, made him taller, better-looking, smarter, and intimidating. He'd become important and respectable. A local celebrity, and he'd even been a guest on *A.M. Pittsburgh*.

Ever since they'd revamped the Bel-Mor and started booking first-rate acts, Moreland considered himself a giant of industry. He even claimed to be friends with Josh Madigan, one of the richest men in the country, and never tired of telling everyone the story about him and Madigan playing eighteen holes at one of Madigan's South Hills golf courses.

Moreland owned and operated one of the biggest and most profitable nightclubs in the city. And everyone coming into it--as well as everyone working there--owed him a great debt of thanks.

And this included Jimmy Russo.

"I really appreciate you coming to see me, Mister Cassman." Jimmy had no choice but to end this quickly. There was no need for Moreland to embarrass the man any further. For an agent, Marc Cassman seemed a nice man. But Jimmy had to face facts. He was stuck here, and there was no need to waste time and energy discussing it. "I know you have my best interests at heart, but I'm happy here."

Cassman stared at him. Jimmy could feel the big man trying to understand what was wrong, why he refused to discuss it. Cassman couldn't possibly know that even if Moreland wasn't standing there, Jimmy would still have to turn him down.

"You're satisfied with how your career's going?"

Jimmy sighed. "Yes, sir."

"There's nothing I can do or say that'll change your mind?"

"Give it a rest." Moreland was giving Jimmy his special glare. Jimmy had seen it many times before and knew how easily the little man pitched a fit if things didn't go his way.

“Thanks anyway, Mr. Cassman.”

The big man nodded and forced a smile. “My office is right on Market--”

“The kid said to take a hike. Didn’tcha, kid?”

“Like I said, it was nice of you to come back and see me.” Jimmy held out his hand.

Cassman took it. “Sorry we couldn’t come to some sort of mutual agreement.”

“Maybe another time?”

“Count on it.” Cassman reluctantly took his eyes from Jimmy and turned to Moreland. “Sorry I took up so much of your time.”

“Can’t blame ya for trying, can we?” Moreland was craning his neck, grinning, thrusting out his narrow chest. “C’mon back tomorrow night. The kid’ll probably have something even better to show you. Right, kid?”

Jimmy remained silent. Cassman gave him one last nod before moving away. As the big man shuffled down the hall, Jimmy knew full well that he’d probably just made the biggest mistake of his career.

“Hey, kid.” Another tap on his shoulder.

He turned.

“C’mon in.” Moreland opened his office door. “I need to give you your allowance for tonight’s work.”

As always, Jimmy forced himself not to kick the pompous jerk right in his scrawny ass.

***

Tiffany followed four giddy customers outside through the front entrance. They were all chattering away about Jimmy Russo's juggling act. One woman said how cute Russo was while her date wondered how a magician could take off his shoes in the middle of a juggling act without anyone noticing.

"It wasn't magic," the second guy said. "Someone working up in the rafters did all the work."

"How?"

"He added the shoes to the mix in the middle of the act. Just dropped them with the rest of the stuff."

"You mean when Jimmy went back onstage after his diamond trick?" the first girl said. "He was wearing shoes. I saw them."

"You sure?" the first guy asked.

"Now that you mention it," she said, "I'm not sure if I'm positive. I'm sure I'm *reasonably* sure, I'm just not *totally* sure I'm positive..."

"Jules, you're a mess."

"What does that have to do with the shoe trick?"

"He took them off way before that," the second guy said.

"You mean he went on without his shoes?" asked his date.

"I definitely saw shoes on his feet," Jules said.

"He slipped them off when the spotlight focused on the beer bottle and baseball," the second guy said. "The spot was on the stuff he was juggling. The light didn't even reach his waist. Since it was dark, we couldn't see anything. That's how they do it. Distraction--not magic."

"Sure looked like magic to me."

"Maybe he was standing near a trapdoor. That's an old building. They've got trap doors and cool stuff everywhere."

"That's another thing," Jules said. "Where'd the beer bottle come from?"

"The guy in the rafters. He had everything ready to go."

"What about the dove? The baseball? The bat?"

"I'm still thinking about that diamond. It couldn't possibly be real."

"What about all those mirrors that just disappeared when he tossed them?"

"Where'd he get them?"

"Pulled them out of his jacket."

"Impossible. No one can carry stuff like that in their pockets."

"I still think it was magic."

"What *are* you, Linda? Twelve?"

It was *magic*, Tiffany wanted to tell them. *Magic from a different world.* But she knew better. People just didn't believe in magic. They refused to accept things they didn't understand.

Anyway, she had more important things on her mind. She had to find Chip. The last she saw him, he was dodging females. His Elvis costume was way too authentic. So were his looks. She guessed that unless he did some quick thinking, he was going to be in serious trouble. Those women chasing him were dangerous.

Tiffany walked over to a park bench and sat down. Two women hurried by, chattering away.

They stopped about five feet from Tiffany's bench. While one of them scanned the street, the other turned to Tiffany. She had a wild expression on her face. Even in the dim orange light of the streetlamp, Tiffany could see the woman's glossy eyes. "Have you seen Elvis out here somewhere?"

"Elvis?"

"That's what I said."

"Costello?"

The other one stopped looking around and glared.

The first one said, "Who the fuck cares about *him*?"

Tiffany shrugged. "Someone has to--"

"Have you seen him or what? Presley--not Costello."

"He's been dead more than thirty years. You must be looking for an impersonator. "

"This guy looked better than any impersonator *I* ever saw."

"It was him," her friend said. "We know it was."

"He's dead," Tiffany said. "Everyone knows that. If he was alive, he'd be eighty by now."

The first one glared. "Who asked ya?"

They both grunted before hurrying away.

"I'll let him know you're looking for him if I see him," Tiffany yelled after them.

Neither responded.

Tiffany sat back and crossed her legs. The streets were busy with traffic. People were running around, laughing, yelling and dodging vehicles.

Small groups huddled at the corner, sharing blunts. A couple of young guys glanced her way but didn't come over. Good deal. She wasn't in the mood for any trouble.

A short, skinny redheaded woman around sixty years old in a baggy yellow tee shirt, black sweats and scuffed white tennies staggered by and abruptly stopped. She squinted at Tiffany. "Tifferoo?"

She sighed in relief. "The coast is clear."

Chip gave the street a quick scan then turned back into himself. "Damn. I thought I'd *never* get rid of them!" He plopped down beside her and ran both hands briskly through his red mop. "They grabbed me in the bar and my life flashed before my eyes. Believe it or not, demons aren't nearly as scary as drunk, horny women. Luckily it was crowded and dark in there, so I just dropped to the floor, rolled underneath a couple of tables and turned back into myself."

"Did it work?"

"It got the women off my ass, but a tall guy with slicked-back blond hair and really tight pants sashayed over and sat down beside me. He wanted to take me to his apartment and do some weird things involving handcuffs, a jar of honey and a gas mask. I distracted him by asking him a question about one of the muscle guys sitting at the table behind him. As soon as he turned around, I made myself into the homeless lady and snuck out of there. How about you? Did you get to talk to your juggler guy?"

"Not yet."

His ears twitched. "You mean I did all that for nothing?"

"As soon as you turned into Elvis and those women started after you, that bouncer closed the door in the hall."

He shook his head. "Mortals. You can't live with 'em and you can't kill 'em because they made it a capital crime." He patted her arm. "You'll get your chance, muffin. He has to go home, so he'll probably be coming out of the building any time now."

Tiffany stared at the brightly-lit entrance. She didn't have a good feeling about what she'd seen outside the office. She didn't like that ugly little guy with the greasy black hair. He looked evil.

But at least she'd been able to get into Jimmy's head. If he was truly a demon, he'd be able to figure things out and would want to get back with her.

But no matter what Chip had said earlier, she was convinced Jimmy was a good guy. Tiffany could tell by his eyes. They were just as soft and as dreamy as Lou's eyes.

Chapter 9

Moreland took his time opening the office wall safe.

He slowly opened the door, pulled out a drawer, grabbed a thick stack of money and carefully peeled off several bills. Then, with his usual smirk, he dropped them into Jimmy's awaiting palm.

Jimmy counted the bills. Ten twenties. Two hundred bucks. Just like the night before.

Something was wrong. He stared at the money with contempt. He saw defeat in his hand. Defeat and frustration. And humiliation. He was so much better than this. He'd just mesmerized three hundred people, rocked their world for forty solid minutes.

Moreland closed the safe and went back to the desk. He watched Jimmy, that smug expression showing so prominently on his dark features. *I did it to you again,* it clearly said. *And you didn't even have to bend over for it.*

Jimmy took a breath to collect himself. "This afternoon you mentioned giving me a bonus if I pulled in a larger audience tonight."

Moreland poured more Scotch into his glass. "Sorry, kid, but the crowd didn't look any bigger than last night."

"I saw a line stretching from one side of the room to the other. Just like last night."

"Last night's line was thicker. More than sixty. Tonight, there were only forty-two."

"Really?"

"Bruno did a thorough head-count. He was standing right there behind the bar. He'd know for sure. And Andy did a check at the door and said two-ninety. That's two hundred for the room, forty-eight in the bar, and forty-two standing behind the last row. Two separate checks couldn't be off. Last night, we topped three hundred."

Jimmy watched Moreland raising the glass to his lips and knew the man was lying. He couldn't be sure, of course. He'd been much too busy concentrating on his act. And the lighting hadn't helped. But he was certain tonight's crowd was bigger; he just couldn't prove it. Bruno would say anything Moreland told him to. Bruno was six-six and went two-fifty, but was intimidated by Moreland. This little bastard knew how to push people around.

Moreland finished his drink and gave the wall clock a quick glance. "It's nearly midnight, kid. Time to head on home. We'll let the drinking folks close the club for us. How 'bout a ride home, as usual?"

Jimmy had no choice. His twelve-year-old Camaro sat in the shop. He had no other way to get back to his Penn Avenue apartment. He'd been forced to rely on Moreland and Bellman to shuttle him to and from the club for the last five days. He didn't have enough cash for a new car. Luckily, the mechanic had been nice enough to keep the car at the shop for ninety days while Jimmy collected the money for the rebuilt transmission. Jimmy hoped he could afford it. Once he paid his rent and took care of his other obligations, he'd be almost broke again.

He followed his boss outside through the back, where Moreland's light-gray Porsche was parked behind the big block building under its roof on sticks next to the exit door and within range of the moving cameras mounted at each corner of the building. Moreland backed out of the space, crossed the gravel lot and took the powerful car up the side street, to the main drag in front of the Bel-Mor. Just before Moreland tore out onto Penn, he stabbed a thumb toward his left, where two figures sat on the park bench in front of the club.

Jimmy glanced to his left. One was the blonde he'd seen in the club. The other, the redheaded guy who'd been sitting with her.

"There are blond bimbos wandering around everywhere tonight, kid." Moreland made a disgusting grunting noise. "Too bad we gotta get you back to your pad. I'd give her a few bucks so you could whip off a piece before bedtime, but since we don't know where she came from, she might give you a little something extra. If you catch my drift. Your contract doesn't allow for a hospital stay, kid. That would cost us money."

Jimmy wanted to belt the sleazy little bastard.

Just as Moreland made the right onto Penn Avenue, the soft, breathy voice entered his head once again:

"*My name is Tiffany.*"

He twisted around in the seat until his back popped. Due to the dimness of the streetlamp, she was out of range, but he could tell she was smiling at him.

Her voice drifted over a second time:

"We need to talk."

"Easy, kid." Moreland chuckled as he raced the sleek sports car down the well-lit street. "You need a bucket of ice water dumped on your lame brain?"

Jimmy barely heard what his boss had just said. He was much too concerned about what the soft voice had just told him.

How did she do that? How did she get into his head?

Was she even real?

No normal person could inject their thoughts into someone else's head. It was pretty clear she was an extraordinary lady. He knew right then that he had to somehow find out more about her.

"Let me out."

"Kid, you're going home--"

"I really like to see that--"

"Kid, I'm your damned boss, and I'm telling you to hold your water!"

Jimmy sat back and forced himself to stay calm. The urge to do something painful to the nasty man beside him was overwhelming. But that would only make things worse. Besides, he'd been there before. Hurting people just wasn't his thing.

"Kid, don't worry about it, okay? This city's got good-looking hookers everywhere. While you're under contract with us, I'm gonna make damn sure you don't pick up anything that'll put you in the hospital."

Jimmy stared straight ahead and decided not to waste any more energy on the contemptible weasel sitting next to him. Strangely, he found that he wasn't as angry as he should be. He had a strong feeling he was going to hear from Tiffany again.

***

Tifferoo was acting weird again, gazing at the sportscar that had crept up the side street next to the Bel-Mor. She didn't take her eyes off it even after it had pulled onto Penn Avenue and became part of the long, jumbled serpent of lights slithering to the next intersection.

Chip had known her long enough to realize something was up. "What's going on, honey bunny?"

She blinked. "Going on?"

Yep, he was right. She had slipped on her clueless expression. He could practically hear the gears grinding inside that beautiful golden melon.

"Don't try pulling that dumb blond stuff on me, princess. Both of us know you're not dumb, so start flapping those luscious lips. I need to know what's going on."

"You're right. You do."

"Great. So we're all agreed. Now…whenever you're ready, I'm all ears." He wiggled them.

"I just told Jimmy who I am."

"When?"

"He was in that Porsche that just took off. I used my head thing to talk to him."

This didn't make sense. "How'd you know he was in that car? It's dark out here, even with the streetlamps. And those car windows were dark."

"It was a feeling I had."

Damn. She was doing it again. "I should've known."

She shrugged. "Sorry. Can't help it. I know you're jealous--"

"Me? Jealous? Now why would I be jealous? Just because I've been a demon for two thousand years, and here you are, dead only a few months and not even a demon, and you can already do more stuff than I could ever do?"

She smiled sheepishly. "Something like that."

"Good. For a moment I thought I was imagining all this."

She moved closer and pushed some heavy gold locks over her right shoulder. He could tell she was about to say something meaningful and tender. Her baby blues were enormous. Even in the dark he could see that dimple in her cheek. He loved Tiffers, but she could be nauseatingly female at times.

"I wouldn't feel so bad if I were you," she said softly. "My powers have gotten us out of some serious jams."

He groaned. Other times, she could be nauseatingly right-on. "I guess you could be right."

"No hard feelings, then?"

"Just don't expect me to get out the beads and sing Kumbaya, all righty?"

She stood. "Actually, we ought to get back to the hotel. I don't know about you, but I'm really tired. I have to think of our strategy in the morning."

"Strategy? We're doing strategy now?"

"I think we should, don't you?"

"Dammit, Tifferoo. You know how bored and confused I get whenever we do strategy."

"I'll be gentle, I promise."

"Just make sure I've got some idea what we're doing. I don't like being a shithead *all* the time, you know."

"I thought that was your thing."

"Every once in a while I like to have a genuine *clue* of where I'm going. I get tired of whacking my head against the wall so much."

"We have to talk to Jimmy. We won't be able to leave Pittsburgh if we don't know what's going on here."

"Yuck. A fate worse than death."

She sighed. "Did *you* have something in mind?"

"Tiffers, when have you ever known me to have something in mind?"

"True."

"But you're right about getting back to the hotel. This time, I suggest we both focus on sleep. I know how you like getting frisky, and I know I can be pretty irresistible at times, but sometimes a guy needs--"

"When was I ever frisky with you?"

"There was that time in Orlando when you--no, that wasn't you. Maybe I'm thinking about that other time--"

"You obviously have me confused with someone else."

"A guy can fantasize, can't he?"

"Sometimes that's all he can do." She started moving away.

"Tifferoosky? Before we head on out, could you please tone it down a tad?"

"Whaddya mean?"

She could really be dense at times.

"There are a lot of folks out tonight, and you look pretty hot. Not that I'm complaining. But I am kinda tired from dodging hysterical females and too chickenshit to step in if we run into a gang of horny guys or street punks."

"Oh." She looked down at herself and closed her eyes. Moments later, her perky puppies went flat. Her honey-blond hair turned dark and frizzy, and her tee shirt and jeans became a loose-fitting sweatshirt and baggy sweats. Her custom-designed red sandals turned into a pair of mud-caked tennies. "Better?"

"Much. But don't get too close. You don't smell so good."

"Is that your crude way of telling me you've finished fantasizing?"

"Just make sure you turn back into tantalizing, titillating Tifferoo, the tough, tangy tart, by the time we get back to the hotel. Otherwise, I won't be able to have my usual wet dreams."

"You're a mess." She swatted his shoulder. "And I'm not a tart."

DAY THREE

Pittsburgh, Pennsylvania

Chapter 10

Braithwaite's Airstream Jet charter, the Falcon 900, carried a single passenger, a man listed only on the manifest as "J. Smith." The plane landed at Pittsburgh International at forty-seven minutes after midnight. The short 98-minute flight had been uneventful, except for the call from Daniel Grove, supplying Andras vital information about the important job at hand.

"Mr. Waite has got several things he wants you to know concerning your itinerary," Grove said.

"I'm listening." Andras, comfortable in his seat, sipped his drink.

"You're going to be met at the airport by a man dressed as a chauffeur. He will take you directly by limousine to your hotel. He's been told nothing but the time he's to pick you up and the route he's to use to take you to your accommodations. He's at your disposable. He will take you wherever you need to be taken. He's a good man and has been well-paid for his services. Is that clear?"

"Yes." This was beginning to sound much like the job he'd been given by Balberith in '63, when he was sent by private charter to Dallas. His instructions for that job were also simple. He was to find a long-range, disposable firearm, pick a secluded spot on Dealey Plaza and fire one shot only into the front of the open Presidential motorcade. He was given a detailed map and a time window, including an escape route and return trip in a specified vehicle to the private airport owned by a Diocese member, who happened to be one of the highest-ranking officials in the Dallas Police Force. The job took just three hours of his time. Andras was back in Chicago that same evening.

"Your accommodations have been arranged," Grove continued. "Once you've been picked up and taken to your lodging, you're free to begin your search. A cellphone has been placed in your hotel room, in the table drawer between the beds. It is a prepaid burn phone and has an untraceable SIM card. You're free to use it as you wish. Questions?"

"Is it equipped with a directory?"

"There is only one number programmed into the unit. It is the only number you'll require. You will not need to contact anyone else."

"Understood."

"You're to find the three individuals requested, use any method necessary to put them on the same charter jet you've been provided, and return to Orlando with them as soon as possible. Is that clear?"

"Yes."

"Mr. Waite wants this mission completed within forty-eight hours."

Pittsburgh was a fairly large city, with a population of more than two and a half million. Forty-eight hours wasn't much time, but Andras had accepted this job and knew better than voice any doubts. "Agreed."

Shortly before one o'clock, after the plane landed and taxied to the gate, Andras went down the ramp and was met inside the crowded terminal by a tall, broad man about fifty years old, with a gray brush cut, small dark eyes and a perpetual scowl. He wore the blue uniform of a chauffeur. The brass name plate over his jacket pocket said DAHL.

"Mr. Smith?" The chauffeur's voice was soft and low-pitched, with a slight British accent.

Andras nodded.

"Any luggage?"

"None." Andras followed the big man outside, where a freshly-washed black limo awaited. Dahl opened the rear door. Andras got in. Dahl closed Andras' door, got behind the wheel and pulled away.

"Where are we going?" Andras figured it wouldn't hurt to know where they'd booked him.

"The Wyndham Grand on Commonwealth Place, sir," Dahl said. "It's one of the best places in Pittsburgh, and in a convenient location."

The Wyndham Grand. He'd never been there, but it sounded nice. Sounded expensive, too. Braithwaite had pulled out all the stops on this venture. "Were you told anything else?"

"I'm to stay with the limo and await instructions by phone, sir."

Andras glanced at his watch. "It's one in the morning."

Dahl eyed the luminous dash clock. "It's one-oh-two, sir."

Grove was right: this man had obviously been paid well. Why else would he willingly wait in a limousine for what could be hours at a time? Judging by the jet, the hotel and its location, Andras guessed huge funds were involved. Braithwaite was probably working directly with the Pittsburgh Diocese. No one else would have such unlimited resources so readily available.

"Were you told how long you might have to wait?"

"However long it takes, sir."

Andras sat back in his seat. He had a feeling he wasn't going to be here long enough to spend much time in his hotel room.

"If you'd like a drink, sir, the liquor cabinet is located in the console beside you. The red button will open it."

Andras pressed the button. A well-lit silver drawer stocked with small bottles, glasses, and an ice bucket slid silently out of the black leather-lined console.

Andras knew then that he was in very good hands.

***

Corporate mogul Joshua Sinclair Madigan nervously paced the spacious living room of his sixteen-room Oakland penthouse suite, obsessing about the call he'd received a few hours ago from Orlando. It was now past seven, and after a vigorous cold morning shower and two large cups of very strong black coffee, he was still moving around like a nervous cat. Using sheer will power, he'd managed to collect himself just enough to make the necessary arrangements resulting from the Orlando call. He knew his orders would be strictly obeyed but also realized his entire world would crumble in an instant if anything went wrong.

As developer of six high-rises in the Pittsburgh Metro area, contractor for a dozen of the city's nearly five hundred bridges, CEO of a software company and sole owner of three prestigious golf courses in the Tristate area, Madigan had been dealing daily with heavy doses of stress for years. Stress was a large part of life and an even larger part of big business. Without it, you achieved nothing. Without its motivation, you never knew who you were, what you were capable of.

At 45, Madigan had built up a solid reputation over the last fifteen years, thanks to his incredible resources and legendary good luck. Tall, good-looking and athletically built, he inspired envy and admiration wherever he went. He'd stopped being humble years ago. A self-made billionaire who employed two thousand people and had daily contact with thousands more, Madigan bowed to no one. But he knew his place when he found himself dealing with someone with the power to turn even the most powerful men on earth into blithering idiots in the blinking of an eye.

Despite the late hour, the call from Orlando should have been a good thing. Madigan had been to Orlando dozens of times in the last fifteen years.

He loved the weather, the skies, the beaches, and the bikinis. He met three of his four ex-wives in the Central Florida area. The golf courses were the best in the state, and with the cooperation of influential friends like Richard Grove, Madigan's business trips always turned out profitable.

However, he'd felt his blood instantly turn cold when Grove's son Daniel called to discuss a matter of major concern regarding Balbor's successor.

A Diocese member for most of his adult life, Madigan fully expected to be contacted about this shift in power. He just hadn't expected to hear about it from Daniel Grove, rather than Daniel's father, a man Madigan had known and respected for years. None of the other Pittsburgh members realized Balbor's predecessor had even arrived until Bob Skyler, Director of PGH/Softwares, Inc., learned about it at a business luncheon organized by the Glaser Group in the Hilton Orlando at Bonnet Creek Resort Lane. When Skyler returned from Orlando last week, he arranged for a quick luncheon at the John Forbes Club to give the members the vital news. As usual, most of the other twelve members were handling business ventures elsewhere, leaving only Skyler, Madigan, H. B. Folsom, and L. Masters Chesney in attendance. Skyler's assessment of the situation had not been positive. Skyler hadn't met Balbor's predecessor, a man calling himself Brett Waite, but mentioned the Group's apprehensions upon learning Waite's plans to sell off large parcels of Florida land to Saudi contacts with terrorist ties.

Madigan was very surprised Richard Grove's son had called, especially at that late hour. And when Daniel mentioned Waite by name early in the conversation, Madigan knew the call was important. Without the leadership of super demons, there could be no Diocese. Without the Diocese, Madigan--as well as the other thousands of super-rich running the world--would be in the same position they were in before making the Pledge.

For Madigan, the Pledge had been a decision he'd never regretted. Since that well-remembered day exactly one year before he'd graduated from Carnegie-Mellon University, his position in life had leaped dramatically. Everything he did from that day forward panned out. His luck consistently ran hot. Decisions were made in his favor. Doors opened for him. People stepped aside, surrendered or vanished. From then on, he could not make a wrong decision. His destiny was forever etched in stone.

Even so, this unexpected phone call had been enough to get Madigan's stress level up to the dangerous level.

"Is this a protected line, Mr. Madigan?" The question was asked as soon as Daniel Grove had identified himself.

"Yes."

"Then I'll speak freely. I understand you personally knew Mr. Balbor."

"He spent a weekend at my penthouse suite a number of years ago, before he moved to Manhattan to open his new offices. I considered him very intelligent and dignified. He was also very demanding and intolerant of failure or weakness."

"I personally never met the man, but my father spoke highly of him. Mr. Balbor apparently provided invaluable assistance to the Glaser Group when he came to Florida and stayed for a month or so in the early seventies, I believe."

Madigan knew to choose his next words carefully. "This Mr. Waite. Can you tell me anything about him?"

Grove's deep sigh made Madigan even more apprehensive. Madigan had learned to interpret phone language long ago. Grove's sigh had transferred fear, caution, and anxiety across the nine-hundred-mile line. Madigan knew right then that Daniel Grove was terrified of his employer.

"Mr. Waite is very demanding, powerful, and extremely intimidating. He's huge--six-six and around three hundred and fifty pounds, with a booming voice, abrupt manner and hair-trigger temper. He doesn't tolerate insubordination and specializes in explosions as a form of relaxation."

"Explosions?"

"Before making me his protégée, Mr. Waite blew up a BMW in the middle of Church Street, while my father and I were having lunch."

Madigan winced. "What was the purpose for that?"

"He said he wanted to make sure we believed who he was."

Madigan wanted to ask more questions but refrained from doing so. As he'd told Grove, this was his personal line, and very secure. However, super demons were notoriously clever and ingenious. They'd have no problem tapping a secure phone line. He chose his next words wisely. "It sounds like Mr. Waite demands results. I admire that, and I assume he rewards loyalty. Balbor did that same thing."

"Everything will be fine as long as his instructions are followed. I can personally vouch for his knowledge and experience. Under his guidance, I've made more money in four weeks than most people earn in ten years."

"What exactly are you doing down there?"

"I'm involved in the escort industry Mr. Waite has set up."

Madigan and the other members had heard rumors that the industry in that area had spiked dramatically in the last couple of months. Being businessmen, they could tell something had changed, especially since the Orlando Police Department had increased their revenues to fight such crime only a year or two before and announced that crime had been dropping as a result.

"In what capacity?"

"I'm running them. When Mr. Waite put me in charge, many of the other outfits in Central Florida went out of business in just a few weeks. Some were bought out. Those who chose to stay are now working for me directly."

"We've heard about the shakeup. He obviously works very quickly."

"Mr. Waite doesn't like wasting time."

"Things are definitely happening. I just read online about the monument the American Atheists have unveiled in front of the courthouse down there in Stark. Did Waite have something to do with that?"

"Mr. Waite makes dozens of calls each day. Many are made directly to Capitol Hill. He also has associates in the Middle East. For the last few days, there have been daily three-party conference calls connected to Washington, D.C."

"Interesting." Madigan wondered if this had anything to do with what Skyler had told them about Waite's land deal ending with an unexpected snag. Going through Syria could be another way of dealing with the Arabs. The new arms deal, obviously. Madigan didn't approve of Muslim terrorist camps over here, but he knew better than voice his opposition with those responsible for making him wealthy. Talking about something like this with a mere protégé would not be wise. Besides, Madigan was more interested in finding out the purpose for the call. "Tell me how I can help you."

"Mr. Waite is sending a representative to Pittsburgh to find three people. This man will arrive at Pittsburgh International by personal charter around one o'clock in the morning. He's to have complete access to anything he requires and taken anywhere he wishes. He's been given forty-eight hours to accomplish his task."

Forty-eight hours to find three people? In a city the size of Pittsburgh? Again, Madigan knew better than raise questions.

"Understood."

"The rep is going by the name Smith. He'll require immediate transportation and an unregistered cellphone with a hookup directly to your private line. Is this acceptable to you?"

"I'll have him met at the airport and taken to a centrally located hotel, preferably one of mine. I'll make sure someone reliable handles the accommodations as well as the cellphone. Everything will be arranged by my personal assistant, who has direct access to every major databank. I also own a security company that handles security cameras and monitors for many of my buildings, as well as those of most of my associates. In other words, we have twenty-four-seven access to just about every face on every sidewalk in a sixteen-block area."

"Excellent. I'll tell Mr. Waite we can rely on you completely."

"Can you tell me a little more about this?"

"As I said, Mr. Waite wants three people returned to him. Two of them are from the Darkworld. The other is a mortal female. We are ninety percent sure this female might have fled to Pittsburgh to be with her uncle, who we understand is affiliated with the fashion business there. His name is Robert Belasco. The niece's name is Ashley Parker."

Madigan clicked the record option on his phone and asked Grove to repeat the names. Once Grove complied, Madigan said, "So there could be a chance they aren't in the Tristate area?"

"Smith has been sent there to find out immediately."

"Tell me about the other two."

"One is a female, the other presumably a male."

"Presumably?"

"There's some question about that. The female is an attractive blonde. Her name is Tiffany LeBouf. Apparently she isn't a demon."

"What *is* she?"

"Mr. Waite won't talk much about it. He said only that she was briefly in the Darkworld. Her partner's name is Chip, who is an inferior. Chip is a short, skinny redhead, and like I said, can be either sex."

"What have they done?"

"They crossed Mr. Waite."

Enough said. "Tell me about the Parker woman."

A pause. "She's nineteen, with long, thick black hair and large dark-brown eyes. She's slender, long-legged and small-breasted. She's also soft-spoken, with dimples and a great smile--" Grove stopped abruptly and cleared his throat. When he spoke again, his voice sounded different. "If she is there, she'll hook up with Belasco. He's successful in his field and has the money and contacts to help her. He shouldn't be difficult to find."

Madigan could tell something was going on. Grove's description sounded personal. Madigan knew better than dig for details. He had all he needed. "And once they're found?"

"Smith will bring them back to Orlando."

Madigan clicked off record. "I think I've got all I need."

"I'll be communicating with Smith on a regular basis until this matter is finished. You can call me at any time. As I'm sure you know by now, this is high priority. Mr. Waite wants these three returned badly."

"I'll get on this immediately and will give your man every available resource."

Chapter 11

At eight o'clock that morning, Tiffany and Chip took the elevator down to the elegant dining room of the Renaissance Pittsburgh Hotel, where they were escorted by a tall, fresh-faced young waiter to a window booth. Over a light breakfast of toast and coffee, Tiffany watched the morning traffic chugging along toward the intersection, while shoppers and well-dressed men and women dodged each other in their frantic haste to reach the light at the end of the block.

She and Chip had been staying at the Renaissance since Ashley moved in with her Uncle Rob, a tall, slender, soft-spoken man in his mid-forties who dressed well and smiled often. He was very grateful to them for keeping an eye on Ashley and offered them a spare bedroom in his Chatham Center penthouse suite for the duration of their stay. However, the prospect of sharing a room with Chip didn't appeal to Tiffany. Instead of trying to explain their relationship, she'd told Belasco that he and Ashley should be allowed to enjoy their reunion privately, and not have to worry about anyone intruding.

Belasco graciously respected Tiffany's wishes. A simple phone call to the Renaissance solved the matter. A four-room suite, used regularly to accommodate Belasco Fashions' international guests, provided the perfect solution. The rooms were comfortable and air-conditioned, with a lavishly furnished living room, two cozy bedrooms and a luxurious bathroom suite. The staff at the hotel was told that Mr. Belasco's two new guests could stay there as long as they wished.

Even though things had gone great so far, Tiffany couldn't shake her uneasiness. Ashley was obviously happy to be with her uncle and eager to start a new life. However, Tiffany just couldn't ignore the fact that Daniel Grove knew where Ashley's mother lived. Daniel had become Breath Mint's pawn and did whatever the demon demanded. Even if Daniel still had feelings for Ashley, it no longer mattered. His spirit now belonged to Breath Mint.

The dreary morning did nothing to help lift Tiffany's spirits. The city of Pittsburgh painted an eerie picture in the early morning hours. Fog clinging to the skyscrapers mingled with puffy mists coming up from the valley, covering the hills with a heavy gray veil. The city itself was smeared with soot, its air saturated with the foulness of exhaust fumes and dirty water slithering up from the Monongahela River. Its darkness and depression mirrored the cold, nerve-shattering hopelessness that had consumed her when the wolf guy had yanked her from the beautiful meadow shortly after her death, into the outer ring of Hell, forcing her into the Valley of Decay.

She knew she was being silly. Pittsburgh was a city much like many of the others she'd seen. Peoria, where she grew up, wasn't much different. Neither was L.A. in the early morning hours. Fog, mist and foulness clung heavily to cities everywhere with the start of a new day. With the exception of the weather, Pittsburgh wasn't much different from Orlando. Mortals lived and worked here. Nothing evil or sinister about it, was there? And if she and Chip hadn't gone to the Bel-Mor the night before, they might have already decided that Ashley was in good hands and that it was okay to leave Pittsburgh.

But they *had* gone into the Bel-Mor. They'd seen a good-looking, well-dressed, charismatic young man woo a capacity crowd with a juggling act that was pure magic. It was the kind of magic no one expected to see in a live nightclub act. It had all the stuff one saw only in dreams, hallucinations, or visions.

But this *wasn't* a dream, a hallucination, or a vision. It was the genuine article, and it happened on a live stage, before their very eyes. Without special lighting, mirrors or fancy props. And both of them knew beyond any doubt that anyone capable of such magnificence could not be mortal.

Their next step was to find out what sort of spirit Jimmy was. Tiffany had seen many since her death and had learned that, despite the common mortal belief that all demons were malevolent, some were not. Chip and Digger both possessed good qualities and would have ended up somewhere else if negative energy hadn't followed them after their deaths. Negative energy wasn't restricted to mortal life.

Negative or not, they had to find out more about Jimmy before deciding if they should leave the city.

"We've got to find him." She turned away from the window. "The sooner, the better."

Chip sat facing her, drinking ice water from the pitcher in front of him. "The juggler guy?"

"Now who else would I be talking about?"

"I don't know, muffin. Sometimes your state of ultimate blondeness makes things downright confusing."

"Stop and try to be serious."

"All righty-rooty, but only if you tell me which I should do first."

"You're boring."

"What does *that* have to do with anything?"

"Work with me here, all right? We've got to find Jimmy Russo."

"Now why didn't you say that the first time?"

Tiffany rubbed her eyes. "I'm saying it now, okay?"

"Nifty. Any ideas?"

"We ask around."

"Now why didn't I think of that?"

"I don't know. Why didn't you?"

He took another huge slug of ice water. "Right now, my brain feels slightly waterlogged. It's tough thinking about anything when your brain's all soggy."

"It's no wonder. That's your second pitcher."

"Water's great for the petals, angel."

"The folks in the kitchen are beginning to talk."

"About me?"

"They keep staring as they walk by."

"They're probably gawking at your perky puppies. I can't blame them. By the way, they look especially delicious this morning."

"Stop it. Everyone's looking at *you,* silly."

He beamed. "It must be my roguish masculine charm."

"Or maybe it's that disgusting plate of stale coffee grounds you've been sucking down."

He turned toward the kitchen. "They keep forgetting my eggshells."

She had a sip of orange juice. "I say we leave here and head straight to the Bel-Mor."

"It won't be open."

"Of course it won't be open, silly. It doesn't open until lunchtime."

"So what do we do? Stand around and look stupid? Or, in your case, hot and spicy?"

"How will my looking hot and spicy help us find Jimmy?"

"You're the one who brought it up."

"We should go on over there and see what we can turn up. We're liable to meet someone who might know him. If we can find out where he's living, that would be great."

"And you actually think you can find out if he's good or bad just by--"

"Yes. I honestly do."

"That's right. I keep forgetting--your nifty head thingy. Why waste time talking to a guy when all you have to do is jump right in there and have a quick look around in his jeans?"

She frowned. "You mean his head."

"That, too."

"In this case, we need to do this quickly. I have a feeling it won't take Breath Mint long to figure out where we are."

Chip's tiny green eyes bulged. "Tifferoo, you aren't, by any chance, picking up anything in the air that--"

"I just don't want to take any chances. Do you?"

"You know me better than that." He finished the second pitcher and picked up the pen lying beside the check on the small black plastic tray at his elbow.

She watched him closely. "Be careful what you sign this time. We don't want anyone calling Ashley's uncle again and asking if someone's wrong with us."

"All I'm doing is signing my name."

"Yesterday you signed your plant genus thing that sounds like Surreptitious Calculator. Lucky for you I caught it in time."

He frowned and his ears twitched. "The name, my delicious but somewhat dense blond beauty, is Cypripedium Calceolus. How long have we known one another? I should think you'd know it by now."

"Hey, it took you forever to start getting *my* name right."

"I found the variations much more entertaining. I have issues, you know." He signed and got up.

She picked up the bill. He'd signed it simply, *Chip*. She put it back in its tray and laid the pen on top. Then she got up.

"Where's my apology?" he asked.

"For what?"

"For butchering my name."

"Get mine right once or twice and I might just think about it."

"You drive a hard bargain."

***

At the corner of Liberty Avenue and 9th Street, *Sexywear Ever* advertised the best and most provocative in evening lingerie. Large-breasted, sexily dressed mannequins decorating the store's large bay window enticed passersby of all ages. Panties and laced bras adorned red velvet-covered chairs between the alluring figures.

Her long black hair a thick shroud sweeping over her shoulders, Danielle Kaminski entered the shop through the back door a little after eight. Dressed in a black leather jacket, skin-tight designer jeans and knee-high black leather boots, she walked right over to the coffeepot with her black leather handbag, which contained a full day's ration of her special brew of Jamaican blend java. She laid the bag on the table, squirmed out of her jacket and hung it on the wooden clothes tree behind the door. Her lavender tank top with the words THE DARK LADY RULES printed in bold white letters over her large round breasts clung tightly to her slender figure. For the next couple of hours, she would tend to important business before going out to the main part of the store, where she'd open up at ten to handle her "legitimate" customers.

These first two hours enabled her to deal properly with her "special" clients: those sneaking in to conduct transactions that would quickly turn devastating if made public. The details of these transactions were kept in a secret journal she guarded with her life. It contained names, dates, times and other details, and sat in a small, compact safe deposit box, which she'd bought several years ago and shoved beneath a loose floorboard about ten feet from the storefront wall. Its location was kept hidden by the heavy rubber mat covering the area behind the counter. Also concealed in the safe were conversations taped from the sophisticated system she'd purchased through a friend working for a South Hills security firm, who'd installed the speakers in hidden places throughout the store.

Digital prints of photos taken of high-profile individuals in compromising positions were stored in thumb drives also kept in her secret box. Danielle had found these photos in the dresser drawer of a fan who'd come to see her nightly when she'd danced at the Club *Risqué* on Liberty Avenue years ago, after leaving home at sixteen. This fan went off the deep end after Danielle repeatedly refused his offers of marriage even after he'd given her his treasured photo collection as a token of his undying affection. For the last ten years, she'd been blackmailing the people in the photos and rarely thought of her infatuated admirer, who'd quietly OD'd in his East Liberty apartment eight years ago.

Being a successful Pittsburgh stripper had enabled Danielle Kaminski, known as the "Dark

Lady" for her raven-black hair, dark-blue eyes and Goth-like inclinations, to amass a long list of victims. These individuals more than tripled the annual income she earned in profits made from her adultware business. A conservative estimate gave her a projected nest egg in the neighborhood of five million dollars over the next seven years, which would enable her to retire quite comfortably a full two years before she turned forty.

She'd learned early on, while growing up in seedy motel rooms with her junkie mother, that the world of secrets was paved with gold. Everyone had them, protected them and lived in constant terror of past sins being discovered. She'd also learned that everyone would gladly pay dearly to keep these secrets hidden, and that the more successful the person was, the more secrets there were to protect.

It was precisely 8:15 when the cowbell above the back door clang. Danielle smiled. Her first appointment of the morning had arrived on time.

His dark-brown hair slightly disheveled, his dreamy dark-brown eyes veiny with sleep, Jimmy Russo shuffled uneasily into the small, cluttered room. He wore a light-blue denim jacket opened all the way. He also wore a red tee shirt, black sweats and scuffed tennis shoes. Judging by the hair and five o'clock shadow, she could tell he had a rough night.

"You look tired." She put some concern into her voice--which, for Danielle, had always been difficult. Concern had never been important for her.

But in this case, she figured it couldn't hurt. "Everything okay?"

He slammed the door shut and stood there silently, glaring as always.

She could tell he wasn't in the mood for pleasant chatter. He never was. But that wasn't the issue. All she cared about was what sort of night he'd had at the club.

She turned on the coffeepot and went over to where he stood beside the clothes tree. She stopped about three feet away and smiled, showing off her bright, polished teeth as well as the silver glitter embellishing her black eye shadow and the many silver rings garnishing her cultured black brows. The two of them were normally about the same height, but her four-inch spikes made her six-three, giving her a notable edge and making her feel superior.

Even though he wasn't quite as broad-shouldered or as muscular as she usually liked her men, she knew he could have his way with her any time he liked. Those bedroom eyes could do serious damage to a gal if she wasn't careful. She understood why he had such power over his audience. But it wasn't only his eyes, it was also his smile. The way those tiny crescent-shaped dimples appeared in his cheeks. It was a real shame he never smiled or laughed when he came for these visits. But she couldn't help that, could she?

No matter. Business was business, and the time had come once again for Dreamy-Eyed Jimmy to cough up her share of his money.

Her right hand came up. Her arm extended out, palm up, her inch-long, black manicured nails nearly touching his jacket.

Without taking his eyes from her, he reached into his jacket pocket. When his hand reappeared, it gripped a slim wad of folded bills. She watched closely as he opened the wad and counted out five twenties. His hands shook slightly; they usually did during these meetings. She couldn't blame him for hating this. Who in his right mind liked pissing away good money? But he had no choice.

His eyes burned at her as he dropped the bills in her palm. He pocketed what was left and stood there, glaring.

"You look like you might wanna do something."

He remained silent.

She shrugged. "Go ahead. Work your magic. Who knows? You might get lucky before someone else drops in." She didn't want him to know about the hidden mikes in that room, or the camera hidden in the vent above the doorway leading to the store.

The darkness in his eyes grew, and she wondered just how much he could do if pushed to his limit. She'd seen his act and knew what he was capable of. This frightened her but also aroused her so much, she could barely contain herself.

"I can tell you're aching to do something," she said, her voice just above a whisper. "I can see it in your eyes, your face."

He took a breath and tried toning it down, but the rage kept fighting to come out. "You don't know me at all."

"Then tell me what's on your mind."

"You know what's on my mind."

"Times are hard. A girl's gotta take care of herself." She blinked. "Too many bad boys are out there, taking advantage of innocent gals like myself."

He puffed. "You haven't been innocent since the day you were born."

"Ouch." He was right but had no idea the hard road she'd been forced to follow since Mommy Dearest started doing tricks for her daily fix just days after little Danny crawled out of her womb. But that wasn't the issue. "Ask your boss for more money. I'm sure he thinks you're worth it."

"If I do, you'll up your cut."

"Like I said, a girl's gotta take care of herself."

"Last night I was offered a contract deal with another agent. This guy actually liked me, even wanted to help kick-start my career."

She wanted to laugh. No way would she let this talent slip through her fingers. "You have to stay at the Bel-Mor. Your bosses want you to stay there. Anyway, you're happy there. I'm happy you're there. From what I keep hearing, no one wants you to leave." She fluttered her lashes. "So I guess you're staying put."

"You're one cold bitch." His eyes burned like simmering coals.

She liked her men hot and frustrated. The trick was getting what you wanted from them without being beaten up, maimed or killed. A girl had to know exactly where that fine line was. And it was tricky. The line sat in a different place with each guy.

"Where's all that charm you dole out when you're on stage, wooing those horny bitches in the audience?"

"I only use it on my *paying* customers."

"I said it before and I'll say it again, baby doll. Do whatever you like. If you really turn me on, I might even lower my cut. It doesn't take much to get my engine running hot. I'm sure you'll be able to find the starter."

"I'd rather suck on a dead cockroach."

"If you're not careful, you might hurt this little girl's feelings."

"I didn't realize you had any."

She glanced at the clock on the wall above her cluttered desk. "We have ten minutes before my next appointment. That's enough time to get me flying." She placed her hands on her hips. "Bring it on over here. Let's check you out."

Before he could respond, she hiked up her tank top. The huge blue butterfly tattoo spanned her chest, covering her silicone boobs. The swirled leafy branch on which the butterfly perched ran down her stomach. It continued past her navel, ending over her shaved pubis to complete the masterpiece. She was proud of her butterfly tatt; it had cost her three thousand dollars and never failed to arouse even her most stubborn client.

"How do ya feel about butterflies?" She was careful to keep her thick blanket of shoulder-length blue-black hair free of the magnificent display.

He blinked, but his expression didn't change. "Butterflies, I like. Body art--especially stuff like that--makes me nauseous."

"Let's see if we can change your mind about that."

"Lady, I don't think you can change my mind about anything."

She smiled. "I believe that's the first time you've ever called me that."

"I was being generous."

"Don't stop now. You could be on a roll."

He watched her silently. She could see the darkness in his eyes and could feel the heat of anger emanating from the inner depths of his soul. He took two slow steps in her direction.

"That's it," she whispered, her body growing hot. "Come closer."

She closed her eyes and felt his hands encircling her neck. She sighed deeply and bathed herself in the excitement of the hot pressure increasing around her throat. She loved it rough and especially loved it when the man applied enough pressure to make her light-headed. Light-headedness produced better orgasms. The surges were hotter and lasted longer. She just had to make sure she could end it before he went too far. She wanted to get off. Not die in the process.

She stared into the fathomless abyss of his dark-brown eyes and saw the red glints. They were always there, hiding amongst the dark-brown swirls, but she only saw them clearly when he turned back inside himself. She had no idea how dark this place was that had taken over his spirit. She only knew that whenever she saw the red glints, he seemed different. It was like a foul darkness had reached out from some horrible place to claim him. It was wonderfully exciting. It stimulated every pore in her body. But she also knew she was treading on dangerous ground. He might lose himself and accidentally send her there.

She wasn't ready to go. Not yet.

The pressure closed around her throat, restricting regular air flow. She briefly saw stars shooting across her vision. She was beginning to lose touch with reality, and the glints in his eyes told her he'd never been closer to the brink than this moment. She managed to get the words out in a hoarse whisper: "You'd better…make damn sure…you don't t--"

The phone on her desk rang, making them both cringe.

He blinked. The red glints vanished from his eyes. He took a step back.

Just then, she noticed his hands. They hadn't moved from his sides.

How the hell had he done that?

You're hallucinating, Danny. You've got to be. He may be a magician, but no one in the world can strangle someone without using his hands.

He'd obviously pulled them away much more quickly than she'd realized. The ringing of the phone had frightened him.

She took a deep breath and forced herself back to reality. She'd check this out later on, when she went upstairs and took the disks out of the camera, as she normally did at the end of each day. Even if he'd actually moved that quickly, had he been able to move faster than the blinking of her eye?

He's a magician. Sleight-of-hand, remember? These guys can go through your pockets while they're talking to you.

She'd also been light-headed. That would explain this, too. She wasn't seeing straight, and experienced a moment of blurry vision. This would clearly explain why she hadn't seen his hands drop back down to his sides.

The phone persisted.

She cleared her throat and forced herself to snap out of it. She pushed down her top, moved rather shakily to her desk and snatched the phone, nearly dropping it. "Sexywear Ever Fashions."

"Is he there?" asked the soft, high-pitched voice.

She took a breath. "Yeah."

"Did he say he was approached last night by another agent?"

"Yeah. But like I told him, we don't want him going anywhere."

"Good job."

"You don't want that either, do you?"

"Of course not. That would be bad for all of us."

"Yes. Both you *and* him."

A groan. "We wouldn't want *that*, would we?"

"No. Neither would he, because I think he's beginning to understand how this game is played. Isn't that wonderful?"

"Tell him we're all proud of him."

"I'll tell him right now." She turned around.

Jimmy Russo had already gone.

Chapter 12

Ashley Parker fixed coffee in front of the tenth-floor window in Uncle Rob's office suite while wisps of morning fog drifted up sluggishly from the river. Early morning in Pittsburgh wasn't anything like Orlando's clear blue skies, fresh warm breeze and bright sun. Here it was chilly and damp, with the sourness from the river hanging heavily in the air.

But she knew she could get used to this place.

The most important thing was that she was no longer being kept a helpless prisoner. What the demon calling himself Brett Waite had done to her was terrifying. But what he'd done to Daniel Grove was worse than anything she'd ever seen.

Daniel was once a sweet, considerate guy who might have become an important part of her life. They'd hit it right off, doing things together and enjoying one another's company as if they'd known one another for years. Daniel even offered to help Ashley move out of her mother's home. For Daniel, the decision was simple. Ashley was unhappy, so things had to change.

For Ashley, the problem was much more complicated. She desperately wanted to start a new life in a new place, where she wasn't forced to watch her mother destroy herself with alcohol. For most people, it was a simple problem with a simple solution. But since Ashley had no money, no credit and no prospects, starting up a religious cult might have been easier.

Daniel's sudden appearance in her life had been almost like a modern fairy tale. A gentle knight in shining armor coming to the aid of the fair damsel in distress. Things would have turned out wonderfully if the demon Mr. Waite hadn't turned Daniel into a cold-hearted bastard who cared only about his own interests and satisfying his master's wishes.

But that was in the past. Despite the hurt she felt from the loss of Daniel as a close friend, she realized it was water under the bridge, as the saying went. With help from Tiffany and Chip, her only true friends, she'd left Orlando. And she no longer had to worry about working as a prostitute for Mr. Waite's escort services or dealing with Daniel and feeling the hatred and evil oozing like an open wound from his decaying soul.

It seemed like years had gone by since she'd first stepped into Daniel's Orlando office, dressed in her best clothes and ready for a bright new career. Her job function, at the very beginning, was simple: answer the phone and relay the message on another line.

A mindless task, to be sure.

She knew he'd offered it to her because he liked her and wanted to keep her close. He also wanted to help her, and her new position would enable her to raise enough money to leave Momma and find her own place.

However, things quickly turned very bad. Daniel came back into her office and in a voice completely devoid of emotion, told her that her job function had changed. She was longer required to answer the phone. She was needed as an escort.

Without another word, he left the room. And never spoke to her again.

Forcing herself back to the present, she went back to her desk and sat down. Her cell lay on her desk blotter, next to the big red coffee mug Uncle Rob gave her when he'd brought her in to explain her new job description, which amounted to answering the phone and directing the calls. Very similar to the job Daniel had given her. But Uncle Rob was no one's pawn, and would never do what Daniel had done.

For one brief instant, Ashley wondered if Uncle Rob could be a member of that group Tiffany and Chip had told her about on the trip from Florida. The "Diocese," they said it was called. As Chip had explained, it was an ancient society made up of the super-rich who'd been given complete reign in this mortal life simply by pledging their souls to the Devil.

"The Diocese?" she'd asked. Something about that name confused her, making her wonder if she'd heard them correctly. "Isn't that a church thing?"

"Demons love playing with mortals' minds," Chip replied. "Confusion and manipulation are what they live for, so to speak. When they were forming the society years before the birth of Christ, many of the demons didn't want to give it a name. They wanted it kept secret so only the wealthy would know about it. However, some of the big boys thought it would be amusing if they named it something that sounded religious."

Uncle Rob could never be a member of such a disgustingly evil group. He'd come up the hard way. High school, college, odd jobs—the whole nine yards. Like Ashley's dad, Uncle Rob's folks hadn't been rich, nor had they experienced unexplained good luck or good fortune. Everything they'd acquired had been earned through hard work, drive and determination.

It took Uncle Rob four years of college, four years of additional study in Paris, and several years of apprenticeship in the garment industry to attain the position he was in. It had taken him years to free himself from college debt. His name in the fashion industry was the result of intense study, hard work, focus and tireless perseverance.

There was no way a man as honest and as respectable as Uncle Rob would deal with demons.

Determined Ashley learn the business the hard way, Uncle Rob had given her this entry level position to introduce her to all aspects of the industry. She could accompany him in a few weeks to a local show and observe the chaotic workings of a live fashion exhibition. Once she got the feel of what went on during these "dazzle displays," as he referred to them, she could go with him when he went to supervise the larger, more publicized shows in L.A. and New York City. She could study any facet of the industry she chose and would have the advantage of on-the-job training to help her get a solid leg up. It would take months to learn just a few of the many flavors of the business, but he'd be there for her and would make sure she had access to all the resources necessary.

Belasco Fashions had been around and doing quite well the last fifteen years, boasting clients and representatives all over the world. Under her uncle's tutelage, Ashley faced a bright future.

She couldn't wait for him to get back from New York. It was kind of lonely being in a strange place, and she still found herself disoriented by the abrupt change in weather and scenery. She'd only seen Tiffany and Chip a few times since she'd settled in with Uncle Rob in his penthouse suite. They'd wanted her and Uncle Rob to have some private time together and didn't want to distract her from her training and study.

She knew better than feel sorry for herself. This was, after all, the best decision she'd ever made. She had to remind herself that even with Uncle Rob out of town, she wasn't really alone. Everyone at the company was friendly and courteous, and incredibly helpful. And even though Tiffany and Chip weren't constantly with her, they were close by.

Uncle Rob called at around 9:00, interrupting her quiet restlessness. He told her a client was coming from New York and would be there sometime later in the afternoon.

"His name is Emile Abramssen, and he's an associate of two of our most prominent French designers." As usual, Uncle Rob sounded rushed. Ashley had only been with him two weeks but noticed that he always moved in high gear. She guessed that in his line of work, he really had to. "Emile customarily meets the designers here before they fly to L.A. He's very influential and knowledgeable when organizing international shows, so quite naturally we want to keep the relationship going. We always have a suite in the Renaissance ready for them, no matter when they fly in. All we need is confirmation of lodging arrangements. The Renaissance has been known to overbook, usually when other conventions are coming in the same weekend. This shouldn't be the case. At any rate, we always inform the hotel staff of our guests' wine and food preferences. Since Abramssen is a Swede, he is extremely particular about his choices. He is a connoisseur of coffee, especially the German brands. And his associates are equally particular with French wines and various *hors d'oeuvres*."

"Will they be booked on the same floor as my friends?"

"Yes. There won't be a conflict, if that's what you're concerned about. My firm has an arrangement to reserve one full floor. Your friends are only using a small corner suite. Don't worry about anything. Just make sure this confirmation has been made. We want Emile's suite ready by the time he and his companions arrive."

"No problem."

"And speaking of your friends... Let's see if we can have them over for an evening at our place as soon as I get back. They both intrigue me—

especially Tiffany. I swear I saw her during one of my Hollywood trips last year. If it wasn't her, it was someone who looks very much like her. You did say she did commercials and a few films, did you not?"

"She doesn't talk much about her career in Hollywood. But yes, she did do some acting before…well, before she left."

"I often wonder about Hollywood. That woman's absolutely gorgeous. She's got ten times the personality of any model I've ever worked with. At any rate, I would like to spend time with them, so let's set aside one night for that. And behave until I get back, all right?"

"I'll try, but I can't guarantee anything."

"Wrong answer." He chuckled before hanging up.

Smiling, Ashley sat back in her chair. Before putting down her cell, her gaze automatically latched onto the directory, where Momma's name was listed. She wondered if she should give her a call. What would she say? *I'm in Pittsburgh, Momma, staying with Uncle Rob in his penthouse suite. I'm learning a valuable trade, and everything is just great. Wish you were here.*

No. That wouldn't work. For one thing, it was much too early. Momma was probably sleeping off a hangover and wouldn't appreciate an early morning call. The last time Ashley called was when they were leaving Florida. The call ended horribly. Momma was so busy yelling at her about the cellphone Daniel had dropped off at the house that she didn't even care where Ashley was, why she'd called, or that it could be the last time they ever talked to one another.

The anger rushed back. She trembled, gazing numbly at the directory. Should she delete the number? Just wipe the slate clean? Erase the source of the stress?

As if by subconscious suggestion, her thumb jerked awkwardly toward the number. In an instant, the name and number would vanish forever. Just a simple tap, and--

Don't, an inner voice said.

Great. Now she was hearing voices.

Ashley sighed. The thought of erasing Momma from her life with a mere twitch of the thumb caused a bubble of hot foulness to settle in Ashley's gut.

She brought you into this world. Yes, she was different then. But so were you. So was everyone. Things change dramatically in nineteen years. People can change in an instant. Can you possibly delete your mother into oblivion? Are you that cold? That unfeeling? If so, you're no better than she is.

No. She wasn't cold or unfeeling. One day, when she was more settled and the mood felt right, she'd call again. Hopefully, Momma would be in a better frame of mind than she was the last time Ashley tried talking to her.

With a sigh, she put down the cell, picked up her mug and got up to fetch a cup of fresh coffee.

Chapter 13

While scattered crowds streamed past the smudged windows of the Penn Avenue Diner, Jimmy Russo huddled over a cup of hot black coffee in a booth and struggled to push away the dark waves of depression slamming through him.

He had to forget about Marc Cassman. Jimmy knew all about agents. He'd been dealing with them for years and knew the games they played. Agents were just lazy crooks leeching off talent for their own personal gain. Moreland and Bellman were two classic examples. Marc Cassman was probably no different; he just had a little more class and finesse than Moreland and Bellman.

Which wasn't saying much.

There were probably one or two good agents in town. Cassman could be one of them, for all Jimmy knew. But he couldn't exactly be sure, could he? Cassman obviously had expensive taste. His Versace suit, professional haircut, imported casuals and Rolex watch spoke volumes. Jimmy had learned long ago that truly honest people rarely spent a lot of money to show themselves off.

But Cassman's appearance wasn't what had impressed Jimmy. The man's manner had actually done the job. He'd treated Jimmy with respect--something he'd never experienced from Moreland or Bellman. Even so, that by itself couldn't be considered the ultimate deal-breaker. Jimmy had seen dozens of agents in action. They all knew how to act in the presence of a celebrity, or potential cash cow.

None of this mattered in the great scheme of things. Even if Cassman turned out to be the world's most honest agent, Jimmy could do nothing about changing the status quo. Because of the contract he'd signed and the predicament he'd found himself in with Danielle, he'd remain at the Bel-Mor as long as he was able to attract capacity crowds.

His insides churned hotly when his thoughts focused on the evil bitch. Each time he found himself in her presence, he wanted to grab her by the neck and strangle her until her big blue eyes popped out of her skull.

Just less than an hour ago, he discovered he didn't need his hands. All he needed was his mind.

He wondered if she realized how close she'd come. If it hadn't been for that damned phone... If it had rung a minute later...

Could he have done it? Could he have actually killed her?

His powers had literally taken over, his anger forming an invisible vise lunging from him, encircling her throat.

It would have been the perfect crime. No prints. No clues. Just a few more seconds would have completed the grisly act. Danielle the evil Dark Lady would have been dead, the life squeezed out of her through the mental power of the gifted magician, Jimmy Russo.

Deep-down, he knew he couldn't have done it. Even if the phone hadn't rung, he would have stopped in time. He was no killer. He was a performer. Magic was his forte, his passion. Taking a life had never been something he'd consciously considered.

Even someone as evil as Danielle couldn't change what he was inside. She'd been destroying him ever since they'd first met, taking from him, draining his life's blood by degrees. But he still couldn't find it within himself to do her harm. Despite what anyone did to him or how they treated him, he could never purposely end someone's life.

The lives lost during his former existence had been a tragic accident. It had caused his own demise, forcing his tortured soul down into the Dark Place. This horrible guilt had darkened his very core, wrapping his spirit in a suffocating cocoon of darkness and sorrow. He'd welcomed his own death, entering the darkness with open arms, never expecting to see light again. And if Balberith hadn't summoned him back many years ago to perform a few unpleasant tasks, Jimmy would have spent eternity wandering the Valley of Decay, sheathed in his own prison of darkness and despair.

He had no clue that a cold, heartless female would find him and imprison him in an even more terrifying darkness in the mortal world.

As the anger raged through him, he closed his eyes and tried desperately to calm himself. *Think happy thoughts. Think about the gig last night. And how they loved you. And tonight. What you'll do. What new magic you'll show this town.*

It relaxed him for a little while, but his thoughts gradually returned to the Dark Lady. He cursed himself for his weakness, knowing he had to focus harder. *Think about something bright and positive. Something that will lift your spirits.*

In spite of what had happened in Danielle's store this morning, of what had been happening to him since that bleak day when he'd first met her, he suddenly felt things might soon change. He had no idea why, just that they would. It was most likely wishful thinking, but ever since last night--

Yes. These strange new feelings had started up last night. It wasn't the discussion with Cassman that had prompted them. It was the beautiful blond woman he'd seen in the hall. And later, on the park bench outside the club. There was something strange and magical about her. He knew the moment he heard her voice in his head that something extraordinary had happened in his life.

He had no idea who or what she was. He wanted to believe she was just a beautiful young woman who'd come backstage to congratulate him on his performance. But he knew she wasn't real—most likely a figment of his imagination. He truly believed that the part of him wanting change in his life had unconsciously fabricated his own special dream, which translated into the dazzling form of a beautiful golden-haired princess.

Or was she an angel?

She certainly looked like one—or at least what most guys would think an angel should look like. He hadn't seen many in life or death, but he had seen his share of demons, and he was certain this gorgeous creature was anything but a demon.

Demons meant darkness, And despair. And hatred. And loathing. This dazzling vision was just the opposite. The moment her image crept into his consciousness, the darkness engulfing his mind lifted like a heavy black cloth, revealing a gem that glittered so brightly, he wanted to shield his eyes.

He couldn't stop wondering who she was, why she'd appeared. Did this have something to do with those poor souls he'd accidentally killed in his former life? Was this some sort of redemption he hadn't counted on? Had he done something that had somehow cleansed his soul without his knowledge?

How could you cleanse your soul without knowing it? How could years of dark, heart-pounding guilt remove the eternal blackness from your spirit? How could anything erase the unforgivable act of sending innocent souls to their death?

He hadn't even been able to sleep properly the night before. He couldn't get the dazzling image of this goddess out of his head. Her beautiful golden hair and big blue eyes filled the picture screen in his mind, and--

"Jimmy, this is Tiffany..."

Her soft, breathy voice had invaded his dreams as well, making him wonder if she was indeed an angel. If she really was such an angel, had she been sent to him for some special purpose? Perhaps to help him cleanse his spirit? Or maybe tell him how he could possibly achieve some sort of personal redemption?

"Jimmy, we need to talk..."

Her voice sounded so clear, even though it had been hours since he'd gotten up. So clear, so close... And it made him warm inside.

"Jimmy, where are you?"

Startled, he put down his coffee cup. His heart raced as he struggled to analyze what was happening. Was he remembering the voice from his dreams? From last night? From the Bel-Mor? The park bench?

Or was this happening right now?

"We have to talk..."

Chills rushed down his limbs. His memory wasn't reproducing her voice. It wasn't that at all. This was happening right here, right now. She was calling him again.

This angel was summoning him, and he needed to find her.

He jumped up from his seat, dumped change on the table and scrambled out of the diner.

***

At 9:30, just as Andras took a corner table in the elegant dining room of the Wyndham Hotel for a quick breakfast, his cell went off.

"Mister Smith?" asked the soft male voice.

"Yes?"

"I'm your contact."

No names. Clever. Braithwaite obviously wanted this done as quickly and as simply as possible. With no traceable trail. "I'm listening."

"My employer was contacted from Orlando several hours ago and told about your trip to Pittsburgh to look for three people who might be seeking refuge here."

"That's correct."

"I've been instructed to give you full access to any resource you require and do whatever is necessary to wrap this up within your forty-eight-hour window."

"We're on the same page, then."

"In case you're wondering, my employer is one of the richest and most influential people in this city, so nothing you require will be beyond reach. I have been his executive assistant for the last eight years and have experience in many different fields. From this moment on, I will be at your beck and call. You will deal only with me, and we will keep in constant contact. Agreed?"

"Agreed."

"Is there anything you need right now?"

"I've been told one of the people I'm looking for could be staying with her uncle, who runs a fashion business in town."

"That information has already been relayed to us. You will be receiving full details shortly. The individual we're talking about is very well known in this town. Is there anything else you need?"

"Can you provide me a less conspicuous ride? The limo's comfortable and smooth, but it is a tad, well, ostentatious..."

"Understood. How long will you be at the Wyndham this morning?"

"I'm having breakfast now. I would like to be on my way within the hour."

"Something more suitable will be waiting for you outside the hotel very shortly."

"Can I have the same chauffeur?"

"If you wish."

Andras pocketed the phone and ordered breakfast.

It took his contact just twenty minutes to provide him with every relevant detail of Robert Belasco's life. Belasco was 45, six feet one and 165 pounds, with light-brown hair and chestnut eyes. A recent photo was emailed to Andras' phone with the other details. Belasco was twice divorced and lived alone in a penthouse suite in Two Chatham Center. He owned and operated Belasco Fashions, in a suite of rooms located in the Fifth Avenue Place building. The company employed nearly two dozen people and participated in international shows several times each year. Belasco traveled frequently, owned a black BMW, did not smoke, fancied himself a wine connoisseur, wore custom-tailored Italian clothes and was fond of French cuisine. He also enjoyed classical music and cooking shows. He was presently out of town and was scheduled to be back the next day, but due to fly to L.A. early next week.

Impressive research for such a short period of time, but Andras noted one major detail missing. He got back immediately with his contact.

"Yes, Mr. Smith?"

"I need everything you've got on Belasco's niece. Her name is Ashley Parker, and I believe she's nineteen years old. I need to know where she might be right now. If she's working for her uncle, I want to know if she's in the building. If so, where. Floor, room, that sort of thing. If she's somewhere else, I have to know that as well. And I'd like to know all this as quickly as possible."

"Yes, sir."

Andras ate his breakfast. By the time he'd left the dining room, his chauffeur was waiting for him out in front of the hotel. The big man stood in front of a dark-blue Lincoln Town Car parked at the end of the concrete ramp.

Andras nearly smiled. These people meant business.

He got in the back and instantly relaxed in the comfortable leather seat. Dahl squeezed behind the wheel and took the quiet, smooth-running machine to Penn and Fifth Avenue. A few minutes later, he pulled over to the curb across the street from Fifth Avenue Place.

Andras scanned the morning crowds swarming in front of the huge building. "Dahl, is there a decent coffee shop in that building?"

"Yes, sir."

"They have lattes as well?"

"Yes, sir, but they're pricey."

"I never worry about stuff like that." Andras pushed open the door. "I'll be right back."

The *Cafe Nirvana* sat at the far end of the spacious plant-filled lobby, sandwiched between a hamburger place and a submarine shop. The lobby and eateries hummed with people bustling about, sipping hot coffee and nibbling on sweet rolls. Andras went over to the machine, poured a cappuccino and took it over to the counter, where a short, skinny young redhead wearing black-rimmed glasses stood behind the register, eyeing the large cup in his hand.

"G'morning." She smiled briefly, showing him two tiny dimples in her cheeks and braces on her teeth. "That'll be--"

"Open the register drawer." He focused on her large cornflower blue eyes. *"As soon as you see the money inside, close the drawer. You'll have the greatest urge to run to the ladies' room."*

She opened the register and immediately closed it. She stared at it a moment, then at him. She looked totally confused. A moment later, she gasped, spun around and raced down the aisle, to the open hallway at the other end of the room, where a sign said OFFICE/RESTROOMS.

Andras was halfway back to the Town Car when his cell buzzed. He fished it out of his pocket and flicked it on. "Smith."

"Parker's in the building, sir. She's working as an office assistant for Belasco Fashions."

"Good deal."

"Anything else you need?"

Dahl held the door of the Town Car open. Andras slid in. "I need a list of Belasco's professional contacts. Associates, clients, affiliates, sponsors--everything. I want this list sent over to my phone as soon as possible."

"I take it you've got something in mind?"

Andras had a sip of hot, foamy cappuccino. "I just thought of one sure way of getting the girl on the charter plane back to Orlando."

Chapter 14

Tiffany was standing beneath the awning of Giovanni's Pizzeria on Liberty Avenue, watching Jimmy as he rushed down the street in her direction. The short, skinny redhead Jimmy had seen with her at the club the night before stood behind her. Jimmy barely noticed him. He saw only Tiffany and her beautiful smile. Her hair, partially hidden in the shade of the store awning, burned like flame. She wore a red short-sleeve tee shirt, jeans, and white open-toed casuals sprinkled with red glitter. Everything about her radiated with warmth, and he suddenly discovered that what happened earlier that morning at Danielle's had dissolved like a puff of smoke swept up in a warm breeze.

He stopped about five feet away and took in everything. Those big, bright blue eyes. The flawless skin. The high cheekbones. The look of spun gold in the thick honey-blond hair cascading down her shoulders. She had the face of an angel, and he found that he could not take his eyes off her.

"Hi." Her voice was soft and low. She held out her hand. When he touched it, a warm tingling danced up his arm, and he trembled.

"Hi." *Damn.* He'd wanted to say something else, something that required actual thought, but his mind had gone blank. He was a performer who faced hundreds of folks each night. He was known for his wit and clever comebacks...

But right now, he couldn't think of a single coherent statement.

"We saw you last night at the Bel-Mor. You really put on a terrific show."

"I'm glad you liked it."

"It wasn't bad." The redhead had stepped into the picture. "Taking your shoes off during your juggling routine was downright terrificoso. I don't think I ever saw anything like that before."

"This is Chip," she said.

Jimmy stared at Chip, trying to make sense of this. They didn't seem like a couple. There was no obvious chemistry emanating from them at all. They seemed separate from one another. Independent. No holding hands, no shoulder-rubbing. No body contact of any kind. He couldn't see the two of them being intimate together. At least, he didn't want to. But nowadays you didn't really know for sure--

"Chip and I are friends."

Jimmy blinked. *Wow*. Had she read his mind? Or was that just coincidence? Her smile told him nothing.

But at least now he knew their situation. However, he realized he should be extremely careful what he thought about in her presence.

"Really close buds," Chip said. "As a matter of fact--"

"Just friends," she said, and Chip closed his mouth and grinned sheepishly.

He had to find out more about this fascinating woman. Even if she hadn't penetrated his thoughts, there was something extraordinary about her. After all, she'd somehow managed to direct him halfway down Liberty Avenue in these busy morning crowds. That alone was an impressive feat.

"I really think we need to…have a talk." He was surprised he was able to get that out without making a mess of it.

"Yes. We do."

"About a lot of things. I'd really like to know how…how you managed to slip into my head last night, as well as this morning."

"Oh, I'm sure you've got some idea."

He could tell by her expression that she knew a lot more about him than he thought. "I'm not so sure."

"I'm more interested in that trick you did last night," Chip said.

"Which one?" he asked. "I remember doing several."

Chip shrugged. "Taking off your shoes in the middle of a juggling act--what else?"

He understood. They knew about him.

Suddenly nervous, he felt a little unsteady and wanted very much to sit down. "There's a nice breakfast place around the corner, about half a block from here. Will that be all right?"

"Perfect."

"As long as they have eggshells." Chip grinned.

"Eggshells?"

"He's just bummed out because he only had stale coffee grounds for breakfast this morning," Tiffany explained.

Jimmy stared at Chip. Something weird was coming out of the shadows. "You must have been a flower in your former life."

Tiffany laughed. Chip went silent.

***

Ashley's line buzzed at ten-thirty. It was Rita, the receptionist who handled the switchboard for Belasco Fashions. "Someone calling from London wants to talk to you, Ashley."

"Are you serious?"

"Yes I am..."

This was very strange. Ashley didn't know why anyone from England would want to talk to her. No one other than Uncle Rob and the handful of employees she'd met in the last two weeks even knew about her. "Is this something Uncle Rob needs to address?"

"I don't think so," Rita said.

"Are you sure? Maybe you should just give them Uncle Rob's--"

"The man is calling from Burberry's. Mr. Belasco has many contacts with them and has dealt with them for years. I believe they all have access to his personal line."

"I don't understand. Why would anyone from London want to talk to me?"

"From what I've been told, your uncle wants you to get your feet wet, and he'd like you to handle as much of the workload as you can. Much of this business requires thinking on your feet, quick decision-making, and

understanding the needs of the clients--"

"He didn't tell me anything about international calls--"

"In case you haven't already been told, more than fifty percent of our incoming calls are from Europe and Great Britain. This would be one of those "getting-your-feet-wet" kind of things. Anyway, this client has been, for some time, representing the agency employing the supermodel Alexia. She's also a friend of your uncle's. He's the first person she looks up whenever she flies over from London."

"Alexia?" Ashley had heard the name but couldn't place it.

"Vandermeer. She's a very tall blonde and has been a principal Victoria's Secret model the last three years. She was just offered a two-picture deal with a Hollywood producer affiliated with Sony and Lions Gate Entertainment. I'm sure you've seen her. She's worked for Dior, Chanel, Ralph Lauren, and has also done modeling work for Oleg Cassini and Gina Fratini."

"That's impressive. But what does this have to do with little ol' me?"

"This caller didn't share any particulars. He wants only to talk to you."

"Are you sure?"

"He mentioned you specifically by name."

This didn't make sense. She thought about it for a moment. It would be just like Uncle Rob to circulate her name around. As he'd told her several times, thinking under pressure was the only way to actually learn anything. And as he'd said more than once, "You learn by making your own mistakes, not by watching others make them."

But she couldn't help feeling nervous and wondered how much damage she could do from one phone call. Possibly quite a bit—especially if she said the wrong thing. After all, she had no idea what this person wanted. And she knew virtually nothing about this business.

If she was asked the wrong thing, or said the wrong thing...

If she made the wrong appointment on the wrong day with the wrong person...

What if she had to verify something before she could commit to it? The only person she knew of who could help was her uncle. Surely her caller wouldn't mind if she put him on hold to ask Uncle Rob a couple of quick questions...

"Can you put this person on hold while I call Uncle Rob--"

"You don't put these people on hold, Ashley."

"All right, then." She took a breath and focused. *Don't panic, now*. She was just gonna have to wing this. What was the worst that could happen?

"You'll be all right. Just be yourself and ask him every question you can think of."

Be myself. Ask questions. No pressure. Sure. No problem. Ashley took another deep breath and forced herself to stay in control. It wasn't like she'd be dealing with someone like Mr. Waite, was it? These were successful, well-educated people. They weren't demons, and they were friends of Uncle Rob. They were very demanding but could also be patient and understanding if the situation called for it.

"I think I might be able to manage this."

Rita had already sent the call over.

"Is this Robert Belasco's office?" The man calling had a low-pitched voice with a strong British accent.

"Yes. Who am I speaking to, please?"

"My name is Nigel Davidson, and I am an executive planner and promoter for Burberry's from their London offices. And you are, I believe, Ashley Parker? Robert Belasco's niece?"

"How do you know about me? Did Uncle Rob say anything? I hope you'll bear with me. I've just started working here, and--"

"I understand completely. You see, Miss Parker--"

"Please call me Ashley."

"I'm sure you're wondering about the nature of this call, Ashley..."

"Yes. I am."

"In a nutshell, one of our top clients, Alexia Vandermeer, is in the process of planning a private fashion event for Mister Belasco and would like to get with you to arrange it in such a way that your uncle has no idea anything is happening."

"A *private* fashion event?"

"Ms. Vandermeer has been associated professionally with your uncle for five years. Mr. Belasco was responsible for getting her a very important contract with Christian Dior--which, of course, opened the door to the three-year Burberry deal she is presently fulfilling. She'd like to show her appreciation by arranging this special celebration and would like to have it held at an appropriate ballroom or convention center you might arrange at your discretion. I understand Belasco Fashions is affiliated with several hotels and convention centers in the Pittsburgh area."

"Is this like, maybe, a surprise party?"

"If you wish to call it that. It shall be rather large, I'm afraid. Approximately forty of Mister Belasco's closest friends, acquaintances and associates in the industry have been invited to attend. There have been two dozen high-fashion models interested in handling the runway event Ms. Vandermeer is presently arranging. Several are already in the states, mostly in the L.A. area. In other words, arranging all this and coordinating it in time will be, well, tricky."

"It sounds really exciting. When does she want to have it?"

"This weekend. Saturday afternoon will be perfect. Ms. Vandermeer will be flying in on her way to Hollywood later on in the week."

"*This* Saturday?" He had to be kidding. "My God. That's not much time."

"Then I suggest we jump on this as soon as possible."

"I'll devote all the time I can to it immediately."

"Excellent. An associate of mine is in town at the moment. He's got a couple of hours free this afternoon. He can meet you wherever and whenever you wish."

Just a few days. Could she do this? Could she really pull this off by herself?

"Ashley? Are you still there?"

She took a deep breath. *I can do this. I can and I will.* "How about in an hour?"

"That will be fine. One thing, though, Ashley."

"Yes?"

"Since this will be a private event, no one but those directly involved should know what is going on."

"I understand."

"Ms. Vandermeer has been very explicit about her instructions. She wants this to be a complete surprise. And she doesn't mind paying extra for whatever additional arrangements must be made. I believe her budget has been set at around a quarter of a million dollars."

"Wow." That was a lot of money. "Mum's the word, then. Where can I meet your associate?"

"He'll be at the Wyndham Hotel until two-fifteen. Room 522."

"I'll be there as soon as I can get away."

Chapter 15

Tiffany, Chip and Jimmy shared a window booth in Val's Breakfast Shoppe on Wood Street. Outside, the dark clouds had lifted. Slices of morning sun peeked through. Tiny bright stars bounced off the shop windows of the buildings across the street.

Tiffany could tell Jimmy was nervous. He kept his eyes on them as their waitress poured steaming black coffee into their cups and placed a giant glass of freshly squeezed orange juice in front of Chip. Once the girl rushed back to the counter, Jimmy turned to Chip and lowered his voice. "Which one of them made you a flower?"

"Olivier." Chip had a sip of orange juice.

Jimmy sat in silence for a few moments. Tiffany could feel the dark images flashing in his mind. He'd gone back to that vile, dark place. "Short, squat dude dressed in black? Wears a hood to hide the scabs covering his face? Drooling all the time?"

Chip nodded. "A nifty description, but he really doesn't look that good."

Jimmy had a sip of hot coffee. He put the cup down and placed his elbows on the table. "Why a flower?"

"He wanted a little color for his rock garden and thought I'd be perfect." Chip ran a hand through his red mop. "He liked the hair. Figured it would blend in with the rocks."

"Asmodeus wanted to turn me into rabbit turds," Jimmy said softly.

"Why?"

"I asked if he wanted me to pull a rabbit out of my hat."

Chip nodded. "That would do it. What happened?"

"Before he could do his number on me, I used my magic to turn invisible and hid from him. I spent my time in the Valley, keeping close to the trees. The supers and subs rarely go there, so I was safe. Then one of them found me. I can't remember which one it was, but I was fairly certain it was an inferior wandering around, trying to stay out of trouble just like me. He told me he'd heard a couple of the subs saying Balberith wanted the magician from New York City who'd been hiding from Asmodeus to go back up through one of the tunnels that led back up there. I didn't believe them, so I stayed hidden. I didn't hear anything for a while, but later on, one of the subs wandered into the Valley and began yelling, saying I should get my ass up there, or stay hidden for the next thousand years." He shrugged. "I just took my chances that this sub was telling the truth. I didn't waste time. I found the nearest tunnel and went back up."

"What did you do when you came back up?" Tiffany asked.

He frowned. "Some things I didn't want to do. But I did them just to stay up here, and kept a low profile. I've been moving around ever since, staying under the radar for the last eighty years."

"When you died, did you reach the Meddaworld?" Chip asked.

"Briefly, but I kept feeling some sort of force pulling me into the woods. Once I stopped resisting, I felt much better. Then I saw the Castle and figured I'd messed up. I tried getting back to the meadow, but my sense of direction was always bad. I guess I wandered into the wrong place. That's when I bumped into Asmodeus. I think he was on his way to the Castle."

"What pulled you into the woods?" Tiffany asked.

"I have no idea. I couldn't shake this heavy feeling of guilt for being in the meadow. It's hard to describe, but I kept feeling like I didn't belong there. I had this overwhelming sensation to hide, to seek the protection of the darkness. I needed darkness to keep me from being seen. Like I said, it's hard to describe."

"You felt like something would happen to you if you'd stayed in the meadow?"

"It's the same sort of feeling you get when you're about to do something, but some feeling inside you tells you not to do it. Has that ever happened to you?"

"I've been there." Tiffany sighed.

"Ditto," Chip added.

Jimmy had some coffee but said nothing.

Tiffany watched him and felt the darkness of the heavy guilt inside him hovering close. He'd done something really bad. But he just didn't seem the type. It probably had something to do with whatever he was forced to do when he came back up.

But something didn't make sense. Jimmy had apparently done something bad when he went down the first time. It had obviously been bad enough to pull him from the meadow and straight into Hell.

"You said guilt pulled you into the Valley?" she asked.

Jimmy nodded.

"Whatever did you do to make you feel so guilty?"

He was silent for quite a while. "One of my magic tricks. It…well, I caused a fire." He fiddled with his coffee cup. "It happened in 1928, in New York City. Several people, they died in the fire."

"What happened?" Chip asked.

"There was this guy who was really big at the time in the New York City area. His name was Hadji Ali. He was called the "Egyptian Enigma," and his specialty was his iron stomach. He was also known as the "Human Waterspout." He'd swallow kerosene and water, then regurgitated the kerosene. He set it ablaze, regurgitated the water and put out the flames."

"Disgusting," Tiffany said flatly.

"Wow." Chip's eyes twinkled. "I wouldn't mind seeing that."

Jimmy frowned. "He was my biggest competition, so naturally I tried competing. But I didn't want to subject my stomach to anything like that, and used props. Needless to say, it backfired, and the building burned down."

"Wow. Kerosene." Chip shook his head. "He must have had a cast-iron stomach."

"Several colleges wanted to study his organs when he died. I'd already died by the time that happened, so I don't know how that ended up."

Chip bent, picked up something from the floor and studied it. It looked like an eggshell with some fuzz on it. He blew on it, popped it into his mouth and munched on it. "You gotta wonder about some guys," she said.

"Constantly," Tiffany said, frowning.

Jimmy had another sip of coffee. "Anyhow, that's how I ended up down there."

The darkness clouding his mind told Tiffany how badly he felt. She knew right then that he wasn't evil. You couldn't be truly evil with such unspeakable guilt weighing down your spirit.

"You didn't purposely do it," she said.

"Of course not. I died in it as well. But I was so eaten up with guilt. Well, it just took over."

This was eerily similar to her own experience, when she'd found herself in that same beautiful meadow, not knowing where she was or what happened, when only moments ago she'd been at that Hollywood pool party. At first, she wondered if she'd blacked out from the strong drink that strange guy had given her. She'd never been a drinker and feared the drink had gone straight to her head. Her first reaction was that she'd somehow wandered into the woods behind the mansion. Then, before she could collect herself and find her way back to the party, she'd become disoriented and felt a surge of panic taking over. She thought she might be losing consciousness again and noticed a thick column of darkness settling in behind her. Before her thoughts could clear, she was pulled into the darkness by the slender wolf-like figure Gutril, and found herself in Hell.

Now that Jimmy had told her his story, Tiffany began wondering if what had happened to her was the result of the guilt she'd felt during those dark days preceding her death. The guilt of leaving her mother with the evil beast Momma had brought into their home just a few years after Dad was killed in the hunting accident that changed their lives forever. Tiffany hadn't wanted to leave Momma alone with such a man--that same monster that had crept into her bedroom those nights Momma hadn't been there to protect her--but she hadn't had much of a choice. She'd done it to survive.

Maybe her being pulled into Hell *hadn't* been a mistake after all. The guilt that had weakened her spirit had permanently stained her soul. It could have been this same weakness that had made her unsteady, edging her closer to the wall of darkness. Otherwise, she would have stayed in the meadow. She might have even eventually found the other place, where the sun always kept things bright, and things stayed warm and wonderful.

The place where the good spirits roamed.

"I have a feeling you know what I'm talking about," Jimmy said.

Tiffany nodded.

"You shouldn't have been down there. Not someone like you."

Tiffany could see the sympathy in his eyes. She suddenly didn't feel so bad. It was then that she knew beyond a doubt that Jimmy Russo was good.

"What about you?" Jimmy asked Chip.

Chip perked up. "I'm a genuine badass--can't you tell?"

Jimmy rubbed his chin. "Then why were you standing in a rock garden?"

Chip smiled sheepishly. "Would you believe I was keeping watch on the Castle?"

Tiffany thought it best to get back to the subject at hand. "What did they have you do when you came back up?" she asked Jimmy.

He looked down at his hands. "They wanted me burning down churches. I did it only once, and it destroyed me. They wanted me to do at least six more, but I snuck away, and they never found me."

Tiffany found herself hating demons more than ever before.

"What about you?" he asked. She could feel his confusion again. "You're not a demon. You can't be."

"I was pulled into the Meddaworld by one of the nasties wandering around." She was surprised that she wasn't as angry as she usually was whenever she went back to that bleak day. Maybe it was because she was now in the presence of someone else who'd suffered the same misfortune.

"You couldn't get away?"

"It happened too fast. I had no idea where I was until it was too late." Doubt nudged her as soon as she'd said it. Had it really happened so quickly? Or had she let it happen? Even now she couldn't remember how much she'd resisted--or if she'd resisted at all--when the wolf guy grabbed her.

"I figured as much. You're not very demonlike."

"Thanks."

"It's pretty obvious."

"I don't think any of us could be demons. Not even Chip--regardless of what he considers himsclf."

"Gee, thanks."

She swatted him. "That was a compliment, silly."

He scratched the top of his head. "Oh. I get it. Gee, thanks."

Jimmy laughed, his deep-set dark-brown eyes beaming. It made her feel good that they'd broken the ice. She even felt her own anger slipping away.

"About your magic act." Chip leaned forward. "Why are you here, rather than New York or Las Vegas, where the crowds and paychecks are much bigger and more meaningful?"

Jimmy stopped smiling and slumped down in his seat. Tiffany could tell something terrible had happened to him. "I just told you about New York. Balberith still has many of his subs and inferiors hanging around. If they recognize me, they'll send me back down. I can't risk that."

“You’re a magician. Can you by any chance--” Chip glanced around to see if anyone was listening “--alter your appearance?”

Jimmy lowered his voice. “I can’t shape-shift. I’m limited to distraction and illusion. Unfortunately, my magic can’t do everything.”

“You’re not using your same name, are you?” she asked.

“My stage name back then was Billy Magic. I was born William Westerman in 1900. But when I died in 1928, the name died with me.”

“And when you came back up?”

“I picked the name Jimmy Russo. It seemed to fit.”

Tiffany had some coffee. “So now all you’re doing is trying to stay in the shadows?”

Jimmy stared at his coffee cup. Tiffany clearly saw his thoughts darken. The image of a slender young woman with long black hair, tattoos, studs and an evil expression on her pretty face had consumed him. The hatred filling his being made her cringe. As Jimmy stared at his coffee cup, Tiffany caught an image of him standing in a dark room, facing the tattooed girl. His hands had become trembling fists.

“Jimmy?”

No response.

“Tifferoo?” Chip moved closer to her on the bench seat. “What’s happening? The boy looks kind of funny.”

“Please tell us what’s wrong.” She placed her hand gently over his.

He stiffened, pulling away. His eyes filled the sockets. He looked like he'd just been awakened from a deep sleep. He ran a hand through his thick black hair.

"Jimmy? Please tell us ."

"I'm…being blackmailed," he said, his voice a harsh whisper.

***

Ashley was about to leave the office when Uncle Rob called.

"I know I just called earlier," he said, "but it looks like I'm gonna be tied up for the next three hours or so, and I figured I'd check in first to see how you're holding down the fort. I've got a conference call in a few minutes, and those can take anywhere from two minutes to two hours, many times even longer. This one will probably run well into the late afternoon. Valentino will be calling from Italy, and Cassini from France, so it's bound to be hectic here. There's a show scheduled for tomorrow afternoon, and everyone's been scrambling around like headless chickens--"

"Everything's just fine here." Ashley couldn't think about anything but the event Alexia Vandermeer was planning for Uncle Rob. She hoped there would be enough cameras around to capture it all. But she couldn't worry about that right now. Uncle Rob might sense something and ask what was going on. Uncle Rob seemed to have a sixth sense about things. "I wish you wouldn't worry so much, Uncle Rob. I'm okay."

"Just making sure you've got access to everything you need."

"Everyone's been just great. Very supportive."

"Anyone call from Europe?"

She nearly dropped the phone. For a moment she wondered if someone was trying to pull the wool over her eyes, or if he and Rita had cooked up some fake drill to test her under pressure.

"Ash? Still there?"

"From Europe?"

"As I told you before, we get them all the time. I told Rita to keep you in the loop. Often something will come up unexpectedly, and I told her to give you anything she thinks you could handle, and if something difficult pops up, she can help you with it. But only if she thinks you can figure out most of it yourself. Get it?"

Ashley took a breath. "Got it."

"You okay?"

"I'm fine. Why?"

"You sound like you've got something on your mind."

"Nothing's on my mind."

"You're sure?"

"Absolutely nothing. Just blank, empty space up there."

He laughed. "Don't sound so proud. People might think you're an idiot."

"I promise I'll try really hard not to sound like an idiot."

"Good. I'll do my best to call later on, but don't expect me to--"

"Don't worry about anything. Just do what you have to do. I'll be here when you get back."

It took her about fifteen minutes to walk to the Wyndham Grand. It was a straight shot down Penn for a few blocks, then onto Liberty and up Commonwealth, where the busy entrance of the hotel buzzed with private vans and limos coming and going, letting off and picking up well-dressed guests.

The huge, comfortably furnished lobby hummed with activity. Porters, diners and visitors darted to and from the elevators, bars and dining room. Everyone was chattering away on cellphones or with one another as they scurried along, hauling briefcases, handbags, laptops and umbrellas.

Ashley followed a small crowd into one of the elevators. She pressed 5 and backed up, until the hard surface of the metal wall pressed against her back. The coolness of the air conditioning made her skin tingle. She took a breath and closed her eyes, forcing her thoughts on this meeting. She was determined to make a good impression and be totally professional. She was, after all, representing Uncle Rob and his company, and everything had to go smoothly.

She kept reminding herself that this wasn't exactly rocket science. All she had to do was discuss the particulars for the shindig with this representative from London. This meant booking the right convention room for the right time and date. She'd brought along the tan leather briefcase Uncle Rob had given her, and it made her feel more self-confident. In it, she'd placed one of the appointment books Uncle Rob had given her, as well as a leather-bound booklet providing a list of every hotel Belasco Fashions had ever used. The booklet contained everything necessary for a booking--locations, accommodations, rates, etc.--and would be all she needed. She'd already decided that it would probably be best to pick one of the places Uncle Rob used the most frequently. This way, the people involved would be more responsive, and would give her *carte blanche*.

If this didn't play out properly, she'd excuse herself and call on Rita for help. She hoped it wouldn't come to that. She wanted Uncle Rob to know he could count on her and that she wouldn't be an embarrassment to him or the company. She wanted his confidence, his faith. She also wanted to convince Tiffany and Chip that she didn't need them anymore and that they could leave Pittsburgh without worrying about her. She was a grown woman and could live on her own, and they should concentrate on their own lives from now on. This move had been intimidating--even frightening--but she hadn't done badly in the two weeks they'd been here. She loved Tiffany and Chip and wanted them to remain in her life. But she knew she had to stop being selfish, and this meant standing on her own and no longer expecting them to watch over her.

She'd started a brand-new career and things were actually looking good, so far. Uncle Rob had even called Dad and arranged for him to come into town to see her in the next few weeks. Ashley wanted more than ever to see her father. She truly hoped that once she was settled and had gotten back her self-confidence, she could call Momma again and try to patch up things.

Maybe life would actually turn out well for her after all.

The elevator stopped on 5. She stepped out into the cool, carpeted corridor. The arrows directed her toward her left, and she went down a few doors, until she reached Room 522. Her heart raced as she brought up her hand and knocked.

A muffled voice from within the room said, "C'mon in."

She pushed open the door and slipped through the doorway. The room was dark, cool and empty. She saw no one.

Something didn't feel right. Her pulse fluttered.

"Is anyone here?"

Silence.

She looked around and noticed how neat everything was. The bed was made and there were no bags on it or anywhere on the floor. Her heart raced, but she told herself not to panic. After all, it was nearly 11:30. Management would have certainly made the bed long before now.

But where was the luggage? She didn't see any sign of life, didn't smell aftershave, or cologne.

But someone had just asked her to come in...

Perhaps he was in the bathroom.

"I'm Ashley Parker," she said uneasily, "from Belasco Fashions. I'm here because Mr. Davidson asked me to--"

She suddenly felt someone behind her. She hadn't heard anything but could tell she wasn't alone in the room. Someone had snuck up to her.

She turned sharply.

A man was standing right there, just a foot away. He was dressed in a good suit, and even though she'd never seen him before, there was something about his eyes. Something cold and frightening.

The tiny red glints. They sat in the center of his steel-gray eyes.

In that same instant, an image of Mr. Waite flashed in her head. Mr. Waite was laughing, and Ashley knew right then that this man had nothing to do with Burberry's, that the phone call from London was not about Uncle Rob or the beautiful model Alexia Vandermeer, and that there was no surprise party. They'd found her, and soon she'd be back in Orlando, facing the wrath of Mr. Waite.

She made one brief, feeble attempt to pull away, but something shot out of the darkness, covering her face. She reached out to pull it away. She couldn't let them take her. Once they found her, they'd find Tiffany and Chip, and the three of them would be taken back to face the horrors of Hell.

Just before the darkness enveloped her, she opened her mouth and took a deep breath to get a good scream going, but the darkness overwhelmed her, making her light-headed. Her scream grew smaller and smaller on its way up her throat, dissolving before it reached her mouth. The growing blackness turned everything numb and empty. Her last thought was of Tiffany and Chip.

She struggled to scream Tiffany's name with her inner voice but felt herself weakening, and heard only silence and more emptiness filling her mind.

A huge blackness swallowed her up.

Chapter 16

Jimmy had expected more of a reaction from Tiffany and Chip.

Judging by their expressions, he hadn't told them anything unusual or shocking. At first he wondered if he'd actually said what he thought he'd said. Had he said the word "blackmail?" Or had it come out differently? He'd been slumped over, staring at his coffee cup at the time. His hatred for Danielle and what she'd been doing to him had made everything around him turn red. Perhaps he'd mumbled something that hadn't made any sense. Or maybe he hadn't said anything at all.

Then he met Tiffany's eyes and realized what had happened. She'd heard him, all right. She'd heard every word he'd said. In fact, as he stared into those clear, beautiful blue orbs, he realized that she'd probably known what he was going to say even before he'd opened his mouth. From what he'd just learned about her, she was also a spirit, and had been to the same place he'd been.

But even so, she was much different. After all, she'd entered his mind several times. She'd communicated mentally with him and even managed to track him down through heavy morning traffic and chaotic street crowds. He guessed it wouldn't have been much of a challenge for her to figure out what was wrong.

"Who's blackmailing you?" she asked softly. "That dark-haired young woman with the studs and tattoos?"

He stiffened. He'd been right. She'd made another quick trip inside his head. "Can you actually see what's going on in my--"

"My ability to read people has been growing."

"You can say *that* again," Chip said, frowning.

She ignored him. "Your mind was filled with her image."

"She's crazy," Jimmy said.

"What kind of crazy?" Chip perked up. "Talking-to-birds-and-walking-around-naked crazy? Or keeping-a-jar-of-eyeballs-under-the-bed crazy?"

Tiffany glared at him.

Chip shrugged. "Hey, what can I say? I was up here briefly in the fifties and late sixties. The fifties weren't too bad, but the late sixties did a serious number on me. I might've inhaled too much, um, incense."

She shook her head and frowned.

Jimmy was suddenly frightened. If Tiffany had seen Danielle, what else had she seen? Had she seen his hatred burst from him and--

"*Yes,*" she said, her voice in his mind this time. "*But that's not important right now. Tell us what happened.*"

Even though he felt totally safe in Tiffany's presence, he found that he was reluctant to open up. He'd promised himself long ago that he'd never mention his predicament to a living soul. It was humiliating and made him hate himself. Each time the dark memory of that dreaded evening lingered in his mind, he wanted to curse himself for his carelessness. His thoughtlessness. His arrogance.

What happened should have been avoided. He should have seen it coming. A successful performer expected such things from his public. He was Jimmy Russo, a magician on the rise. Although he'd perished in a fire he himself had caused more than eighty years ago, his cunning and sense of self-preservation had enabled him to return to mortal life. It was a shame his intelligence couldn't shield him from his own masculine desires.

"Please tell us," Tiffany urged once again in her soft, caressing voice.

Three months ago, not long after he'd arrived in Pittsburgh from New York City, he visited a club called The Attic on Liberty Avenue. The marquee outside advertised live nightly entertainment and also included short comedy acts on weekends.

Jimmy went in and immediately saw the place in utter chaos. Their main act hadn't shown, and the audience was clearly agitated. The management was in a panic, combing the audience for talent and making calls to find someone to fill the fifteen-minute gap until a replacement act could be found and brought in. Jimmy went backstage and offered to fill in. They were so desperate that they agreed to let him go on without even asking his name or references. He went on stage, did a few jokes, and even slipped in some impressive magic, which included stealing a pair of laced pink panties from one of the waitresses as she passed the stage.

The audience loved him. The manager of the place was so impressed with his act that he asked Jimmy back the following night. When he returned, he was given the opening twenty-minute spot. He did a fresh routine, adding some juggling with his mike, six shot glasses, a chair and a customer's walking stick. The crowd went crazy. He was asked to come back the next night. By the time he'd arrived, the place was so packed, people stood in the aisles during his entire act.

After that third night, a party of more than twenty people waited for him backstage, asking him to go with them to a private residence on Penn Avenue for a celebration. He was taken aback by the attention and agreed to go with them. The party was being given by someone named Danielle, who'd sat in the first row all three nights he'd performed at the Attic.

The large apartment was packed. Everyone was standing around with drinks or blunts, or huddled over a table, sharing lines of coke.

Danielle gave Jimmy two strong drinks. He wanted to stop after the second, but she insisted he have a third one. She'd fixed all his drinks and stuck close to him the entire evening. She made him feel like the most important man on earth. He could do no wrong. She was a sexy, good-looking girl, and he enjoyed her attentions as any other man would have. The prospect of having sex with this raven-haired beauty had filled his mind since he'd arrived at her party. He didn't want to screw things up by drinking too much.

To please Danielle, he had one small sip of this third drink. It didn't take long for him to realize that he shouldn't have had it. The numbness that quickly overpowered him convinced him he should have listened to his gut.

"Did you black out?" Tiffany asked. "Or are we talking about something else?"

"I wasn't sure. Not at first, anyway. I thought maybe it was because I really didn't want that third drink and it was my body's way of telling me I was an idiot for even taking it in the first place. I was trying really hard not to get drunk. I thought Danielle and I…to be blunt, I wanted to get lucky after everyone had left. I thought Danielle felt the same way. At least, that's how it seemed to me. She was constantly right beside me, rubbing against me, touching me. All that sexy flirty stuff a girl does that turns a guy on. But it didn't happen like that."

"What *did* happen?"

Not long after he'd taken that one sip of that third drink, Jimmy collapsed on the couch. He had no idea how long he was out, and when he woke up, everyone but Danielle had gone. She was sitting beside him, talking softly, almost in a whisper, holding his hand, stroking his cheek. Her face was just inches away.

"What happened?" he'd asked, his throat hot and dry.

She didn't say anything. His first reaction was that she'd also had too much to drink. Her face seemed distorted, her eyes much larger than they should be. As he watched, her eyes moved down from his face, an inch at a time, and he soon noticed what she was looking at.

His trousers were unzipped and unbuckled, his shirt open.

His heart thrashed as he frantically zipped up. She sat there smiling, obviously enjoying his dilemma. He asked her what happened again, and she laughed and told him to guess.

"We did it?"

"Not exactly..."

He knew he was messed up, but he couldn't believe he'd been so drunk that he'd actually had sex with someone and couldn't remember. Had he blacked out completely? What had she put in that third drink?

Danielle had done something horrible to him. There was something in her eyes that frightened him. Judging by the coldness he felt coming from her, he decided that he didn't want to know. He only knew that he wanted to get away from her. He'd been in the presence of evil before and could tell that this woman was just as evil as anything he'd encountered in the deepest darkness of Hell itself.

Then, just when he decided to get out of there, she moved closer, until their thighs were touching. Her coldness made him tremble. "We need to talk, Jimmy."

"I have to leave. To go home and sleep it off..."

"You need to stay here. That is, until I tell you to leave."

"What?"

"You belong to me now." Her face was only inches away. "You're a star. *My* star."

She wasn't making any sense. How could he be anyone's star? He was a magician. He was good but was no star. What was she talking about?

"I do magic tricks."

"You're a star. I just saw you in a movie."

"A *movie*?" He still had no idea what she was talking about. But something in her eyes told him he didn't want to find out.

Her gaze never left him as she picked up the remote from the coffee table and pressed a button. The big widescreen TV filled the room with brightness. Images emerged. The scene took place in someone's bedroom. Three figures-- Jimmy and two naked young girls--were engaged in sex in the bed. A camera had been positioned somewhere near the ceiling and looked down, showing Jimmy's face and body as well as the girls tending to him.

"How young were they?" Tiffany asked uneasily.

"Too young," he replied flatly.

"Where'd they come from?" Chip asked. "They were obviously too young to show up at a party like that."

"Danielle was kind of vague about the whole thing. I figured they were probably brought in later on and paid for what they did. They looked around fourteen or fifteen but obviously knew what they were doing. As I watched the film, I could tell they'd done all that before."

Tiffany lowered her voice. "What happened once you saw the film?"

"It shook me up, of course. My whole world had just caved in, and I knew she fully intended to use that film to blackmail me. I had no idea what to do. All I knew was that I'd just met an evil bitch who now owned me, and if I did or said the wrong thing, she'd send that movie to some scary people. Based on the number of people who'd been at her place, I suspected she had a lot of connections. She might have known every single sub or inferior wandering around in Pittsburgh. I knew I was toast. From that point on, I couldn't do anything to rock the boat. There were people in New York City who'd been looking for me for a long time. I was responsible for two major fires that killed dozens of people who had friends and relatives, and neither case was ever solved."

"What did she want?" Tiffany asked. "Was this just simple blackmail?"

"She said all she wanted was a little security. She wanted me to stay in town. She told me about this new place that was looking for good acts. The Bel-Mor. She said she knew the owners and could arrange for an audition. All I had to do was perform, give her a fifty percent cut, and I wouldn't have anything to worry about."

"There was no way you could've snatched that film?" Chip asked.

"She'd made copies. She had it on digital as well as glossies. There were obviously at least two cameras in her bedroom."

"She was busy," Tiffany said.

"She handed me two glossies and a thumb drive. She said the copies were in a safe place."

"Did you look at the thumb drive?" she asked.

"I took it to an internet café the day after that happened. It's authentic, all right."

"I guess Tifferoo and I now know what sort of crazy this lady is," Chip said flatly. "Just who is she? Is she from down below?"

"Her name is Danielle Kaminski. She's got a shop on Liberty. It's called Sexywear Ever. And I'm pretty certain she's mortal."

Tiffany turned to Chip. "I have a feeling she's done this to other people."

Chip shifted in his seat. "I'm picking up vibes in your tone, muffin."

"What vibes?"

"They're telling me that you're thinking of looking for another butt to kick."

"Then I guess you read me right." She turned to Jimmy. "I think we'd like to pay this lady a visit."

Jimmy gawked at her. "You mean you can actually *do* something about this?"

"We're not making any promises. But I'll certainly try."

"How come *you* didn't handle this?" Chip asked Jimmy. "You have powers, you know."

Jimmy shrugged. "Not the ones that matter."

"Can't you read her?" Tiffany asked.

"I can't read anyone." He shook his head. "Hard to believe, isn't it? I can't shape-shift or read minds."

"Join the club," Chip said flatly.

"Stop being a baby," Tiffany said. "Like I told you before--" She stopped talking and closed her eyes.

Chip gently tapped her shoulder. "Tiffers?"

No reply.

"Is she all right?" Jimmy asked.

"I'm not sure. She always acts like this when she picks up something."

"Picks up something? You mean like when she was communicating with me?"

"Tifferoo can be pretty frightening. Sometimes she's a regular Geiger counter. Keep spoons and other metal objects away when you see her acting like this. Like I said, she's scary."

Tiffany snapped out of her trance. She looked like she'd just seen a ghost. "It's Ashley." Her voice was a whisper. "I just heard her voice. She sounded terrified."

PART TWO

Rounding Up the Victims

Chapter 17

Andras left Ashley Parker lying on the big double bed in his hotel room. She lay on her back, her arms at her sides, her eyes closed. She looked very peaceful. She would remain in this state until he released her from the spell after they touched down in Orlando.

He fished the cell out of his trouser pocket.

"Yes, sir?" asked his contact.

"Parker's now ready for transport."

"Excellent. Did you have any difficulty?"

"I never have any trouble when I know where someone is. For me, it's merely a matter of where to set the trap."

"Where are you and what are your instructions?"

"I'm in my room at the Wyndham Grand. I'll need someone here as soon as possible, with a suitably sized packing case. Will this be a problem?"

"Not at all. We're on excellent terms with the Management and Staff. I'll handle this immediately."

"I'll also need someone in uniform to wheel the case out of this room, down the freight elevator and out to the loading dock. From there, the package will have to be transported to the airport and loaded onto the plane."

"I assume you won't be accompanying the transport, will you, sir?"

"I have to stay back and make arrangements to collect the others. The plane will be standing by until I'm ready to make the return trip to Orlando. I'll let you know when I'll need another transport."

"Very well, sir."

"Will this be handled professionally? I mean, should I stick around to make sure--"

"There will be no need for that, sir. You can be assured this will be properly handled. We're using only our best and most reliable personnel for this venture. Will there be anything else?"

"That should do it."

Andras pocketed the cell. Before he left the room, he glanced at the Parker girl. *One down*, he thought with a nod. *The other two should be no problem.*

Mortals were so easy to hunt down. It bothered Andras that they almost always offered very little challenge.

Hopefully, hunting the blonde would provide him with more excitement than what he'd just experienced with Parker.

***

Tiffany used her cellphone to call Ashley.

No answer. Ashley's voice came on, asking her to leave a message. She tried again and listened to the same message. Something was very wrong.

Ashley would never ask Tiffany to leave a message after she'd just summoned her.

For the next couple of minutes, she sat staring at the phone, wondering what was going on. What she should do next.

"Try Belasco's company," Chip suggested.

She punched in the number Ashley had given her last week. After two rings, the receptionist's soft, friendly voice came on. "Belasco Fashions, how may I direct your call?"

"I'd like to talk to Ashley Parker."

"I'm sorry, but Ms. Parker isn't in at the moment."

Tiffany sat back and took a breath. As soon as the dreaded words sunk in, she realized she'd been right. Ashley was in trouble. But she shouldn't panic. It wouldn't solve anything and would only make things worse. If Ashley did need her help, Tiffany had to keep a clear head.

She took a moment to collect herself. *Breathe. Stay calm.* "She's not answering her cell," she told the receptionist.

"Miss--"

"She always answers her cell--especially when she knows it's me. This isn't like her."

"Miss, I assure you Ms. Parker is presently--"

"Listen." Despite her efforts, Tiffany found it difficult to keep her composure. "My name is Tiffany LeBouf. I'm Ashley's best friend. We came up here from Florida and--"

"Miss LeBeau, if you'll please leave your message--"

"I need to talk to her *now*, and it's Le*Bouf*. With an *F*."

"Miss Le*Bouf*, I'm sure you realize Ms. Parker has been working here--"

"Of course I know where she's working. We came up from Florida. Didn't I just say that?"

"Yes--"

"And didn't I say Ashley and I are best friends?"

"I understand how upset you may be that she isn't answering her phone, but--"

"No. You don't. You can't possibly understand how upset I am. You have no idea what could be happening right now. If you did, you'd understand why I'm so upset. You'd probably be upset, too. Ashley could be in trouble, and as I promised her a long time ago--"

"Miss LeBouf, if you'll just calm down, I'm sure you'll realize that you're worrying over nothing. Ashley told me less than an hour ago that she'd be taking an early lunch break, and that she might be a little late getting back, so--"

"Did she say where she was going?"

"No, but like I said, I really wouldn't worry. She's been very busy lately, and her uncle--who's also her employer--wants her to handle as much work as she possibly--"

"What sort of work? And I *know* who her employer is, thank you."

"Whatever comes up, he'd like her to handle it without interference. He wants to see what she can do by herself."

Tiffany felt her pulse flutter as she took another breath. "What came up?"

"I'm not at liberty to discuss this--"

"Listen to me." This was not getting her anywhere. She knew right then that she was not going to learn anything through conventional methods.

"Yes?" The receptionist sounded impatient.

Tiffany closed her eyes and focused. "*What was the last thing she told you*?" she sent through the line.

Silence.

"Please. This is very important."

A pause. Then: "She said, "I'm leaving now, Rita, and I might be a little late getting back.""

"What else?"

"I asked her where she was going, if she needed directions."

"What did she say?"

"No, thanks, I know what I'm doing."

"Was she distressed in any way?"

"No. In fact, she seemed very excited."

"What happened before she told you she was leaving?"

Another pause. "There was a phone call."

The back of Tiffany's neck grew warm. "*Go on."*

"It was an international call, from Burberry's in London."

Burberry's? Interesting. "*What did they want?"*

"They wanted to talk to Ashley."

Tiffany sat up. Something was wrong. She had heard of Burberry's when she was living in Hollywood. They handled the biggest models and designers. She totally understood why they'd need to call Belasco Fashions.

But why would they want Ashley?

How did they even know about her?

"Why?" she sent to the receptionist.

"They said it was personal."

"Had they talked to her before?"

"That was the funny thing about this. I'm sure Burberry's didn't know anything about Ashley."

"Didn't that strike you as odd?"

"Yes, but as I told you, Mr. Belasco wants her to start taking responsibility on her own."

Tiffany trembled as she clumsily pocketed the phone.

"Tifferoo? What's going on?"

She barely heard him. She closed her eyes and sent over a message to Ashley:

"Ash, if you can hear me, tell me where you are and what's going on."

Silence.

"Ash?"

Nothing.

"Ashley? This is Tiffany. Please tell me where you are."

Silence.

"Ash? Are you in trouble? Please send me something. Anything. I'm worried!"

Silence.

"Tifferoo?"

Tiffany opened her eyes. Everything was blurred. She couldn't remember where she was or what she was doing. She rubbed her eyes and took a couple of deep breaths. When her vision cleared, she found herself staring at a nice-looking dark-haired guy sitting across the table. He was staring right back at her and looked uneasy. They were sitting at a window booth in a restaurant. She vaguely remembered who he was and why they were here, but somehow that didn't matter.

She slid out of the booth and heard a familiar voice behind her. She turned. A skinny body and a thick unruly mop of red hair approached her.

Her eyes had gone blurry again. She rubbed her temples. The faint, indistinguishable red shape gradually turned into Chip.

"Tifferoosky, what's happening? Where the hell are you going?"

She sighed deeply and forced the panic away once again. It went away more sluggishly this time. "Ashley's in trouble." She didn't want to waste time with explanations. Ashley needed their help now. "I'm going to her building and find out what's going on."

"Right now?" Chip asked.

"You got it." Tiffany spun around. Dodging waitresses and customers, she bolted across the crowded room, to the glass doors.

***

As Dahl, gazing straight ahead, sat stiffly behind the wheel of the Lincoln, Andras relaxed in the back seat and watched the crowds moving across the street. Most of the street traffic appeared to be shoppers. Others, especially those leaving the building, were well-dressed men and women moving quickly, their briefcases, laptops and umbrellas hopping along with them.

Andras consulted his watch. It was slightly after twelve. Just thirty minutes since he'd snared Parker. Right at this moment, someone would be fitting her snugly into a packing case. She'd then be pushed safely down the hall, placed in the freight elevator, taken down to the loading dock and shoved into the trunk of the awaiting transport vehicle.

Right now he was more concerned what would happen across the street. It shouldn't take long for the others to show themselves. Daniel Grove had told him the three were close friends. Once the other two discovered Parker missing, they'd hurry to her workplace to see what was going on.

The heavy lunch crowd could become a problem or an advantage. Crowds were desirable when planning something requiring confusion and distraction, like his Dallas assignment in '63. He didn't think he'd need chaos right now but decided to prepare for it, just in case. He also needed to find out the ground rules for this area. A good hunter always prepared himself in an unfamiliar setting.

He pulled out his cell and punched in the number.

"Yes, sir?" came the familiar voice.

"What's the security situation on Fifth Avenue? I'm on Liberty at the moment. Confine the area to the block between Stanwix Street and Fifth."

"Are you referring to Fifth Avenue Place, sir?"

"Yes."

"There are cameras situated outside approximately two dozen stores to monitor that grid. Fifth Avenue Place is equipped with state-of-the-art security monitors. Some are motion monitors, others visual, with split-screen models also being used. Some are programmed to switch angles at frequent intervals at anywhere from five to thirty seconds, to monitor the vulnerable areas more efficiently."

"Is there a camera watching the outside entrance facing Liberty? I'm about a hundred yards up from that corner."

"Both ends of the street are being monitored. Stanwix on the far side, and Fifth on your end. This is a standard, seven-twenty-four procedure--"

"Your people were given a description of the three I'm looking for, correct?"

"A written one, sir. Other than Parker's Florida driver's license photo, we haven't received photos for the other two."

"Can I assume you've also been given this written description?"

"I have it on my laptop screen."

"Tell me exactly what it says."

"One blond female, between twenty-two and twenty-five years old. Five-feet-five, 115 pounds. Blue eyes, shapely and trim. One redheaded male, approximately the same age. Green eyes. Height and weight similar to the female."

"Sounds good enough."

"Would you like me to arrange to have someone watch for them specifically from one of the assigned monitors in that section, sir?"

"That would be a good idea. I have a feeling they'll be here very shortly."

"Since Parker is employed at Belasco Fashions in the Fifth Avenue Place Building, I assume you'd like this agency monitored as well as the front entrance of the building itself?"

"You may also want to have all other entrances and exits monitored as well."

"Very well, sir. I'm on it."

"I want to know the instant they're spotted, and would like footage immediately sent over through my phone."

"I'll make it happen."

Andras pocketed the cell, sat back and closed his eyes. It wouldn't be long now. Good thing. He was getting hungry and wanted to take a quick trip to the steakhouse halfway up the block. He craved a huge steak *tartare* with raw egg, capers and onions. A good hunt always stimulated his appetite.

Raw meat sharpened the hunter's senses.

But that could wait. Business first.

Chapter 18

Tiffany squeezed through the heavy lunch crowds clogging up Liberty Avenue. She had no idea if Chip or Jimmy Russo were behind her and didn't care. The only thing that mattered was Ashley--where she was, what had happened.

As she forced her way through the slow-moving groups, she kept alert, focusing on everyone she passed. It was frustrating to see so many females with long dark-brown hair. Many of the women in the crowd had the same body type. There were even several young women with the same sort of face as Ashley, and Tiffany had to restrain herself from rushing over for a closer look. She knew that if Ashley saw her, she'd immediately yell Tiffany's name.

As she fought the crowd, she called out mentally for her friend.

"Ashley, this is Tiffany. I'm looking for you!"

Silence.

"I'm on Liberty Avenue right now. In just a few minutes I'll be in your building, asking around."

Silence.

"Ashley? Can you hear me? Please answer me--"

Someone tapped her shoulder and she cringed. "Tifferoo?"

Chip and Jimmy Russo were standing right behind her. As the crowd slithered around them, Chip jabbed a thumb toward his right, where a street vendor stood behind his wooden booth, selling a bouquet of fresh flowers to two elderly ladies.

Despite her inner turmoil, she joined them. They moved away from the crowd and gathered at the corner of the liquor store just a few yards away from the flower vendor.

"What's the problem?"

"We'd better talk." Chip looked solemn.

She didn't have the time to stand here and argue. She had to find Ashley. Chip knew that, knew it very well. "Listen. I've got to--"

"We know, Tiffers. But before we go anywhere, we've got to know what's on your mind."

"You know what's on my mind. I've got to find Ashley."

"Righterino, but you're not going about it the right way."

"What way is there? I'm going in the building and ask about her."

"It's a big building, Tifferoo. You could get seriously lost in it. So could we. So could anyone--especially if you don't know where to look."

"I know it's a big building. I also know which floor she'll be on."

"But she isn't there right now, is she?"

"That's why I'm going in there. To make sure."

Chip ran a hand through his thick red mop. "And once you find out she's not there, then what?"

She couldn't believe she was listening to this. Ashley was missing, and instead of wanting to help find her, Chip coaxed her over here to talk about stuff they already knew. "We're wasting time, Chip. My friend is missing and I've got to find her!"

"We know," Chip said. "We were right there in the breakfast place when you had that moment."

She felt her composure crumbling. She had to keep it together. Chip wasn't the enemy. Neither was Jimmy. But she couldn't hold back the panic if she wasn't allowed to look for her friend. She had the feeling that for every moment they wasted, they were letting Ashley slip further away. "She's in trouble. I think someone's got her."

"You can't know that for sure."

"I heard her voice back at the restaurant. She sounded terrified. I just tried getting back with her two minutes ago. I heard nothing. If she could answer me, she would have. She can't. This tells me she's unconscious, under a spell, or--"

"We'll find her, Tiffers."

"I can't do it as long as you're keeping me here, can I?"

"You don't know if anyone in there actually knows what happened," Jimmy said.

"I'm going to talk to that Rita lady again."

"Who?"

"The company's receptionist. I grabbed some images from her while I had her on the phone back there, but I think I might be able to find out even more in person."

"What if you can't?"

"Ashley wouldn't have left that office without letting anyone know where she was going."

"What if everyone's at lunch?" Jimmy asked.

"If I don't learn anything right away, I'll come right back out."

"Let me guess. You don't want us to come in with you, right?"

"I think I can do this faster by myself."

"And what do we do while you're in the building?"

"Keep an eye on the crowd. If we're lucky, I'm worrying for nothing. If she shows up, give me a yell. I'll hear you."

"And if she doesn't?"

"I'll be fifteen minutes. Can you entertain yourself for fifteen minutes?"

Chip blinked. "You really want an answer to that?"

She wasn't in the mood for his warped humor right now. "Are you gonna wait out here for me or what?"

Chip waved her on. "Go do your thing, grasshopper."

Tiffany spun around. Just before she darted down the street, she changed her stylish open-toed casuals into silver high-topped running shoes with arch support designed for speed and ankle stability.

***

Andras' cell went off at 12:21.

"They're across the street from you," his contact said.

Andras sat up sharply and pushed the button that lowered his tinted window. The crowds and traffic were relentless. People clogged the streets, crossing between stopped traffic while drivers inched through intersections against the light. Several blond women hurried down the street. Andras counted at least eight. Although he couldn't see them clearly at that distance, he noted that they were dressed smartly. This told him nothing.

"Tell me where I should be looking," he said to the cell.

"We're picking up the scan from one of the monitors across the street facing Fifth Avenue Place. The monitor is fixed on the third floor of the bank building about half a block up from your position. It's equipped with a zoom lens. It's a private security monitor, and from what we're seeing, the people you want are standing at the corner, in front of the liquor store next to the building."

Andras could see only crowds and passing traffic. "The crowds are making this impossible. Send me the scan."

"It's coming right over."

Ten seconds later, Andras' display lit up. The images were microscopic, but he could make out three figures standing at the corner.

"I see three people. Who are they talking to?"

"I just sent a zoom-in order to the security agency. These people work quickly. It should only take a few minutes for a positive ID."

"There's no time. How soon can you get someone over there?"

"I can have a unit from the Police Department sent there in three minutes. That area is hot for drug buys, purse snatching and muggings, as well as traffic accidents. The police rove there all the time anyway. I'm surprised I don't see a cruiser there right now."

"No cops. Too much publicity. This has to be done quietly."

"How about the DEA? We've got people there as well as Undercover Crime. Plainclothes cops would be much less conspicuous. All they'll need is someone reporting a drug buy. We can even supply a photo of any one of several known dealers to get them there faster. I have a list available."

Andras rubbed the back of his neck. Braithwaite wouldn't want anyone else knowing about this. With cops involved, things turned messy in just minutes. "I don't know how much time we've got. And we have no idea how long they're gonna be there."

"I'm guessing they're planning to go inside the building to ask about Parker."

"In that case, they already know Parker's disappeared. They might have tried calling her."

"If they know she's missing, why are they outside the building? They might have called Belasco's company and inquired about her. The company wouldn't know where she is, would they?"

"I was very careful about my strategy. If they know Parker's missing, then they also know something's wrong. I'm wondering why they're standing there. And who's that third guy? That *is* a guy, right?"

"It's a male, sir. We're still waiting for the ID."

"We need to grab them before they go inside. That's a huge building, and if they think someone's after them, they'll hide and we'd have to evacuate the damned building to find them. That would be a giant fiasco and would take the rest of the day. We'll have to arrange something else. Besides, an evacuation or fire alarm will attract the police and the Fire Department, as well as the fucking media and a crowd. Sending in a security team will attract attention as well. Does the building have its own security department?"

"Of course, but you're right about the unwanted attention. Hold on. I'm in the process of contacting an individual we use from time to time for rush jobs. He lives in the area and knows how to get things done. I just texted him."

"I take it he's reliable."

"And very discreet. He's expensive, but he'll get the job done."

"That's no problem. What does he usually charge?"

"For something like this? I'd say two thousand would get his attention."

"Offer him five for this. How fast can he get it done?"

"It depends on where he is at the moment."

"You realize we might have only seconds to act here."

"Understood, sir."

Andras watched the display. The blonde had turned around and began moving away very quickly. "Shit. She's leaving."

"Copy that. She's heading straight for the building."

"What about the other two?"

"They haven't budged. I need an order, sir. As quickly as possible."

The blonde dodged crowds as she ran toward the building. Something just didn't make sense. There were supposed to be two of them, not three. They'd either picked up someone along the way or just stopped to talk. If they knew Parker had disappeared, they'd be in a hurry to find out what happened. They wouldn't stop outside the building to talk to a stranger.

That didn't matter right now. The blonde was running toward the building while the redhead and the dark-haired guy stood outside. It wouldn't take long for her to find out no one knew where Parker had gone. Once the blonde found out, she'd hurry back outside to rejoin her friends.

This should be a good thing, but Andras knew better than take anything for granted. The blonde was obviously very bright and knew how to put things together. Her guard would be up. And since she had powers no one could explain, she remained extremely dangerous.

"Sir?"

If only they knew who that other guy was...

But that didn't matter, either. Andras had been sent here to grab Parker, the blonde, and the redhead. The redhead was now within reach. If Andras could grab him, the blonde would be out there by herself. Once she'd discovered her friend was also missing, she'd panic--which would make her vulnerable. She'd lose her focus and would make mistakes. This would make her much easier to catch.

"Have your contact snatch the redhead. Once the blonde's inside, we might have at least ten, maybe even fifteen minutes, to arrange for a team to snatch her on her way out."

"What about the third man? I'm still waiting for the ID."

"Not interested. If he gets in the way, deal with it. Just don't attract attention."

"I'm on it."

***

Tall, darkly bearded and menacing in his leather jacket, tight leather pants and black biker's boots, A. J. "Brush" Conley stopped by the bargain DVD bin on his way to the cash register. He began scouring the stacks to see if there was anything he could add to his personal collection. Something with Jet Li, Jackie Chan, or Steven Seagal. Presently he owned more than 200 actioners: Clint Eastwood, Jackie Chan, Bruce Lee, Steven Seagal, Chuck Norris and Jet Li. It was time to enjoy another movie marathon for the coming weekend, with Sara Jane coming over for the festivities, along with a case of Bud and whatever toys she decided to bring over from her porno shop on Liberty.

Sara Jane loved kick-ass movies, but she always brought over a couple of bondage flicks from her store for variety. She tended to get frisky after about an hour of non-stop action and made no bones about what was on her mind. She merely got up during the movie, picked up her black leather overnight bag and went into the bathroom. Fifteen minutes later, she came out wearing her skin-tight leather outfit, black leather mask and black leather boots with six-inch spikes and told him to mute the volume on his 55-inch widescreen.

Brush always enjoyed the abrupt change in the program. Like all men, he appreciated it when a hot, provocatively dressed lady tossed him handcuffs, twenty yards of clothesline and a bright-red ball gag, and told him to get to work, and not to bother being gentle.

Brush was a lot of things, but gentle wasn't among his vices.

After just a couple of minutes of browsing, he discovered that he was wasting his time. Except for a couple of "Dirty Harry" actioners he already owned and a Lee Van Cleef Italian B-western, everything in the bin dealt with mindless tripe. Bored teens of both sexes turning into the world's stupidest idiots at summer camp. He'd be better off going back to the computer in his East Liberty townhouse and ordering his flicks online.

Conley's cell went off. He fished it out of his pocket and read the display. His pulse pounded. This caller was important. Anonymous and well-connected, with political ties. He called only when he needed something important done immediately. These jobs were dangerous, but given his employer's position, there was little risk of incarceration, and the money was very good. The only drawback was that if you fucked up or didn't meet the deadline, you'd better leave town, change your name and have major cosmetic work done to your face.

But the money was well worth the risk.

He moved over to the end of the aisle, away from wandering customers. When he was alone, he flicked on the cell.

The computer-generated voice said, "Are you available?"

"Yes."

"What is your location?"

"I'm in a drugstore on Penn, between Fifth and Sixth Street."

"Two men are on Liberty & Fifth, outside the liquor store across from Fifth Avenue Place. One man is a short, thin redhead, mid-twenties, with green eyes. Grab him in the next ten minutes without anyone noticing and detain him until someone comes for him. Five thousand dollars will be paid for this."

Five K. That was a lot of jack. Especially for what sounded like ten minutes of his time. It made him wonder how far up this one went. But he knew which questions not to ask, and that was definitely one of them. "Where do you want him detained?"

"The alley. Make sure you're at least a hundred feet away from the main street. Someone will be there very shortly to collect him."

"I take it you don't want him hurt."

"Affirmative."

“And you want this done in the next ten minutes?”

“Affirmative.”

Five grand for ten minutes’ work. That was even better than knocking someone off, or transporting a trunk of illegal meds across the state line. “And you don’t want anyone noticing anything?”

“Affirmative.”

“I’m your man.”

Chapter 19

Her thick gold mane leaping behind her like dancing flame, Tiffany dodged the crowds in her quest to reach the front entrance of the big building at the corner.

"Am I seeing things?" Jimmy asked Chip, "or is she wearing different shoes?"

"I can't really tell if you're seeing things," Chip said, "but Tifferoo's definitely wearing different shoes."

"When did she change them?"

"Most likely when she was talking to us."

Jimmy scratched the back of his neck. "Any reason she did that?"

"She changes her shoes all the time. I've seen her wear six different pairs in one day."

"But why this time?"

"Knowing her as I do, I'd say she can probably move faster now."

"Ah. I see."

"Tifferoosky has a thing about shoes."

"Obviously." Jimmy turned back to the building. Tiffany had almost reached the entrance. Once he'd stopped staring at her shoes, he found that he couldn't stop gawking at the rest of her. He reminded himself that, like him, she was no longer a mortal. But somehow it didn't matter. She was a feast for the eyes. He couldn't stop imagining how that enchanting figure would look unclothed--

Stop it. This was not the time for such thoughts. Their good friend had gone missing. He'd seen the look of horror in Tiffany's eyes at the restaurant and felt the despair filling her being just as intensely as if it were happening to him. He wanted to help them but had no idea what he could do. He didn't know Ashley Parker, but he'd heard of Belasco Fashions and could ask someone who knew something of modeling agencies if they could help. Marc Cassman, for instance. Jimmy knew better than ask Bellman or Moreland for *any* sort of help or advice. Whatever dealings he'd had with those two had always backfired.

But he had to do something. Tiffany had recently offered to help him with his Danielle problem. He wouldn't be able to sleep at night if he didn't try and return the favor.

He pulled out his cell and checked his directory. Besides Bellman and Moreland, Danielle was listed, but only because she'd told him to add her to his list. Marc Cassman was also included. On a whim Jimmy had transferred Cassman's card info to the directory last night, after Moreland had driven him home. Jimmy had been tempted to toss the card, but after those two strange encounters with Tiffany at the club, he found that he wasn't as depressed as usual and felt his luck might change.

But whatever happened, he had to find out what was going on. When a friend of yours disappeared, it could mean drugs, the Mob, or illegal trafficking. He couldn't see these two involved in stuff like that, but something serious was going on, and it would be foolish to involve himself without knowing the facts.

"We need to talk about this." He stared at Chip as he pocketed his cell.

"About what? Tifferoo? The Ashley babe? The two of us standing out here, not knowing what to talk about? Or did you want to delve more into Tifferoo's shoe obsession?"

Jimmy was beginning to understand why Tiffany's patience frequently wore thin with this character. "Let's start with Tiffany and see where it takes us. Think she'll be back in fifteen minutes?"

"Tifferoo's usually good to her word, but if something strikes her fancy while she's inside, she's liable to be gone longer."

"Strikes her fancy?"

"Say she's reading some vibes from the receptionist. If she picks up something else, she'll stay there until she discovers what's going on. Tifferoo's a curious babe. She doesn't like it when something's going on without knowing what it is."

Jimmy found himself growing more fascinated with the woman by the second. "Can she really pull vibes from people?"

"She did it to you back at the restaurant, didn't she?"

"She sure did."

"And last night, at the club?"

"It felt like she jumped right into my head and started talking."

"Tifferoo's had the gift almost as long as we've been up here."

Jimmy still found it intriguing how she'd got him talking about his problems. "I never thought I'd ever talk to anyone about that business with Danielle. Talking to Tiffany is like being injected with truth serum."

"Tell me about it."

"You, too?"

"Like I said before, Tifferoosky's downright scary. She looks at you with those big baby blues and that dazzling smile, and before you realize it, she just took a quick browse inside your head."

"How does she do it?"

"No idea. She doesn't even know. It really tears me up that I was down in that black hole for two thousand years and can't do stuff like that. She went down there for fifteen minutes and now she's got as many powers as most of the subs I've seen."

Jimmy sighed. He didn't want to ask, but he had to know. "She can't be a demon. *Can* she?"

"Does she act like one?"

Jimmy smiled. "She's about as un-demonlike as anyone I've ever seen. I think she's more like an angel than anything."

"There you have it, then."

He searched Chip's eyes. "Then *that's* what she is? An angel?"

"I wouldn't go that far. She *was* down below, after all. Angels usually aren't sent down there. They'd want to clean it up and make things pretty, and what fun would *that* be? First thing you know, they'd make the demons take showers, watch their language and prance around the Valley wearing beads and flowers and singing folk songs." Chip tilted his head. “Come to think of it, that would really be something to see.”

Jimmy couldn’t tell if Chip was serious or just being his usual impish self. But they were getting off the subject. “You seem to know her better than anyone. What would you say she is?”

Chip puffed. “One of those babes every guy dreams about from the time he first discovers he’s got something seriously interesting hopping around loose in his undershorts.”

Jimmy felt his patience jumping ship again. “What I *meant* was, where did she get her abilities?”

Chip sighed tiredly. “Like I just said, we don’t know.”

“But you two are friends. You must have--”

“I have no idea.”

“And she had these powers when you guys were in Florida?”

“That’s why we got in so much trouble down there. Tifferoo did a serious number on the super’s pals when they came over from Egypt to buy up some land.”

“Balberith’s replacement?”

“Braithwaite.” Chip’s voice dropped at the utterance of the name. “He’s in Orlando right now. He’s probably gonna make a move north pretty soon. He’ll head for a big city, set up and move on.”

“It could be several years before he makes it up here, then.”

“It depends on how long it takes him to find enough subs and inferiors to handle each place. But it doesn't matter. By the time he gets here, Tifferoo and I will be long gone."

"What about your friend Ashley?"

"We haven't figured that out yet. Tifferoo has always been nervous about leaving her here. Tifferoo hates demons and will kick their asses if she gets the chance. That's why we looked you up. We had to find out what kind of spirit you were and what you know about the situation here."

"And if I'd been bad?"

Chip chuckled. "Tifferoo would've kicked your ass."

Jimmy smiled at the prospect. "That really doesn't sound bad at all."

Chip turned solemn. "You'd think differently once you woke up and found yourself back down there."

Chip's expression made Jimmy reconsider his reaction. It also made him wonder just what happened in Orlando.

"This "trouble" you just mentioned. What happened?"

"It'll be better for you if you didn't know. But like I said, it's only because of the Ashley babe that Tiffers and I are still here."

Jimmy felt a wave of sadness settling over him. The prospect of Tiffany leaving brought about a sudden depression. He couldn't imagine anything much more unpleasant than meeting such a beautiful creature just to see her walk away forever.

"You're stuck on her." Chip's voice snapped him out of it.

"P-Pardon?"

"I can see it on your face. She got to you."

Jimmy felt himself reddening. Chip gave one the impression he was stupid, but this sudden observation suggested otherwise to Jimmy. "I-I don't know what you mean…"

"Guess what? You got to her, too."

Jimmy blinked.

"Let me put it a gentler, subtler way. I'm a genuine asshole. In other words, I don't normally do gentle or subtle, so you can take this morsel to the bank. Tiffers fell for a guy in Ohio when we first came up. She fell hard, and when it happened, she wore the same glossy blank look for him as she did when she saw you last night at the Bel-Mor."

Jimmy tried hard to read his expression. Was it possible Tiffany did in fact like him? Or did she just feel sorry for him? His Danielle story had obviously made Tiffany angry. He hadn't considered the fact that she might actually be attracted him. Women generally found him sexy and exciting, but he suspected this was due to his status as a performer. He knew what hype and celebrity did to people's heads.

"You don't think this is because I'm a performer who does magic tricks, do you?"

"Are you trying to ask me if Tifferoosky is dazzled by your celeb status?"

"I guess I am."

"For your information, Tifferoo was an actress before she died. Flash and glitter never impressed her much. In other words, if Hokeywood didn't get her engine going, I'd say your local status isn't doing it, either."

"What sort of actress was she?"

"She did commercials and a few other things. Minor parts, mostly. She didn't have time to get a decent career started because some idiot accidentally killed her by giving her a spiked drink. Otherwise, she might've--"

A huge leather-clad blur exploded from the crowd, grabbing Chip by the collar and Jimmy by the arm. Jimmy caught a heavy mix of *Brut* cologne and B.O. Before Jimmy could pull away, the blurred leather mass shoved him directly into a knot of passing shoppers.

Jimmy brought up his arms to protect his face. His right hip slammed into someone's briefcase. The pointed toe of a woman's high heel caught him on the instep, and a tingling splash of fire scrambled up his leg and sent him sprawling. He rolled over to the curb and caught a glimpse of a gray SUV screeching to a halt. Gasps and shrieks echoed up and down the block. Adrenaline forced him to his knees. Instinct and fear told him to get out of the way of traffic. Ignoring the throbbing pain in his right hip and ankle, he pushed himself to his feet, turned and hobbled back to the corner.

More than a dozen people had stopped walking to watch, but the majority of the crowd paused only for a moment. Dazed, Jimmy struggled to analyze what happened. Someone in a hurry? If that were the case, why not just push him out of the way? A pickpocket, maybe? Jimmy checked his pockets.

Cellphone, wallet, keys, money. Everything was there.

But something strange just happened.

The loud roar of the SUV behind him nudged him back to reality. He elbowed his way back to the liquor store, where he and Chip had been standing just moments earlier.

Chip was gone.

***

Tiffany stepped into the crowded elevator. Others filed in, pushing her toward the rear of the car. When the car was filled, the *ding*! of the bell announced the closing of the doors. They began to close, and she noticed that the light on her floor had already been pressed.

In the next moment, a voice exploded in her head. It was Chip, and he sounded frightened.

"*Tifferoo! Help! Someone just grabbed me--*"

Silence.

Pulse pounding, Tiffany reached out clumsily for the DOOR OPEN button and quickly found that her arm was two feet too short. The doors eased shut. The skinny young guy standing beside her snickered and moved closer. Tiffany caught a whiff of onions. "Ya need longer arms, lady."

Tiffany glared at the closed doors and concentrated. "*Open right now!*" her mind commanded.

The car stopped moving. The doors eased open.

Surprised and relieved, Tiffany elbowed her way toward the front of the car. She turned back to the young man, whose gaze remained riveted to the opened doors. “I guess I didn’t need my arms after all. By the way, you need a breath mint.” She slipped through the widening opening, bolted out of the car and dashed through the crowded lobby.

It didn’t take her long to reach the glass doors. She pushed them open and charged outside. Her adrenaline in overdrive, she dodged the crowds easily, ran down the street and stopped abruptly at the end of the block, where she’d left Chip and Jimmy at the corner not five minutes earlier.

Jimmy was standing where she’d left them, looking around dazedly while the passing crowd veered around him. He paled the moment he saw her and hurried right over. His hair was mussed, his dark-brown eyes glazed and out of focus. His clothes were dirty. Dark, wet circles covered his knees and elbows.

“He’s g-gone,” he croaked, his arms held out. “He just disappeared! We were standing right here, talking. And suddenly this huge *thing* comes out of the crowd, grabs me and tosses me out in the street!”

Tiffany could tell he was in shock. His dark eyes were glazed. He could hardly look her in the eye. He obviously felt incredible guilt for whatever had happened.

She had a pretty good idea what had happened. First Ashley, now Chip. It wasn’t rocket science.

“What did you mean when you said huge thing?”

He nodded.

“Jimmy?”

He kept nodding.

"Can you hear me?"

More nodding.

She sighed. "Did you know you have what looks like a smashed French fry stuck to the toe of your shoe?"

More nodding, but he didn't take his eyes off her.

"Do I have to slap you?"

The nodding continued. Jimmy was obviously in a much worse state than she'd thought.

"I don't *want* to slap you."

He continued nodding. "Uh-huh..."

She sighed and clasped her hands together. "You're really making this tough for me."

"Uh-huh..."

"Darn it." She reached out, grabbed his shoulders, and shook him vigorously.

He blinked, shook his head and rubbed his eyes.

"Now *talk* to me, okay? We need to figure this out rationally."

He took a deep breath, then another. His color started coming back.

"Now tell me what happened."

He rubbed the back of his head. "A big, ugly bearded guy in leather. He just came right out of the crowd and rushed at us. Sucker was as strong as an ox. He grabbed me by the arm and tossed me into the crowd. Like I was a football or something. I was rolling out into the street before I even knew what the hell was going on. Damn. I was almost run over!" He gawked at her and nearly smiled. "*That* would have been fun, trying to explain."

Tiffany did a quick probe of Jimmy's brain. The image of a tall guy with a thick black beard, leather jacket, leather pants and boots filled the picture screen in his head. She also caught a glimpse of a gray SUV screeching to a stop, and someone's tan briefcase jumping out of nowhere. But there was no sign of Chip among the images.

"Where was Chip during all this?"

"He was standing right over here, where you left us."

At first she wondered if Chip had done one of his tricks to escape. His distress call instantly dismissed that theory. This had obviously happened too quickly for him to react. "And he just disappeared?"

"By the time I picked myself up and came back here, he was gone."

"How long did all this take?"

"A few seconds, maybe. Thirty, tops, from the time I rolled out into the street to the time I came back and found him gone."

Tiffany's head swam with wild images. This had to be connected with Ashley's disappearance. Now she had to find out if the big leather guy was a demon. And where he'd taken Chip.

"And where did this huge guy come from?"

Jimmy threw out his arms. "He was just here. Right *here*. Like he'd come around the corner and--"

"This corner?" She pointed.

Jimmy nodded.

Tiffany hurried over to the curb.

About fifty yards down the street, a dark-blue Lincoln Town Car had just pulled away from the curb and went north, toward Penn Avenue. As it moved away, a tall, leather-clad figure walked away from the curb and headed straight for the alley running perpendicular to the apartment building on Fifth.

***

This was the easiest money Brush Conley had ever made since graduating high school nearly twenty years ago. When he returned from Saudi, he did three quick hits for the Lombardi brothers in South Hills. Each hit had taken just a few days of his time, but considerable research and several hours of surveillance had also been required. Finding and purchasing the appropriate weapon through the appropriate dealer was tricky. Feds, DEA and ATF agents seemed to be everywhere nowadays. Investigating the premises and checking cameras and security had nearly gotten him arrested. Dusting a Federal employee was not easy or safe. The money was fantastic, the risks extremely dangerous.

Not so in this case. It took just five minutes of fast walking to get to the corner. It didn't take much effort at all to push the other guy out of the way, grab the redheaded mark and disappear around the corner with the victim tucked safely under his arm. To make the job even easier, the two men had been talking to one another and much too distracted to notice him. And to top it all off, both were relatively small. The dark-haired guy didn't go much more than one-sixty or so, the redhead no more than one-twenty. Conley regularly handled three times that much weight in the gym.

The redhead hadn't even noticed what was happening until it was too late. He was too busy watching his friend rolling out into the street. Conley simply wrapped an arm around his skinny neck, picked him up by the waist and hauled him around the corner, away from the crowd. The victim didn't squirm much, not with the huge corded arm gripped tightly around his throat. He gasped and sputtered. Conley eased up slightly on the pressure but kept his grip firmly around the man's tiny waist.

About a quarter of the way up the block, Conley sensed someone following him. His gut instinct, still strong from Saudi, had kicked in. Shoppers were no doubt coming up behind him. This didn't pose a problem. Shoppers were usually lost in their own little world and cared only about being mugged. If they got too close, he'd tell them to get lost. His size usually sent people scurrying. But sometimes that wasn't even necessary. Nowadays, people didn't want to get involved. You could get hurt or worse by sticking your nose where it didn't belong.

Still carrying the redhead, Conley spun around. A dark-haired dude in a pricey dark suit approached him. He didn't have the look of a cop, but his eyes were strange and kind of spooky looking. He seemed more interested in the redhead than Conley, the way he was staring at the little guy. The phone call had mentioned the alley, so Conley suspected this could be the dude making the pickup.

Briefly Conley wondered if he was connected to the Mob.

Why would the Mob be interested in this sawed-off runt?

It was stupid to waste time sweating over this. For five K, there was no reason to question anything. He'd seen some really goofy-looking politicians in his day.

A dark-blue Lincoln Town Car pulled up silently behind the man, stopping at the curb.

"I can take it from here."

"Be my guest." Conley eased up his grip on the redhead's neck.

The other man reached out and touched the redhead's arm. The redhead immediately went limp. Like one of those inflatable dolls when you let the air out.

Wow. This dude was goddamned scary. It wouldn't be a very good career move to get on his bad side.

The dude turned. His driver had already circled the Lincoln and opened the rear door. The dude bent, carefully pushed the redhead in and slid into the seat beside him. The driver closed the door, circled the car and got back in. The Lincoln immediately pulled away from the curb and sped quietly up Fifth.

Fucking weird. Conley nervously turned toward the alley entrance. He'd seen some strange shit in

Saudi--more than any one person should ever see in his lifetime. But that was to be expected when you went sneaking into the desert at night, looking for Taliban.

But this was America. His home. Touching a guy and turning him into a fucking zombie?

Best forget about it. For all he knew, this could be one of those secret programs the Government always seemed to be working on. Besides, there were more important things to think about. His bank account, for example. Time to pop on over to the Internet café and check out his balance.

Five thousand smackeroos just to pick up some guy so some scary dude with weird eyes could turn him into a zombie, shove him in the back seat of a Lincoln and ride off into the sunset?

More than my feeble mind can wrap itself around.

Conley crossed the walk and stepped down off the curb.

"Excuse me," a soft, breathy voice behind him said.

His senses alert once again, Conley turned around.

A sensationally hot-looking blond chick approached him from Liberty Avenue. The dark-haired guy Conley had just tossed out into the street was walking beside her. He looked pissed, too. His clothes were pretty dirty. Briefly Conley wondered if the guy was going to retaliate. He didn't think that would be wise. Conley was half a head taller and at least eighty pounds heavier.

But that didn't matter. Only the babe mattered. She looked kind of pissed, too.

Maybe they were a couple, and she wanted Conley to apologize. Or maybe she was the one who wanted to retaliate.

Baby, I just made five K in the last ten minutes. I'll apologize to your guy if you want. Or maybe we could duke it out. I'll even let you get in a few licks.

"Help you?" He couldn't stop gawking. Her honey-blond hair, those yummy melons and that hot, shapely figure were doing a serious number, heating up his juices.

"You can tell me something." She drew closer.

Conley had grown more excited than he'd been in a long time. This babe made Sarah Jane and all the other bimbos he knew look like drowned cats.

"I'll tell you anything you like, baby." *I'll do anything you like, too. Especially if it involves getting you out of those clothes.*

When she was just five feet away, her big blue eyes began to glow.

Every thought in Conley's head vanished like a puff of smoke.

Chapter 20

Dahl turned left onto Penn and took the Lincoln just half a block, just before a multi-vehicle snarl at Stanwix & Penn brought traffic to an abrupt halt.

Andras sat back in his seat and took a breath. There was no reason to get uptight. Two-thirds of his job had been completed. The inferior sprawled unconscious in the seat beside him and did not move. Like Parker, he would remain in this silent state until Andras released him.

It was time to stay focused and keep things moving. He couldn't let traffic problems dictate the outcome of his mission.

Andras fished the cell out of his pocket and pressed the button. "I'm going to need another transport," he told his contact.

"I can have another packing case sent to any location you desire within fifteen minutes."

"I'll have my driver take us back to the Wyndham." He checked his watch. "It's now twelve-forty-five. Meet us at the loading dock behind the building at one. We'll drop off the package and you can have your people take it to the airport. I've got to leave immediately and hunt the blonde."

"I don't think that'll be necessary, sir."

Andras stiffened. "What did you say?"

"I'm watching one of the monitors. The woman you're looking for is with a dark-haired male, and they're walking up Fifth Avenue. It looks like they're approaching the man who just gave you the redhead."

Confusion rocked through him. "I thought we both watched her run into the building not very long ago."

"Well, she obviously came back out. The male with her probably told her what happened."

This didn't make sense. If she'd gone inside to ask about Parker, why would she come right back out? She had no idea the redhead was being snatched. Even if the other guy had called her immediately, it would have taken her precious minutes to get back on the elevator, take it down to the ground level and run back outside. And the crowds would have made her progress even more difficult.

"Are you sure that's her? We both saw her go inside. If she went in to ask about Parker, she should still be in the building. I don't think her friend had time to contact her. Even if he did, no one can move through a building that size that fast. Elevators don't move very quickly. It would take much too long to get to Belasco's floor, get back in the car and take it back down. And with all those stops, she should still be inside. We're obviously missing something."

"Well, I'm watching her and her friend walking up Fifth, and they're both moving pretty fast."

"Did you find out who that guy is yet?"

"Still working on it."

"Send me a visual. I have to see this for myself."

"Sending."

Ten seconds later, the image appeared on the display. Damn. His contact was right after all. The blonde and her friend approached the tall, bearded man Andras had just met with.

This made no sense at all. How could she find out about this so quickly?

"Any instructions?" his contact asked. "The way I see it, you don't have time to drive to the Wyndham. If you want to nab her, the time to do it is now."

"You're right." Andras' pulse hastened. "Keep an eye on them. We're turning around. In the meantime, I'll need both ends of Fifth Avenue blocked. How quickly can you get someone to do it?"

"I can have three men covering that block in less than five minutes."

"Do it, then. If I let her get away now, I might not have another chance while it's still daylight. Make sure your men are pros. I don't want a media circus out there, and I sure as hell don't want her hurt."

"We use only good, capable men, sir."

Andras clicked off and pocketed the cell. He didn't need any chest-thumping right now, he needed results. "Dahl, take us back there."

"As soon as I can, sir, but with this traffic--"

"I don't care about the fucking traffic. We need to get back there now!"

***

As Tiffany faced the big bearded guy, she saw the same expression she'd seen hundreds of times before. It showed clearly in his eyes and body language and was something she'd been familiar with all her life.

When a man experienced this emotion, it quickly consumed his soul. Life as he knew it ceased to exist. His job, his wife, his children, even his home and all his worldly possessions. Everything vanished in one hot instant. He'd become oblivious to the outside world and was convinced that the only thing in his life that really mattered was the woman trapped in the crosshairs of his vision.

When she'd first seen glimpses of it as a child, it scared her. She wasn't yet aware of what it was, nor had she been told what it meant. She originally feared something was wrong with her. Why else would so many boys and men stop what they were doing and stare at her like that?

Mom and Dad hadn't helped. They'd both decided to shield her from the negative side of life until they thought she was old enough to understand. All this changed, of course, when Dad died. It wasn't long after that when Tiffany discovered what a terrifying place the world could be for a girl.

But once she saw how desperate men became when their lust took over, she realized she'd learned one of the most important lessons in life. She also learned that this masculine weakness invariably brought along fear and confusion with it, creating a wonderful advantage.

It gave the woman a feeling of extreme power.

Although she was no longer mortal, Tiffany had learned that this power remained with her, and that a generous portion of it had transformed into something much greater than she could ever imagine.

Now was the perfect time to use it to its full advantage.

"What's your name?" She latched on to his steady gaze.

"C-Conley." His deep-set brown eyes dropped to her breasts, then her hips, before returning to her face. She knew right then that he was at her mercy.

"Is that your first or last name?"

"Everyone calls me Brush. Or just Conley."

"Brush?"

"It's a nickname."

"Have any idea who I am?"

"You're one hot babe." He made a feeble attempt to smile, but his facial muscles would not cooperate. He'd already lost control.

"Thank you, but I've got some questions to ask. Before I ask them, I've got to tell you something."

He began to drool.

"That little redheaded guy you just carried up this street. He's my best friend."

His eyes had turned glossy. He was already fantasizing and had developed an erection. Further conversation would be pointless.

She decided to probe his thoughts. "*Who contacted you?*"

"Never tells me his name. God, you're hot--"

"What were you asked to do?"

"Grab the redhead and pull him off the street. I wasn't supposed to attract attention. Damn these jeans, they're gettin' really tight..."

"What were you supposed to do then?"

"This other guy took him from me."

"Show me his face."

The image of a grim-looking, dark-haired man in a dark suit flashed brightly. The tiny red glints in the centers of the man's eyes told her the most important detail of this. Chip had been turned over to the well-dressed man, rendered unconscious and pushed in the back seat of a dark-blue Lincoln Town Car.

"Anything else?"

"You're just about the hottest chick I've ever--"

"About the job, you idiot." She forced herself to stay focused even though she wanted to do something nasty to him. *I'm not a demon*, she reminded herself.

"He tells me what he wants done, when, where, and how much it pays."

"How much did this pay?"

"Five grand."

That was a lot of money for so little work. Breath Mint wasn't sparing any expense to get them back.

"That's all you know?"

"Yep."

"You have any idea where the man took my friend?"

"Nope."

Since she was in his head, dealing with his natural thought processes, he had no choice but tell the truth. However, she didn't appreciate what he'd done with Chip and decided to teach him a lesson. *"Tell you what, Conley. If you take that five grand out of your bank account and donate it to St. Jude or the local ASPCA, I won't come back and make you suffer."*

He grinned stupidly. His left eye twitched. "*S-Suffer?*"

Tiffany sighed. This jerk's hormones had made him stupid. She sent over an image of him tied naked to a chair with razor wire and bleeding freely, while a spaced-out hooker shaved his genital area with a rusty machete.

"Like that."

Conley trembled.

"You can go now. And don't forget that donation."

Conley turned stiffly on his heel and shuffled toward the alley.

"Get anything?" Jimmy asked. "I assume you did that mind thing Chip told me about."

She wondered what else Chip had told him. It wasn't important right now. "Just the make of the car and the face of the demon that was sent here for us."

"What's he look like?"

"Close your eyes." She sent him the image.

His eyes snapped open. He grinned. "Wow. That was really cool. You should have your own act."

"I've got better things to do. But now we both know who we're looking for. And who's looking for us. By the way, this isn't your problem, so I suggest you leave right now."

Jimmy didn't budge.

"You're not moving."

He smiled. "I haven't known you and Chip very long, but I already consider you my friends. Besides, you offered to help me with my Danielle problem. I'd be a jerk to turn my back on you, right? And who knows? I might just be able to help."

Tiffany just smiled. She'd been right about him after all.

They turned and followed a small group of shoppers back down the street toward Liberty.

Tiffany soon felt the waves of depression and anger settling around her. First Ashley, now Chip. Her instincts had been right about staying in Pittsburgh. Despite their caution, Breath Mint had found them. In just two weeks, the super had found out where they'd gone, sent a demon here to get them and grabbed two of them.

How did he find out?

Ashley's mom, obviously. She knew Ashley's uncle, knew where he lived. Once Daniel Grove told Breath Mint about her, questioning her would have been easy. Tiffany could only wonder what the demon had done once he got the answers he'd wanted. Had he killed the poor woman? Done something horrifying to her mind?

She didn't want to imagine what could have happened. Watching the demon destroy innocent people had been a horrible experience. Those memories had smothered her soul with a heavy darkness she knew would never go away.

But now she faced a situation even more dismal and hopeless. Ashley and now Chip were gone, and Tiffany had no idea where they were or how she could get them back.

She might have to use certain powers she'd promised herself she'd never resort to. These powers separated her from the very demons she loathed. She'd assured herself many times that as long as she didn't use them, she could never consider herself a demon. But now that she found herself racing against time to find her friends, she realized that she might actually have to get down and dirty.

As they approached the end of the block that brought them to Liberty Avenue, the dark-blue Lincoln Town Car pulled up to the curb across the street.

Tiffany stopped walking. Her pulse thundered.

Jimmy stopped moving as well. "That's the car, isn't it?"

She scanned the buildings across the street. Several moving cameras silently scanned the streets. The messenger obviously had others working with him. The Diocese, no doubt. As Chip had explained it, demons used mortal representatives everywhere.

There could be dozens of them in this city. They were rich. They employed hundreds—perhaps thousands—of others.

She finally began to understand what they were up against.

"What do we do now?"

"I wish I knew."

Just then, the rear window of the Lincoln lowered.

Chapter 21

From the back seat of the Lincoln, Andras carefully studied the crowd activity. Heavy foot traffic came from the direction of Fifth Avenue, as well as steady crowds moving east and west on Liberty. Reckless jaywalkers added to the chaos.

Two figures stood at the corner, facing Liberty. The passing crowds made an ID difficult, but Andras saw thick blond hair and a shapely figure. The dark-haired male standing closely beside her was about half a head taller than she was. Both were watching the Lincoln.

Andras' gut told him she was the one they were looking for. His heart sputtered as he whipped out his phone and thumbed the appropriate button. "I'm looking at her right now," he told his contact. "She's right across the street, staring at the Lincoln."

"I've just received an ID on the male. He goes by the name Jimmy Russo. He's a local celebrity. A magician. He's been working at the Bel-Mor club on Penn Avenue for the last month. Apparently he's well-known in the area, and--"

"I don't give a rat's ass about him." Andras gripped the phone tighter. They were wasting valuable time. The blonde and her companion could easily blend in with the crowd and disappear. "Focus on that street corner. Like I just said, the two of them are just standing there, staring at this car. Unless they're waiting for a bus or taxi, they won't be there much longer."

"Zooming in."

"While you're doing that, tell me about those men you just sent out. Are they anywhere in the area? I know they're not gonna be visible, but I would like to know what they're doing."

"We haven't heard from them yet. They were ordered to report as soon as they arrived at the location. They probably haven't gotten into position. It *is* the lunch hour, and the area's pretty congested."

Andras found that he'd been sweating. The coppery taste of blood filled his mouth. His spiritual form of the hunter always intensified during a hunt. This same thing happened in '63, when he'd first glimpsed the Presidential motorcade coming into full view on the straightaway.

But he'd been much more in control back then.

Now, unfortunately, he found himself at the mercy of unseen mortals operating modern state-of-the-art technology. Andras was in charge, but had no control over what was being done. If just one of these morons touched the wrong button, entered the wrong command or mistyped a coordinate, the whole thing would blow up in their faces. Andras would be the one facing Braithwaite to explain what happened.

"I don't care about the congestion. She's right across the damned street, and I want her taken in the next five minutes. I don't even care if anyone sees what's happening. As long as a TV crew doesn't catch it and put it on the evening news, this needs to go down right now."

"I think we should remain cautious until the men get into--"

"We can't expect her to just stand there and wait, dammit." The urge to send an eardrum-shattering jolt through the line had become overwhelming. Best hold off. It wouldn't be a good move to create problems with the Pittsburgh Diocese.

"If the men move too soon, she might disappear. The crowds--"

"She already knows Parker's missing, and the guy with her just told her about the redhead. Her guard was already up even before she went to talk to your guy. For all we know, she got him to spill his guts."

"I doubt he told her anything. He's a good man. We've been using him for years."

Good man. Andras had heard that same phrase many times before. It was almost always spoken prematurely.

"Didn't it bother you that she hunted him down so quickly and spent nearly five minutes talking to him?"

"I was a little nervous about it, but like I said, he's good. He's a former Marine, did two tours in Saudi. He obeys orders, doesn't ask questions, does his job and keeps his mouth shut. He's got a good, steady gig with us. I don't know if he was ever captured or interrogated, but with his extensive training, I wouldn't think a good-looking woman would be able to make him talk that easily. Not when he was just paid five thousand dollars for a simple job he knew almost nothing about."

This didn't make Andras feel any better. According to Daniel Grove, the blonde was dangerous and had powers no one knew about, including Braithwaite. Andras knew better than take unnecessary chances.

It would be best to handle this himself. It could be tricky, but he was confident he could do it. He'd been doing great work for nearly a century. Besides, a hunt was no problem at all when your prey was in clear view.

"I'm gonna do this myself."

"But my men should be getting into position as we speak..."

"Let them work. If she somehow slips by me, they'll nail her."

"You don't know what she's thinking. She might turn around and head back up Fifth."

"I'm thinking worst-case scenario. If she found out anything from your Marine, she'll know her friend is in this car. That's probably why she's watching it right now. But this could actually help us. While she's distracted, I might be able to walk right up to her. Meanwhile, your men can cover her in case she does something weird. Whatever happens, don't take your eyes off those monitors."

"But sir--"

"Those are my orders." Andras pocketed the cell. Beside him, the redhead continued snoring softly. "Dahl, watch our passenger here. Make sure he doesn't go anywhere."

"I've got my taser, sir." Dahl held it up. "Fifty thousand volts."

Andras grabbed the door handle. "Wait fifteen minutes, pull out of here, circle the block and come back down Fifth. I should have another passenger ready by the time we meet again. I'll need you to pull over to the curb on Fifth and have the trunk open and ready. I might have to carry her. I won't want too many people seeing me."

"Yes, sir."

Andras waited for slow-moving traffic to block the blonde's view of the Lincoln. As soon as the light at the intersection created a snag, he inched the door open and slipped out.

***

When traffic began slowing down, Tiffany's view of the Lincoln was blocked by a shiny black SUV. More traffic inched past. A PAT bus stopped behind the SUV.

Tiffany didn't want to lose sight of the Lincoln. It had only been a few minutes since Chip had been snatched. Breath Mint's messenger hadn't had enough time to take him anywhere. But she knew better than confront the messenger. He could probably put her under a spell with a simple touch—as he'd done to Chip. Then he could take them all back to Orlando.

She knew better than try to guess how many others were involved and decided it best to assume their enemies were everywhere. The cameras and monitors across the street and down the block all seemed to be pointing in her direction. The camera focused on her from the bank building across the street told her what she needed to know. There were cameras everywhere. On Liberty. And Penn. And Fifth. In the buildings, as well. In nearly every store she'd gone into. Even in the smallest shop, a camera bolted to the ceiling was aimed at the front door. Anyone with enough money and Internet access could hook up to any camera in the city.

So why was the Lincoln still there?

Or was it? The SUV, the PAT bus, and a dozen other vehicles obscured her view. The Lincoln could have already left its spot, crept through the snag and turned down a side street, for all she knew.

About a minute later, traffic resumed. The SUV and bus eased away.

The Lincoln remained there.

"It hasn't moved," she said softly.

"Strange," Jimmy said.

"Not really." The reason for this had suddenly become evident.

"What are you thinking?"

"Someone wants us to stay here and watch it."

"If you're right, this is a trap."

"I'm pretty sure it is."

"Any ideas?"

"You see that camera pointed at us across the street?"

"I noticed it about two minutes ago. If we really are being watched, it doesn't matter what we do, does it?"

Tiffany studied the crowds wandering up and down the sidewalks. "Maybe, maybe not."

"I'm open to suggestions."

The heavy, rapid-moving crowds hadn't yet thinned out. They had maybe twenty minutes or so before the lunch crowd went back to work. Right now, confusion might be the only ally they'd need.

"I think we should split up."

"How's that?"

"What better way to lose a tail than in heavy crowds?" Out of the corner of her eye, she caught the familiar figure emerging from the crowd about fifty yards from them. He slipped behind two businessmen and kept out of sight, but Tiffany could tell it was the same man whose image she'd pulled from Brush Conley.

"That's him, isn't it?" Jimmy asked.

"I'm afraid so."

The figure stayed invisible as it kept behind the crowds moving in their direction.

Slick, she thought. *He's definitely hunted before. I have a feeling he's gonna be in our faces long before we realize it.*

Jimmy moved closer. "You sure you want to split up?"

"I can't think of anything else that'll work."

"Where do we hook up again?"

"I'll find you. Let's try for half an hour from now."

"You sure?"

"Trust me."

"I do." He touched her hand.

A spark shot up her arm. "Later." She tossed him a quick smile.

A group of a dozen or so teenage kids passed. Jimmy moved forward and quickly fell in step with them.

Her nerves jumping erratically, Tiffany watched the next group approaching. She still couldn't see him but guessed that he was probably much closer than she hoped. She decided she had fifteen seconds, tops. She glanced to her right. A large knot of middle-aged women approached, moving in the other direction.

Think, Tifferoo!

Chip?

Her imagination, most likely. Chip had been placed under a spell and could not communicate. In her panic, his influence had obviously penetrated her mind, forcing her to rationalize, to concentrate on changing the situation.

Change. *That* was the key.

Yes. She *could* change if she wanted to. She'd been so frightened and confused that she hadn't been able to think straight. But now that she'd finally snapped back to reality, everything became clear again.

She glanced across the street.

The Lincoln was gone.

Panic rocked through her, but she forced herself to focus. *Do something. Do it now, before it's too late*!

Just as the group was about to pass, Tiffany fell in behind them. They were all busily talking among themselves or eyeing the stores they passed. She quickly changed her honey-blond hair to a reddish brown. At the same moment, her form-fitting light-blue tee shirt turned a light-green, her faded form-fitting jeans into baggy gray sweats. She made her breasts two sizes smaller and altered her shapely figure to that of a skinny, small-breasted street girl.

The messenger passed the liquor store and carefully scanned the passing group. His eyes drifted onto her and immediately shifted, moving toward his right as he eyed the women behind her.

A few steps later, a member of her group--a short, heavyset woman wearing thick, black-rimmed glasses--tapped her on the shoulder.

Tiffany turncd.

The woman squinted at her.

Tiffany smiled. "Hello."

The woman nodded and kept staring.

"Something wrong?" Tiffany asked.

The woman took off her glasses and began wiping the lenses vigorously on her sweatshirt. She put them back on, glanced briefly at Tiffany again and turned to face the front.

About ten yards later, as two of the women left the crowd and went into a leather store, Tiffany casually turned around.

At the corner of the liquor store, the messenger scanned the crowds.

Chapter 22

Keeping in the center of the fast-moving crowd, Jimmy headed east on Liberty. He felt guilty about leaving Tiffany but realized it was the right thing to do. When someone was looking for two people, finding them was much more difficult after they separated.

The messenger sent by Braithwaite was good. He'd already taken Ashley Parker and Chip and also managed to triangulate Tiffany's position during the city's chaotic lunch hour. It was obvious that he was being aided by other people, and that these people could find whoever they chose.

Jimmy knew right then that he and Tiffany could not afford to make any mistakes.

He decided to start working on his own strategy. If he went three or four more blocks, he could duck into one of the stores and watch the street activity from the storefront window. He'd stay hidden for the half-hour Tiffany had suggested. With her unique gift, he knew he'd see her again in no time.

Keeping with the crowd, he crossed the intersection of Liberty and Sixth. He began wondering if Tiffany was safe. If she'd been able to slip away, as he'd done. If she'd found a place to hide. He'd hated leaving her and felt a burst of rage climbing up his back each time he imagined the messenger finding her. But he reminded himself that this was her idea. There hadn't been time to argue. Besides, Tiffany could take care of herself.

Even so, he found that he couldn't stop agonizing over this. If the demon found her, she and her friends would be taken back to Orlando, and Jimmy would never see her again.

A cold wave of nausea ripped through him. He'd never met anyone like her before and knew he'd never see anyone like her again. He found himself helplessly drawn to her and could not stop thinking about her for more than a few seconds at a time. She was the woman every man dreams about. The woman every man wants in his life. His career in show business had put him in contact with hundreds of females, many of them beautiful, classy, intelligent ladies…but not one of them could hold a candle to Tiffany.

Unconsciously he began slowing his pace, barely noticing the crowd as it surged on ahead. Running away just didn't feel like the right thing to do anymore. However, going back to Tiffany felt more right than anything else. He had to get back to her and didn't care about the consequences. His safety no longer mattered. What good was being safe if you were miserable?

"*I'm coming back, Tiffany,*" he thought, hoping she'd be able to pick up on his feelings. "*I'm going to help you get your friends back.*"

He stopped walking and stood there, the crowd veering around him. He had to do this. There was no other way. Together, they might even find a way of getting rid of the demon.

Just as he started to turn around, a feeling of cold dread washed down his back.

Was it the fear of being caught? Of walking into a trap?

Or was it something else? Something he couldn't explain?

It didn't matter. He had to help Tiffany and didn't care what might be waiting for him when he got back.

He turned around and froze.

A tall, broad-shouldered man in a dark-blue uniform faced him just six feet away. A silver badge pinned to his shirt pocket winked brightly. A nametag stamped with a name he couldn't quite make out stretched across the flap. His right hand rested on the Pachmayr grip of the automatic jammed in the holster above his right hip. Dangling from the man's left hand, a pair of silver handcuffs glistened in the afternoon sunlight.

Behind him, an unmarked van, its tires lightly scraping the curb, crept up to them like a stalking black cat.

The cold dread easing down Jimmy's back made him tremble all the way down to his toes.

"You're coming with us," the man said in a firm voice. He held out the cuffs. "If you'll just turn around slowly and place your hands together on the back of your head, we won't have to use the taser gun."

***

Standing near the front entrance of Fifth Avenue Place, Andras forced himself to think rationally while the crowds streamed steadily past.

Where the hell was that blonde? She was right here with Russo just two minutes earlier. Now she was gone. And so was Russo.

How the hell was this possible? Madigan's people had been monitoring the entire block. There were cameras everywhere. Additional men had been sent to watch both ends of the street. There was no conceivable way those two could have slipped away.

The crowds continued. There was just too much activity to be able to keep an eye on things. People entered and left buildings, crossed against the light, got out of cabs and other vehicles and ran across the street. It would have been easy for Russo and the blonde to blend into a passing horde of shoppers or businessmen and vanish.

There were too many blondes out there making things even more difficult. She undoubtedly knew that and would use it to her advantage. She was indeed one bright bitch. She'd made her move the moment she saw him turning his attention away from her--

No. He hadn't taken his eyes off her from the time he'd gotten out of the Lincoln. He was a trained hunter--a skilled tracker. Once he spotted his prey, he focused on it until he captured it. He'd never lost his quarry before. He did, after all, possess the finely tuned hunting instincts of both the owl and the raven.

Something else had happened to upset the works. This had become a giant shell game with too many females with the same hair, looks and figure popping up. This modern age had evolved into a giant beauty factory. As each decade passed, mortal females grew more attractive. Fifty years ago, a beautiful woman was a rare gem. Nowadays they were everywhere. Just ten minutes earlier, as he sat in the Lincoln, he'd watched them parading down the street in droves. Was it any wonder he'd lost track of her?

It was vital to rethink his approach. He wouldn't accomplish anything by standing here, agonizing over his mistake. He had to get back on track.

He whipped out his cell. "What happened, and where the hell are your men?" There was no need to be polite. They were running out of time.

"I'm replaying the tape on the monitor and adjusting it to three-quarters speed to determine where they might have gone. My men are also in the area, checking things out."

"We're losing time."

"Yes, sir. We're aware of that."

"If she got away from us that easily, there's no way we'll be able to find her again. Not soon, anyway. I wanted to be on that charter by suppertime. As it is now, I may have to stay here another night. Another day will give her too much of an advantage. I have to be back in Orlando by tomorrow at midnight."

"I understand. As I just said, I'm working up a frame-by-frame replay of the last five minutes, and I'm seeing a glitch that could explain what happened."

"What sort of glitch?" This was not the time for a technological fuckup. Andras hated technology. It wasn't dependable and always seemed to cause more problems.

"There's a point in the images where the crowd grows really thick and out of focus. The pixels are distorting, making the images blur and soupy-looking. And when the crowd temporarily thins out and the images clear up, both of them have already disappeared."

"Pretty fucking bad when you're watching something frame-by-frame and it looks like something's missing."

"There's no way this could have been doctored or tampered with. There were obviously just too many pixels for the images to handle clearly."

"They were watching the crowd, waiting for their moment."

"They obviously found one."

"Where does this leave us?"

"We've got monitors up and down that street. We'll find her."

"I'm really beginning to tire of all this. I'm getting the idea that grabbing two of them will be much better than all three."

"How's that, sir?"

"I think I should cut my losses and take the two of them back to Orlando. If the three of them were that chummy, I say wait and let nature take its course."

"What about the blonde?"

"She already knows her friends are missing. If she's as bright as everyone says, and I'm pretty damned sure she is, she knows this is all happening because I've been sent here. She'll put two and two together and figure out where they are."

"What if she doesn't want to fly down there after them?"

"From what I've been told, she's the loyal type. I can't see her turning her back on her friends."

"Hold on, sir. I'm picking up something from one of my men."

Andras went over to the corner of the brick building and continued scanning the crowds on both sides of the street. Then he turned toward Fifth Avenue. The Lincoln crept down the street, keeping close to the curb. He frowned and felt a fresh billow of heat racing down his back. He and Dahl could be putting the blonde in the trunk right now.

His contact came back on. "I just received word that one of our men nabbed Russo about three blocks down from where you are."

"They found him that fast?"

"Yes, sir."

"Good." Maybe all wasn't lost after all. They now had something they could use to bargain with. "Bring him over to my location on Fifth. I can definitely use him."

"Do you think you can get him to cooperate?"

"I could care less about his cooperation. I have something that'll work much better."

***

His wrists cuffed behind his back, Jimmy sat in the back seat of the van and stared uneasily at the two uniforms in the front seat.

Anyone could tell they weren't cops. Their uniforms looked legit, but they didn't act like cops. They hadn't said a word to him after they'd cuffed him and shoved him in the vehicle.

These two probably worked for the demon. They might even know the big guy who'd grabbed Chip. If so, they had nothing to do with the Police Department. Jimmy had been arrested in New York City a couple of times in the old days, before he'd died in the fire. Although each arrest had been for a minor violation, he clearly remembered how they'd treated him. Cops told you why you were being arrested. They couldn't just pick you up off the street, cuff you and toss you in the back of a van. Nowadays they were even more thorough. They asked lots of questions while patting you down and searching your pockets. They also told you your rights and where they were taking you.

However, he had more urgent matters on his mind.

They'd been monitoring him since he left Tiffany and came this way. If they'd been able to catch him so easily, they'd also picked up Tiffany. He had to do something quickly to scrap their plan.

Slipping away would be his best option. It would take precious time for them to pull over. Even more time to find him again in the crowds. They might also have to call in backup to circle the area to find him and get him back in the van.

But even if he did get away, what would it accomplish? There were so many others involved in this. It would only take them a few minutes to get someone else here. How would any of this help Tiffany?

Something else occurred to him. He wanted to curse himself for not thinking of it sooner.

Why did these two want him?

It took him only a moment to figure it out. They obviously hadn't found her yet and wanted to use him as bait to lure her to them.

If so, things would turn horrific very quickly. He'd been in Hell and knew something about demons. He wouldn't stand a chance during an interrogation. Some demons used torture to satisfy their sadistic cravings. However, most were lazy, relying on their mental skills for manipulation. He would be put under a spell. Then they'd plunge into his brain and take whatever information they needed.

But how valuable was he? Other than seeing Tiffany last night for the first time and reconnecting with her earlier, he knew nothing about her or Chip. He knew she was dead--but so did the demon. He also knew she had powers no one else could explain. And that she could read minds.

This was the one fact that frightened him. If the demon already knew about Tiffany's powers, he wouldn't need Jimmy at all. But if he *didn't* know, anything Jimmy said about her would be very bad for all four of them.

Something else occurred to him, and this frightened him even worse. The demon didn't know Jimmy was a spirit. Putting him under a spell would be just as bad as Jimmy telling them about Tiffany's powers. The demon would quickly learn all about him. The fires, Danielle, the underage girls.

Taking a couple of deep breaths, he concentrated on making his hands small enough to fit through the openings in the cuffs. Silently he slipped them off. Then, keeping his arms locked behind his back, he placed the cuffs gently on the seat behind him.

A cellphone buzzed quietly. The passenger fished a cell out of his jacket pocket, opened it and held it close to his ear. He whispered into it, snapped it shut and shoved it back in his pocket. Without turning to the driver, he said, "Fifth and Penn."

Jimmy's heart sputtered. They were taking him back. The messenger probably wanted to question him.

Subtly he eyed the passenger door. No handles. That didn't matter to a gifted magician determined to escape from a confined space. Unless the windows were lined with metal, he could produce something hard and solid to shatter the glass.

He decided to wait for the next light. When the van began easing to a stop, he'd pull a brick from his jacket pocket, break the window and leap out. The heavy traffic would prevent these two from getting him. They'd have to pull over and--

"*Jimmy? Can you hear me*?"

Her soft, breathy voice nearly made him gasp.

He'd totally forgotten all about her powers. He wanted to kick himself for being so stupid. With her help, he didn't have to take any risks. He wouldn't even have to escape from the van.

He closed his eyes and sat back in the seat. "*Tiffany?*"

"*Where are you?*"

"*Two of them just picked me up. I'm in a van on Liberty. They're taking me back to Fifth and Penn.*"

"*How'd they find you? I told you to get away.*"

"*I felt really badly about leaving you and turned around to come back.*"

"*That's really sweet, but you're an idiot.*"

"*I know.*"

"*How far are you from there?*"

"*I figure around fifteen minutes.*"

"*I'll meet you there. And Jimmy?*"

"*Yes?*"

"*Don't turn stupid on me again, okay?*"

"*I won't.*"

He struggled to keep from smiling as he quietly slipped the cuffs back on.

Chapter 23

The Lincoln eased halfway down the block and stopped at the curb.

The phone still pressed against his ear, Andras circled the big car and kept an eye on the street activity. "While I'm waiting," he told his contact, "tell me a little about Russo."

"He's been working at the Bel-Mor on Penn Avenue. He specializes in magic tricks and also juggles."

"You told me that before. Is that all you've got?"

"I can get more, but it'll take fifteen or twenty minutes."

"How long will it take to find out where he lives?"

"I can get in touch with his employer at the Bel-Mor. That should only take a moment or two."

"Once you get him, transfer him over to me."

"Will do."

"By the way, any idea where your men are? I know it's only been a few minutes since they picked up Russo, but I'd like to know how much time I've got before they bring him here."

"The latest coordinates say they're about five blocks away. In this traffic, they should be delivering him in fifteen minutes, tops."

"If you can get hold of someone from the club right away, that'll be just great."

“Right now, I’ve got several people working the lines--wait a minute. Hold on. Someone’s calling in.”

Andras leaned against the side of the Lincoln and watched the hordes of passersby. It was a quarter past one. The lunch crowds weren’t quite as hectic, but scattered groups wandered up and down the block, many of them attractive young women in nice-fitting clothes. Several glanced his way, but he knew the blonde wouldn’t be foolish enough to show herself. Someone as bright as she was, wouldn’t get close enough for him to see. Even if she knew for a fact that her friend was being held captive in the Lincoln, she wouldn’t put herself in jeopardy by letting Andras see her.

About two minutes later, his contact came back on the line. “I’ve got Douglas Moreland on the line, sir. He’s one of the Bel-Mor owners and is very anxious to know what’s going on.”

This was good. When someone was anxious, you’d already won the battle. “Conference him in, then hang up. I’ll call when I need you.”

Click. “Ready to go, sir.”

“Moreland?”

“Yeah, I’m Doug Moreland. Who the hell’s this?”

Andras frowned. The man sounded like a thug. “My name is Smith, and I’ll make this brief. I’ve come here to--”

“Smith?”

“Yes. Smith.”

“Listen…Smith--”

"*Mister* Smith to you."

A groan. "Whatever. Listen here. What's this have to do with Russo? He's my biggest moneymaker, and some joker I never heard of calls me out of the blue two minutes ago and tells me my boy's been picked up by the fucking—"

"Listen to me, Moreland."

"Wait one fucking—"

"I said listen, dammit, or you'll never be able to open your nightclub again."

"What the fuck are you—"

"You heard me." Andras put some genuine fear into his tone.

Silence.

"Do I have your attention now?"

A pause. "Yeah."

"And will you shut up long enough to hear what I've got to say?"

Moreland sighed. "Go 'head."

"Long story short. Your client was seen with someone I'm interested in, and I need some questions answered."

"What's this all about? Who's this…who the hell are you interested in? Maybe I know him."

"It's a woman, and let's just say she's important to my job and leave it at that."

A chuckle. "A chick, eh? Listen. Russo's a chick magnet. Babes love the guy. Ever get a good look at him? He's got that hair thing goin' on with the curl over one eye. Looks like dynamite in a good suit, and has those dark eyes and lashes chicks drool over. You know the drill. How the hell am I s'posed to know—"

"I'll make this simple. I need to know everything I can about this woman. And if this means bringing in your chick magnet moneymaker and detaining him for three or four days, that's exactly what I intend to do—"

"Wait one fucking minute--"

"Or three or four *weeks*, if you keep pissing me off."

"Listen to me. You can't do that!"

"I not only can, I will. I already have him. If you don't start cooperating, you're not going to get him back. Not any time soon, that is."

"He's got an iron-clad contract!"

"I don't do contracts. And if it'll make things plainer, I don't do attitudes, either."

Another sigh. "Listen, fella. This is America, for Chrissakes. We got rights here. All kinds of fucking rights. Something tells me you ain't no cop or Fed, so whatever you're doing ain't right, and if you think I'm gonna just stand here and let you fuck me like this—"

"You're absolutely right. I'm not a cop or Fed."

"Then what the hell--"

"I'll let you figure that out for yourself."

Silence. Andras could tell Moreland was furiously trying to work out some sort of angle. Moreland's type screamed angles.

"I've got connections, buddy-boy," Moreland finally blurted out. "All kinds of connections. I know lawyers, bankers--the works. I own a *club*, dammit. It's one of the biggest and most successful places in the Burgh."

"That's fine. I'll let your connections talk with mine when we've finished here."

A pause. "And who might you know? I been living in this town all my life. My wife's family happens to be a Hunt. Ever heard of 'em? There was this major traffic accident a few years back. You mighta heard of it. It involved a PAT bus, a cop car, and--"

"If it'll make things simpler, I'll have my connection talk to them when we've finished this unpleasant little chat. His name is Madigan. Josh Madigan. I'm sure you've heard of him. I can't say for sure if he's heard of you, though. I've been dealing with his right-hand man all day, but your name never came up. I only heard of you for the first time just a couple of minutes ago, actually."

Silence.

Andras could tell he'd hit pay dirt. Everyone in the city knew about Josh Madigan.

It was time to add a little more pressure. "In the meantime, I strongly suggest you start cooperating."

Moreland cleared his throat. It took him two tries to get the words out. "And if I do?"

"I get what I want and you get your moneymaking chick magnet back. Simple enough?"

"All right, all right. Whaddya want?"

"Where does Russo live?"

"He's got a place on Penn Avenue. A two-roomer. He's been living there since he started working at the Bel-Mor."

"I need the address."

"You just told me you got him, right? Just ask him."

"I want his apartment checked out while I'm questioning him. The woman I'm looking for could be staying there. Get it?"

"What if she ain't there?"

"Then I guess I'll have to ask him where she might be, won't I?"

A pause. "This chick. She wouldn't be a blond fox, would she? Lots and lots of hair? Big knockers? Nice bod?"

Andras stiffened. "How would you know that?"

"I think I spotted her last night, when I was taking Russo home. She was outside the club. She seemed real interested in him."

"You didn't see her any other time?"

"I mighta seen her outside my office after last night's show, but I ain't sure that was her. There were a lot of 'em out there. But if she's the one you're looking for, I wouldn't count on Russo givin' her up. She's helluva piece. I wouldn't blame the boy for stashing her somewhere safe."

"I have ways of finding out things. Especially things people want kept secret. Just give me five minutes. It's all I need."

Silence.

"You still there, Moreland?"

Silence.

"Moreland?"

"I don't seem to remember where…I have Russo's address--"

Andras gritted his teeth when ripples of heat began whipping down his limbs. "You don't want to mess with me."

"Listen, Mister Smith—or whatever the fuck your name is. If I say I can't remember, what the fuck you gonna do? It ain't like you can force me to--"

Andras sent a jolt of fire through the line. It wrapped tightly around Moreland's neck. When he heard the loud choked gasp on the other end, he said, "Is this helping you remember, Moreland?"

More choking.

"I can make it tighter, if that'll help."

More gasping and choking. Moreland was struggling to say something.

"Want me to ease up a little?"

Another gasp. "*Mmmm*...*hmmmm*!"

Andras relaxed some of the pressure. "Can you remember now?"

Moreland sounded like he'd just run a mile at full speed. He choked, gasped loudly and cleared his throat. "What the *fuck*?" A cough. "Wh-What hap-*happened*?"

"Have you found the address yet? Or do I have to apply pressure to some other portion of your body? Your testicles, perhaps?"

Moreland cleared his throat and coughed wetly. "F-Found it," he whispered, his voice raspy.

"Now that wasn't that difficult, was it?"

"N-No. Not diff-difficult..."

"Good. Now give me the address, and when you're done, I want you to hang up, walk right over to the first person you see, and punch him in the face."

Silence.

"Did you hear me?"

"Well yeah, but why should I--"

"No questions. Just give me the address. I'm in a hurry."

***

Still a flat-chested redhead in loose-fitting clothes, Tiffany crossed the street with the crowd at the intersection of Liberty and Stanwix.

It had been five minutes since her mental exchange with Jimmy. If he'd been right in his calculations, she had about ten minutes to get back to Fifth.

She had no idea what to do once she reached Fifth. Her disguise would keep her safe, but she had to somehow rescue Jimmy and Chip without getting in harm's way herself. Since she didn't know how much her powers had increased, she didn't want to risk going up against the messenger. Breath Mint would never send an incompetent demon for a job like this. She feared this one was more than powerful enough and possessed at least as many powers as she had. The biggest problem she faced was to help her friends before the demon had the chance to see her and place her under a spell.

Two male teens in faded jeans, baggy sweatshirts and athletic shoes strolled up the walk toward her, sharing a blunt. Both wore their dark hair very short on the sides and long on top and in back. Their pockmarked faces were covered with studs. The tattoo of green tombstones encircled the slender neck of the boy on her right. His friend sported a large red swastika tatt on his neck directly over his protruding Adam's apple.

The boys didn't slow their gait or move out of her way. Tombstones lowered the blunt from his mouth and blew a thick cloud of gray smoke at her. His glazed eyes immediately lowered to her flat chest.

Tiffany veered to her right to circle them.

Tombstones sidestepped, blocking her way. "Get away, skank."

Skank?

She backed up. She really didn't have time for this. "I'm *trying* to, but--"

"Fuck you." Swastika edged around her.

"Don't touch 'er, Randy," Tombstones said. "You'll catch somethin'."

Tiffany tried veering around them the other way, but Swastika sidestepped, blocking her path once again. "Get the fuck away, you ugly crack whore."

The first one elbowed her, slamming her into the brick wall of the building. A wall of bright pain raced up her side. She doubled up and waited for the onslaught of heat to subside. As she collected herself, the two thugs made pig noises and blew more smoke at her.

When the throbbing pain in her side finally ebbed, she slowly straightened. She caught her reflection in the store window on her right. She did look like a junkie. But that was no reason to be verbally and physically assaulted.

A knot of anger burned in her gut. She stole a quick glance at her watch. She now had about seven minutes to get there. She spun around. Her anger taking hold, she turned into her old self for one brief moment.

The boys gawked at her. Tombstones backed up stiffly. Swastika made loud gurgling noises.

"What the fuck? What's…goin' on?" Tombstones' jaw quivered.

"Dude, this is fucked up. Seriously fucked up!"

"This blow, man. Where the fuck didja get it?"

"Was that necessary?" Her face instantly returned to that of the dirty redhead. "Slamming me into the wall?"

Neither could reply. Their eyes lowered as her breasts suddenly vanished.

Still watching them, Tiffany lowered her voice. "Why don't you two just turn around and take a walk into traffic?"

Like automatons they turned around stiffly, crossed the walk and stepped down from the curb. Traffic roared by, missing them by inches. They both screamed, holding out their arms to shield themselves while fighting furiously to back out of the way. A Dodge Ram pickup swerved around them, nearly slamming into Swastika and barely missing oncoming traffic.

A PAT bus came into view, heading straight toward them.

Tiffany watched in fascination. In precious seconds, the two would fly in the air like rag dolls, screaming as the bus turned them into--

Not *a demon*... Not *a demon*...

Reality snapped her out of it. "*Turn around. Now*!"

They spun around quickly. Arms flailing, they scrambled back onto the curb.

The bus roared past, horn blaring.

The boys dropped to their knees and huddled together at the curb, shaking, heaving and clutching one another while sobbing hysterically.

Another wash of anger surged through her. She'd almost let two arrogant street punks turn her into a demon.

She took a few deep breaths. *Calm. Think of what you're doing, what needs to be done. Chip. Jimmy. Ashley. You need to focus on your friends and forget about the idiots wandering around the city.*

With a deep sigh, she resumed her journey down the busy street. People steered clear, giving her space. The only one who didn't turn away was a homeless man standing at the corner, grinning at her through his gray beard as she hurried past. Hopefully, everyone would forget her very shortly. Complete anonymity had become her most important ally. She didn't want to take the chance of being seen as herself in someone's monitor. It was bad enough that she'd turned briefly into herself back at the corner. But those two jerks needed to learn a valuable lesson.

A few minutes later, she reached the corner of Fifth and Liberty. She went around the corner and stopped cold. The dark-blue Lincoln Town Car sat at the curb halfway up the hill. The messenger stood beside it, talking on a cellphone.

***

The man sitting amidst the sea of monitors in the brightly lit room stiffened as he was getting up from his seat.

It had been a long, tiring afternoon. He'd been glued to his chair since eight that morning. Except for a couple of quick potty breaks and some moo goo gai pan and egg rolls brought in from the Chinese place on Liberty Avenue, he hadn't taken his eyes off the screens. But now it was well past one, his shift was over, and his replacement was overdue.

Still, the strange sight on the monitor made him lower his butt back into his seat.

The skinny redheaded woman roughed up by the two street guys near Liberty and Stanwix just moments ago had somehow looked totally different for just a second or two.

The blonde. She'd looked just like the blonde.

He studied the computer-generated photo on his other screen. The same hair, the same face, the same clothes.

It was her, all right. The woman they'd been looking for all morning. They hadn't been told much about her at all. Just that she was a "PI," or Person of Interest, and was being sought by some VIP no one had the authorization to talk about.

In this case, such info meant anything from a drug smuggler, professional hitter, politician, or the daughter of a diplomat--although this lady didn't look much like any of those. In fact, she looked like a babe he'd seen in a commercial last year, hustling perfume. He and Nathan had immediately gone into the various databases they used for tracking, but all they could find was a marked resemblance to a young Hollywood actress who'd O. D'ed at some party a few months earlier in Beverly Hills. Since the actress hadn't been well-known and several VIPs had been at the party, the news item was quickly quashed. Brad, his supervisor, had said that women looking like her were a dime a dozen out there in Hollywood. It really didn't matter who she was. The official word was that they weren't to do any further investigating in this. The VIP just wanted her found. Case closed.

But the fact remained. He'd just seen something really weird on the monitor and had no idea what was going on. Was he seeing things? How could a woman suddenly change into someone else for just a few seconds? It couldn't happen, but it did. He saw it. Only moments ago, he saw it.

He knew how the eyes worked when they were tired and needed rest, when they'd been staring too long at one thing. When they fixed on thousands of pixels, slews of images. They rebelled, lied to you, told you all sorts of weird things.

He took off his bifocals and rubbed his eyes vigorously. They'd betrayed him, obviously. Maybe the glasses were the culprits. He hadn't replaced them in two years. He no doubt needed a stronger prescription. In this business, you had to stay on top of your game. When you stared at pixels and digitals all day long, eyestrain became common. It also became your number one enemy. To do your job effectively, you had to make sure your eyesight was clear and sharp.

Nonetheless, fatigue had definitely set in. Hell, he'd been sitting here all morning and half the afternoon, his eyes glazing over more than a dozen times as lunchtime approached.

Things like this happened all the time. At JSM Security, half the guys on the monitors had developed eye problems. You couldn't possibly stick to this job very long without something breaking down.

He put the bifocals back on and went back to the monitor. Sure enough, the woman was gone. He checked the other four monitors at his station. The screens buzzed with street activity, but the image he'd seen two minutes ago was gone.

He attacked the keyboard and started up a replay program. He decided to go back two minutes and watch it again, this time at a slower speed. 75% would be about right. Once he found the right frame, he could perform a zoom, freeze it and record from there. He'd save it, clean it up, sharpen it and attach it to his email program. Before sending it off to Brad, he'd replay the entire two minutes. If they could do this quickly enough, they might be able to find her again.

His phone rang. It was Brad.

"Yes, sir?"

"Wrap it up. You're finished for the day."

"But I might have something here."

"What is it?"

"Well, it's kind of hard to explain."

"What are you trying to say, Milton?"

"Well, I'm pretty sure I saw the woman we're looking for."

"Just *pretty* sure?"

"The camera was half a block down and she was standing beside an awning. There were crowds moving past, but I'm confident it was her. It was only for a second or two, but--"

"A second or two?"

He was beginning to think he'd made a mistake by telling Brad. He glanced at the photo stuck near his monitor and for a second wondered if he really *had* seen her. Maybe he'd only *thought* he had. After all, he'd been glancing at the photo ever since they gave it to him. And it was no wonder. The woman was one of the hottest babes he'd ever seen. Several times during that first hour, he'd caught himself staring at those big blue eyes, wondering if he'd ever be lucky enough to meet someone who looked like that. Then he began wondering what she was like. If she was even approachable. A while back, one of his college chums had met a Hollywood star at one of those wild parties out there on the West Coast but said the bitch wouldn't even look him in the eye. She was so stuck on herself that--

"Milton? You still there?"

Snap out of it. "Like I said, sir, it was crowded, and she was probably a hundred yards away. I saw her on Liberty and Stanwix, about a block from McDonald's."

"What direction is she going?"

"That's just it. I don't know."

"You lost her?"

"Not exactly, but--"

"Then where is she?"

"Well, like I just said, the crowds--"

"Milton, did you see her or what?"

He knew better than tell Brad that the woman he might have just seen could have well been imagined. Brad didn't like complications and might even send him to the eye doctor if he thought something was wrong.

This had to be phrased just right. "Yes and no. She just appeared, then she wasn't there anymore."

"Did Nathan see it?"

"He's on break."

"What about Powell?"

"He hasn't come back from lunch yet."

A pause. "How long have you been there by yourself?"

Milton glanced at the clock. It had been more than half an hour, but he knew better than tell Brad. They didn't want anyone on his own longer than twenty minutes at a time and might go back to those weird shifts that everyone hated. Besides, he didn't want to get anyone in trouble. "About fifteen minutes," he said.

“Wait till Powell gets there, then go home and rest your eyes.”

“But I think I might be able to sharpen up this image a bit. It might explain what—“

“Once Nathan or Powell gets back, go home. See ya tomorrow, eight o’clock sharp.”

“Yes, sir.”

Chapter 24

Twenty-two minutes after Jimmy was cuffed and shoved into the van, the driver turned left, onto Fifth Avenue. When the last of the crowd crossed the street, the dark-blue Lincoln came into view. It sat halfway down the block, resting against the curb. A man in a dark suit stood behind it, talking into his cell.

As they approached, Jimmy saw him more clearly. It was the man whose image Tiffany had shown him before. The demon that had shoved Chip into the back of the Lincoln.

The van slowed, pulled over to the curb and coasted the last twenty yards, stopping about fifteen feet from the rear bumper of the Lincoln.

Jimmy gazed uneasily at the vehicle straight ahead. The tinted window revealed no one inside. Chip was no doubt lying in the back seat under the demon's spell. Or dosed with a strong drug. Jimmy expected the two uniforms to escort him directly from the van and shove him into the back seat of the Lincoln next to Chip.

His thoughts whirred as he struggled for some sort of distraction. He could easily use magic to delay the inevitable but knew he should wait until he'd heard from Tiffany. She could already be in the area, assessing the situation.

A long line of pedestrians crossed the street farther down on Liberty, while smaller knots moved up and down the sidewalk on both sides of Fifth.

There were more than a dozen young blondes among them, but no sign of Tiffany.

Even if she was close by, it would be much too dangerous to let anyone see her. He hoped she knew what she was doing and that she wouldn't risk her own safety. That would be stupid, and he couldn't see her doing anything stupid. But even faced with these odds, she wouldn't let them down. She told him she'd be here. That was all he needed to know.

Briefly he wondered if the messenger had questioned Chip. That wasn't possible. There hadn't been enough time. It hadn't been very long at all since the big bearded guy in leather had snatched Chip, and less an hour since Jimmy and Tiffany had split up. The messenger had been much too busy tracking him down while trying to get a fix on Tiffany. It took too much time to slip into the mind of someone under the influence of a sleep-induced spell.

Even so, Jimmy understood the predicament he was in. This messenger had been sent here to get quick results. For such a job, a subordinate would be needed. Subordinates excelled in mind control and thought manipulation. The messenger would have all the answers he required just minutes after Jimmy was brought to him.

Jimmy had no chance of surviving this. In minutes, the messenger would know Jimmy was a spirit, that he'd been in Hell, and that he'd been hiding amongst the mortals for nearly a century. He'd learn about the fires, about Danielle, and about the sex session with the underage girls. After learning all he needed to know about Tiffany, the messenger would send Jimmy back down to face Asmodeus and the other supers.

A cold knot of fear had gathered low in his gut. If Tiffany didn't get here soon, he was going to have to work some serious magic.

The van shook as the two front doors pushed open.

An icicle rushed like gunfire up Jimmy's spine. His thoughts raced. "*Tiffany, please get here!*"

***

Tiffany crossed the street and joined a small group of middle-aged female shoppers heading north, toward Penn Avenue. When she saw the big utility van stopping behind the Lincoln, she veered off to the right and stopped in front of a window facing the apartment building. She took off her tennis shoe and made a show of checking it for a pebble, but in reality she was watching the reflection of the activity across the street.

She directed her thoughts directly to the van:

"Jimmy? Can you hear me?"

"Damn!" came the nervous reply. *"I never thought I'd ever hear your voice again!"*

"I told you I'd meet you here. I always keep my word."

"I know, but this is really scary. They pulled me right off the street and brought me here. I think the messenger's about to question me. "

Darn. If that happened, it would ruin everything. The messenger would learn about

Jimmy and this would turn ugly. *"We can't let that happen. What are they doing right now?"*

"They're about to take me out of the van. Where are you?"

"Close."

"I don't see you."

"It doesn't matter. I can see you."

"Any ideas?"

"We need to cause a distraction to keep them away from the Lincoln."

"And how do you suppose we do that?"

She watched the crowds in the reflection of the window. Most were in a hurry. But since there were a lot of them, it could be all they needed to cause enough commotion to enable Jimmy to get away. *"You're going to do it."*

"Me?"

"You."

"How the hell can I possibly--"

"Think of something, but do it quickly. We don't have much time."

"Look, I'm scared and can barely remember my own name. How can I--"

"Jimmy, listen to me."

"But I don't think...I don't know if—"

This was no time for him to freeze up. *"Jimmy, you're doing it again. If you don't want me to slap you the next time I see you..."*

"I'm listening..."

"*Good.*" She had to force him to keep his cool. After all, he was a performer, and a really good one at that. He knew how to think on his feet, and had nearly as many one-liners at his disposal as Chip. There was no reason why he couldn't shine now. Too much was at stake.

"Jimmy, you're probably the best magician I've ever seen."

A pause. *"Well, thanks, but I don't see how that has anything to do with--"*

"Like I said, we need a distraction. A big one. You're a performer. And quite possibly the world's best juggler. Put on a show and get as many people as you can to come over and watch. I know you can do it. Understand?"

***

"Yes. I think I do."

Jimmy knew what she had in mind, but it didn't make him less scared. But it didn't matter. He wouldn't let Tiffany down.

But even with his magic helping him, this wouldn't be easy. The messenger had access to money, connections, monitors and cameras. The city's resources would be totally available to Braithwaite and the Diocese. Without Jimmy's help, Tiffany didn't stand a snowball's chance.

The big uniform pulled open the rear door. "Time to get out." He jabbed a fat thumb at the Lincoln.

Jimmy tried focusing on the task at hand but quickly found it impossible to concentrate. Fear had already set in. All he saw was the uniform standing there, watching him, the other uniform getting out, and the messenger standing behind the Lincoln, the cellphone in his left ear as he watched the van.

Jimmy couldn't succumb to the fear. He had to do what Tiffany had asked him right now, before these two could shove him into the back seat of the Lincoln. Once that happened, he belonged to the messenger. Everything about Tiffany—as well as himself—was up for sacrifice. The messenger would simply reach inside his head, find whatever seemed interesting, and pull it out. Jimmy and Tiffany—as well as Chip and Ashley—would be at the mercy of the super demon.

"Quit stalling." The big man grabbed Jimmy's upper arm and pulled. The sudden wrenching movement sent a stabbing of pain up his arm, and he nearly toppled out of the van. He brought out his left leg and slammed his foot onto the pavement. Then he gazed into the uniform's arrogant eyes and realized in that single moment that the fear had left him. Anger had replaced it. And with the anger, the knowledge that this uniformed bully—as well as his partner, the messenger, and the people walking up the sidewalk—now belonged to him.

"You're probably the best magician I've ever seen..."

Yes, Tiffany, he thought, the confidence thundering back much quicker than he'd ever imagined, *I am pretty damned good.*

While lowering his other foot to the pavement, Jimmy removed the cuffs. He then straightened and brought his arms out from behind his back.

The uniform gasped. He obviously had no idea what had just happened. Jimmy should have grunted into an awkward standing position with his arms pinned behind his back. But that did not happen. Jimmy's arms were free. This made no sense. Those were standard, regulation police handcuffs. You couldn't just slip out of them like that. No one could. Houdini himself would have had a bastard of a time getting out of those damned cuffs.

Jimmy held them out and winked. "These were a tad too large. As you can see, I've got dainty wrists. Do you happen to have a smaller pair I might use?"

The big man took a step back and nearly tripped. He gawked at Jimmy, then at the cuffs dangling from Jimmy's left hand. His partner had already started circling the front of the van.

Jimmy grinned and handed over the cuffs. The other man took them and eyed them stupidly. A weird whining sound trickled out of his throat.

It was time for the show to start.

Jimmy slipped past the astonished guard and stood in the middle of the street. His hands began moving in a slow piston-like action. In the blinking of an eye, three red rubber balls slightly larger than golf balls magically appeared, each jumping a foot in the air, one right after the other, in perfect cadence.

"What the fuck..." The second uniform watched in awe. His partner hadn't taken his eyes off Jimmy. His chin rested on his breastbone. The cuffs dropped from his grasp, clinking to the pavement.

Jimmy added a rubber ball each time his right hand pushed the preceding ball in the air, until he was juggling a dozen of them. As he worked, he backed up, edging over to the curb behind the van. Then stepped carefully onto the sidewalk.

The second uniform circled back around and stopped about fifteen feet from Jimmy, watching in fascination. His glazed eyes moved up and down in unison with the dancing rubber balls.

"That's fine, Jimmy," Tiffany's voice said, *"but you need to step it up. The crowd isn't big or rowdy enough."*

Jimmy forced himself to concentrate on the balls dancing wildly in front of him. There was no need to scan the area. Tiffany was obviously close enough to see him. *"How?"*

"Use your own judgment. Don't forget, we're both already playing with fire. Nothing you do can hurt anything."

Fire. Of course. Why hadn't he thought of that?

"Get ready to be impressed."

"I'm ready."

Just then, a flickering flame appeared on each ball as soon as it touched his palm. One by one, each ball danced with flame as it jumped into the air. Tiny tongues of fire swirled and flickered vivaciously in front of him, creating an unusual display that caused several passing vehicles to stop abruptly. The uniform closest to him gasped and shook his head. "Son of a bitch..."

People rushed out of stores and stood at the curb, watching. Others stopped walking and just stared. A dozen more vehicles came to a sudden stop. Passenger doors swung open. Windows lowered. Heads peered out of windows and above opened doors. People came out of stores and just froze, hypnotized. Everyone within the block gawked helplessly at Jimmy as he stood on the sidewalk, juggling dozens of flame-covered red balls.

Jimmy risked a glance at his audience. There were at least forty people shuffling toward him. Others were getting out of their cars and standing there, mesmerized. There was no sign of the messenger. People had swarmed closer to the two vehicles, hiding him from view.

It was time to add even more confusion to his act. As he juggled, he purposely dropped one of the balls. Its flame immediately went out as it hopped away, smacking the uniform squarely on the nose.

Taken completely by surprise, the big man gasped and took a couple of quick steps backward. The heel of his shiny black shoe slid down from the curb. He fell backward, landing on his butt. Jimmy then turned slightly to his left and dropped another ball. It hopped over the roof of the van, to the other uniform, whacking him between the eyes. He fell backward and numbly watched as the ball hopped past him and skittered beneath a vehicle.

During the next two minutes, the crowd had grown. Jimmy dropped several more balls. They leaped onto the hood of the van, one right after the other, hopped down onto the hood, into the street, bounced off a vehicle and ricocheted off the side of the pickup truck behind it. Two small kids ran wildly after them, yelling and screaming. A slender young woman in gray sweats and a black pullover and hood trotted down the sidewalk after a ball. Jimmy lobbed another, then another, making sure the number he kept in motion did not change.

The street erupted in chaos. Horns blared as motorists turned onto Fifth and discovered traffic at a standstill. Small groups of young thrill-seekers squeezed between vehicles, jumped onto bumpers and darted across the street to snatch a bouncing magic ball.

A crowd had congregated between the van and the Lincoln. Jimmy tossed a dozen more rubber balls into the middle of the street. People leaped after them. Jimmy directed six more balls to hop across the roof of the van, into the crowd flocked behind the Lincoln.

As the crowd fought one another, Jimmy caught a glimpse of a skinny redheaded woman heading straight for the Lincoln. The crowd moving across the street hid her from view, but he caught sight of her again as she disappeared behind a small bunch in front of the Lincoln.

"Get out of here, Jimmy. Now!"

Jimmy lobbed a dozen more balls. They dropped to the macadam, bouncing wildly. As a final *coup de grace*, he tossed two dozen balls high into the air. Just as they began their descent, he dropped his arms and scrambled into the closest group. The crowd went berserk, elbowing and slamming into one another to retrieve the final onslaught.

Oblivious to everyone, Jimmy disappeared in the crowd.

Chapter 25

Surrounded by excited, unruly mortals, Andras couldn't believe Russo had turned the entire block into total madness. He'd just lost sight of Russo, making this situation even worse. The crowds, traffic, and the resulting chaos had made it impossible to see anything on the other side of the utility van.

Out of the corner of his eye he caught sight of a skinny redhead moving away from the Lincoln. He watched her for a few moments but didn't sense any suspicious vibes. She'd probably just been crossing the street when he noticed her.

Slipping past a small group scrambling after half a dozen bouncing rubber balls, he moved over to the side of the Lincoln. Another line of gawkers crowded around it, but he could see Dahl sitting behind the wheel, his Taser gun in his right hand. The inferior remained motionless in the back seat.

Using his powers, Andras shoved people out of the way and slipped through the staggered mass. Throngs of idiots fought furiously for those cursed balls--pushing, shoving and elbowing one another. The damned things flickered with flame as they hopped, the flame dying the moment someone grabbed it.

The crowd had pinned the two uniformed guards helplessly against the side of the van. Using his powers to clear the way, Andras walked right over and got in the guards' faces. He grabbed each by the collar and shook them vigorously. "Remember me?"

They both squinted at him, trying to focus. After a few moments, they both nodded.

"Find Russo and bring him back here right now. I haven't seen him come my way, so that probably means he's headed toward Penn Avenue. Got it?"

They both nodded.

"Make sure you don't come back without him. And stay the hell away from anyone with a camera or microphone."

"I don't know if…if we can get the van out of here, sir." The driver frowned at the people running around. "Not in this crowd."

"Go after him on foot. I'm going back to the Lincoln. As soon as we can, we're getting out of here. Something tells me if we're not out of here in the next couple of minutes, we'll be seeing camera crews for days."

"We'll find him, sir."

"See that you do. Call your boss the instant you track him down. He'll get with me immediately and you'll receive your instructions from there."

The guards backed away, shoved people out of the way. They began jogging down the street.

Andras edged back to the Lincoln. He fished his cell out of his pocket and switched it on. "I guess you know by now that we lost Russo."

"We've all been watching. What happened, anyway?"

"What do you *think* happened?"

"I saw him get out of the van and hand over the handcuffs to our driver. Then he went right into a juggling act. We didn't think the block would turn into such pandemonium so quickly."

"You know how stupid people are. They see something strange, get curious, go brain-dead and turn into an instant mob of worthless flesh. In the middle of the fucking street."

"Russo's actually very good. I can understand why he's so popular at the Bel-Mor--"

"Save the reviews for someone who actually gives a rat's ass. But since you brought it up, he's *too* fucking good."

"How's that, sir?"

Andras had never seen a mortal magician perform such feats. Not without props, lighting, mirrors, or assistants. Questioning him was going to be extremely interesting.

"Just thinking out loud. We've got to find this clown and get the hell out of here."

"You're right, sir. And we've got to work fast. Two Nine-One-One calls have already been made. I estimate police involvement in the area within ninety seconds. There's a squad car three blocks east, on Penn. It's already turning around. Another car's a couple of blocks farther down, on Liberty. It's responding as well."

"I've just sent the two uniforms on foot pursuit after Russo, but I don't think they'll be able to find him in the next fifteen or twenty minutes. How quickly can you send a car to my location?"

"What do you have in mind, sir?"

"I've already captured two of them. The way things are going, I don't want to lose either of them. To make sure nothing else happens, I want you to bring a car over here right now, pick up the redhead and take him directly to the airport."

"But--"

"You can watch us on the monitors, as you've been doing all day. As I just said, I don't like how things have been going and don't want to tempt fate. Understand?"

"Yes, sir..."

"My chauffer's going to take me to the nearest coffee place. I'm going to enjoy a cup of good, strong coffee and wait for you to pick up the redhead. Once you pick him up, take him to the airport and put him on the plane. I'll wait here for half an hour while your boys look for Russo. If no one shows, I'll leave for the airport and wait another half-hour. If I don't hear from anyone by three o'clock, I'll have no choice but leave for Orlando." Andras moved closer to the passenger door.

"I'll have someone there directly, sir. Meanwhile, we'll find Russo. We've got influential people with the Pittsburgh Police. I'll have them issue an APB as well as a BOLO. They'll treat it as an emergency. I'm confident they'll find him very quickly."

"I hope you're right." Andras opened the door and slid in the back seat next to the unconscious inferior. Luckily, traffic had already begun moving again. "Let's get out of here, Dahl. This place is beginning to piss me off."

"Yes, sir."

"One second." Three teen males wrestled with one another across the street. *You're not doing it right*, Andras thought, grinning darkly. *You need to stop acting like little girls and put some serious punch into it.* He sent a surge of heat in their direction, and in seconds the boys were kicking, punching, elbowing and stomping one another.

Andras applied the same spell to four other groups. Within one minute, more than a dozen people lay bleeding on the pavement.

"There." Andras nodded in satisfaction. "Now the cops actually have something to deal with."

"All right, Mr. Smith?"

"Yes, Dahl. I feel much better."

Dahl started up the engine and inched away from the curb.

***

The 7-Eleven at the corner of Sixth and Penn was fairly crowded. Several people flocked the register, checking out display items on the counter while waiting to pay for their purchases. Others wandered down the aisles, touching things and picking up others. A couple of teen boys, their faces covered with studs and pimples, huddled near a comic book tree.

Jimmy paused behind the glass door, watching the street. Street traffic and pedestrians scurried by, but no sign of the two uniforms. He could almost feel them out there, looking for him. After all, he'd slipped away from a demon. No one who did something that reckless should expect to kick back and relax for the rest of the day. He suspected that all he had to do to test his theory was go back out there. He'd undoubtedly run into them in just a few minutes.

He had to remain alert. He wasn't dealing with normal people. He was dealing with demons and the super wealthy. When he thought of it, he suddenly realized that there really was no noticeable line separating the two. The rich had amassed its wealth pledging allegiance to the Dark World. As a result, this had become their world, and there was very little Jimmy could do to keep them from snatching him again.

But with Tiffany's help, he sensed that he stood a far better chance of keeping them at bay.

One last glance at the street told him the coast was still clear. Jimmy went down the aisle, to the rear of the store. The refrigerated shelves spanned the back wall, extending to the hall leading to the exit door. Beer, milk, soft drinks and other perishables crammed the icy shelves. The hall led to a door marked RESTROOM. A door marked MANAGER faced it on the other side of the hall. At the far end, a large solid metal door braced shut with a heavy-duty lock sat directly beneath the flickering EXIT sign.

Jimmy tried the restroom door; it was unlocked. He went inside. The small, dark empty room smelled strongly of Lysol. He locked the door and flicked on the light. Feeling unsteady, he went over to the sink, poured water from the tap and doused his face. The cold water immediately snapped him alert. He splashed himself again and washed his hands. His heart was fluttering madly, but he knew he'd be okay once he took a few deep breaths.

He'd done it. That was the main thing. He not only escaped, but he'd caused enough commotion on Fifth Avenue to--

What had he accomplished with that impromptu spectacle? Had it enabled Tiffany to reach the Lincoln? Was she able to rescue Chip? Take him away from the messenger without being captured as well?

Or had his efforts caused more problems?

He wiped his face with paper towels from the dispenser and suddenly realized that although he'd saved his own skin, Tiffany and Chip might not have been so lucky. He'd gotten away, but that didn't mean they had. And if they hadn't, that meant they were both now in the hands of the messenger.

But she'd told him to get away.

Get out of here, Jimmy, she'd said. *Now*!

She'd been clear about it. She'd meant it. She wasn't the type to say something she didn't mean.

But it still made him feel guilty.

What if the messenger *had* caught her? What if he'd spotted her when she approached the Lincoln? What if he'd put her under a spell, tossed her in the back seat with Chip and made off with them?

I'm safe. That's what matters.

He stared at his reflection in the filmy mirror and suddenly hated himself more than ever before. Right now, he hated himself even more than when he'd caused those fires that had sent himself and innocent people to their deaths.

You're despicable. You escaped the messenger, but you did it at Tiffany's expense. She could be on her way back to Orlando with Chip and Ashley while you're standing here, safe and cozy in a locked bathroom. You should be ashamed of yourself. If you cared about her as much as you think you do, you'd be getting your sorry ass back to Fifth Avenue this instant.

Yes. He was going to do that. He was going back there and find out what happened, and if those two uniforms caught him, that was his problem. He was a magician, wasn't he? He'd gotten away from them before. As far as he was concerned, he had no choice. He could never look himself in the face if he didn't help the beautiful woman who'd just saved his own skin.

Jimmy turned away from the sink and took one step toward the door. Then he heard her voice.

"You okay?"

His pulse hammered at the wonderful sound. It took him a few moments to collect himself. *"I'm fine. For now."*

"That was some really terrific juggling you did back there."

"Thanks. Are you okay?"

"I'm fine."

This was terrific. This was great. This was terrific *and* great. Tiffany was fine. Warm relief shimmered through him. He leaned against the door to steady himself. "*Where are you?"*

"Can't talk too much right now, but it looks like I'm about to rescue Chip and Ashley."

"That sounds great. What can I do?"

"You can make sure you stay out of sight and don't get caught. They're looking for you right now. "

"Who is?"

"Everyone. Those two big guys, the messenger, and whoever he's been communicating with. They're using cameras and monitors everywhere. I'm pretty sure these people are watching the streets and the stores. Can you stay out of sight?"

"I think so. I'll try, anyway."

"Good. I'll let you know when we can hook up again. "

Smiling, Jimmy left the bathroom. By the time he'd left the store, he was wearing a green baseball cap, wraparound sunglasses and carrying a red umbrella in his right hand, with a newspaper tucked under his left arm.

***

Andras sat in the back seat of the Lincoln, enjoying a cup of black coffee he'd grabbed at Dunkin' Donuts on Market Square.

Just two minutes earlier, a black Oldsmobile had picked up the unconscious inferior, put him in the back seat and then left immediately for the airport. Andras had watched closely as the two big men carefully picked up the little redhead as if he weighed nothing, placed him in the back seat of the Olds and pulled away in less than two minutes' time.

Good deal. Two out of three were now in the bag.

Now it was time to put the lid on this irritating assignment.

At least the coffee was hot and strong. Best enjoy it before something else happened to screw up the works. If he didn't hear about Russo by 2:30, he'd have no choice but order Dahl to take him straight to the airport. Flying back to Orlando without the blonde was something he didn't even want to think about, but if he could also take Russo with him, his chances of enticing the blonde back to Orlando would increase considerably. This way, Braithwaite could deal with the others while he had his men look for the blonde in Orlando.

At 2:08, his contact buzzed him. "Good news, sir. We just found Russo."

Andras sat up sharply. "Where was he?"

"They found him on Sixth and Penn, near the 7-Eleven. He was trying to blend in with the crowds. We picked him up two minutes ago. He's already in the van."

"Was there any problem?"

"He offered no resistance."

That didn't make sense. Judging by Russo's performance and how he'd escaped, Andras couldn't understand why he'd surrender just an hour or so afterward.

"That's strange," he said. "After what he put us through, why would he just give up?"

"He could be exhausted. Maybe he's smart enough to know we'll get him eventually, so he might as well just give up."

"Maybe." Andras didn't believe that for a moment. However, this wasn't the time to question their good fortune. "Anyway, that *is* good news. Keep close to him. Make sure he doesn't change his mind and attempt another escape."

"We've got two guards sitting with him in the van. If he tries to get out of the cuffs, the guards have orders to Taser him."

"Just make sure he stays reasonably healthy." If these idiots damaged Russo, Andras wouldn't be able to find out anything about the blonde. "I need him for questioning, and he has to be alert when the time comes. If he's hurt, I won't be able to get the right answers."

"Agreed. Where would you like him delivered?"

"The airport, of course. Once I question him, I'll find out where the blonde is and give you instructions where to collect her. If we're lucky, we should have all four of them ready for transport before suppertime. I'll see your people at the airport in about half an hour."

"They'll be there, sir."

Andras clicked off and immediately called Daniel Grove in Orlando.

"I've got Parker and the redhead."

He heard Grove sigh. "What about the blonde?"

"I'm getting to that. I'm also bringing down a local juggler who's mixed up in this mess."

"How is he involved?"

"The others befriended him."

"Is it necessary to bring him here?"

"Maybe, maybe not. If he can tell me about the blonde, I'll no longer need him, and he'll be disposed of."

Grove groaned. "That's kind of harsh."

"It's necessary."

"You said you've got Ashley?"

"I picked her up first."

"She's...not hurt, is she?"

"Not at all. She's sleeping, like the inferior. She's already on the plane. The inferior is presently being taken there as well."

"So then, what about the blonde?"

"She slipped away from us, and we haven't been able to find any sign of her. This is why I decided to bring in the juggler. If I don't learn anything from him, I'll bring him and the two others down with me."

"Mr. Waite isn't going to like that, you know."

"This could actually be a good tactic. The blonde will undoubtedly return to Orlando on her own volition. She doesn't strike me as the type to desert her friends. And the juggler might give her further incentive."

"How does he figure into this?"

"I'm fairly certain they were getting close."

"Then you could be right about this new angle."

"That's what I'm hoping."

"But we're still not out of the woods. Mr. Waite's the one who has to sign off on this."

"I suggest you ask him immediately, before I get on the plane."

"I'll get right back with you."

Andras sat back in the seat and finished his coffee. He wanted a strong drink but decided to wait. If Braithwaite agreed to these new terms, Andras would soon be boarding and wouldn't have to worry about going back for the blonde. Hopefully, Braithwaite would see this his way. Andras didn't want to stay here any longer than necessary. He wanted to get back to Chicago and resume manipulating politicians. He enjoyed manipulating them. He loved it, actually. Next to causing riots, manipulation was his favorite pastime.

About three minutes later, his cell went off.

It was Grove. "Mr. Waite approves of your plan and says you should interrogate Russo. He wants you to bring Russo and the other two with you on your way back to Orlando. He's certain the blonde will come back to help her friends, so don't worry about spending any more time up there than necessary."

Andras sighed in relief. "We'll be on our way in the next hour."

Chapter 26

Tiffany sat in the back seat of the van, her wrists locked behind her back. She wanted to smile when saw the reflection of Jimmy Russo staring back at her from the rearview mirror above the dash.

Once again, she found herself totally in awe and somewhat frightened of her growing powers. It had only been a month or so since she'd died and returned to the world of the living. In those early days, all she could do was change her cup size and alter her clothes and footwear. But it wasn't long at all before she discovered she possessed more powers. In the last few weeks, she'd developed the ability to not only read someone's mind, but also communicate telepathically with them.

She could also shape-shift. Somehow that seemed even more fantastic than all the other stuff. And she intended to use it to find her friends.

Just minutes ago, when she spotted the two uniformed men heading her way on Penn, she knew just how she could fix this. The best way was to have these men take her to the messenger. During Jimmy's impromptu juggling routine on Fifth Avenue, she'd seen Chip lying unconscious in the back seat of the Lincoln. She hadn't had enough time to wake him or slip into the car without the driver alerting the messenger, but at least now she knew where he was. This in itself convinced her she could rescue them. She knew it wouldn't be easy. To do it, she'd have to show herself as Jimmy.

She closed her eyes and focused. Then opened her eyes and looked down at herself. She was wearing the same outfit Jimmy had on during his juggling act. Everything from his shirt, jacket and jeans, and the tennies he'd worn at the breakfast shop this morning.

She moved quickly down the street, separating herself from the crowd and approaching the guards directly.

They stopped cold, gawked at her, then at each other, then at her again. When they realized who they were looking at, they reddened and clumsily went for their guns.

Tiffany tried not to laugh as they ordered her to turn around and put her hands behind her back.

The important thing was that she'd done all this without getting anyone else involved. And in doing so, she'd be reunited with Chip and Ashley. She knew that she'd soon be facing the messenger. She had no idea how powerful he was. She only knew she'd have to be extremely cautious.

She could worry about that later, when she was back with her friends. She'd faced demons before; this would be no different.

For now, she should just sit back and enjoy the ride.

"Cuffs too tight?" the guard on her right asked.

She knew better than tell them anything. Best let them think they'd done their job. "I'm fine, thanks."

The guard on her left watched her closely, a sneer covering his rough bulldog face. *Try something.* His thoughts rang loud and clear as he gripped the Taser fastened to the side of his belt. *Piss us off and you'll be dancin' to the tune of fifty thousand fucking volts.*

She wondered what the Taser could do to someone not of this world. She decided not to tease him. It would delay her rescue attempts and embarrass him in front of his partners.

"That sure seems like a lot of volts to be dancing to," she said, smiling.

"Damn straight. Matter fact--" He gulped loudly and froze in his seat. For the longest time he just stared, his bulging eyes fixed on hers.

Tiffany's smile did not waver.

***

From the window booth in Valli's Bar & Grill on Penn Avenue, Jimmy kept a sharp eye on the street while sipping a dark beer. He still wore his baseball cap and sunglasses. His umbrella lay on the table beside the mug, the paper on the seat beside him. He knew he was no match physically for two huge armed guards but had no intention of making it easy for them if they found him and tried to haul him back to their van. He could do some interesting things with an umbrella most people couldn't even imagine.

But he saw nothing but the usual street traffic. No one in uniform. No van. No Lincoln Town Car. Not even an unmarked vehicle, cops, or anyone glancing at shop windows. It was nearly three. The evening rush hour would start shortly, and the city would become a madhouse again.

So why didn't he see anyone in uniform walking down the street?

The answer was simple. Tiffany had done something else to get him off the hook. Of that, he was certain. But what did she do? And had she put herself in jeopardy?

I'll let you know when we can hook up again.

He hadn't heard from her in nearly half an hour and was getting worried. She should have contacted him before now. If she was in trouble, it was because of him. He had to help her, but this time he wouldn't let her talk him out of it. He had no intention of sitting here, swilling beer, while she was out there, putting her perfect ass on the line.

He closed his eyes. "*Tiffany?*"

Silence.

"Tiffany? Can you hear me?"

"I'm here."

The sound of her voice made his heart leap. Warm relief shimmered through him. He felt his face stretching into a stupid grin. He'd found her, and she was still able to communicate. It meant she was all right. It might even suggest she hadn't been captured.

Or did it?

There was one sure way of finding out.

"Tiffany, what happened, and where are you?"

"You're safe, Jimmy. Don't worry about them coming after you anymore, okay?"

He didn't like the sound of that. It sounded so final. And it convinced him even more than she'd done something to put herself in jeopardy again.

"What do you mean?"

"They stopped looking for you."

He didn't like the sound of that, either. He knew they wouldn't stop looking unless they had a good reason. "*Tiffany, what did you do?"*

"It's not important."

"Yes. It is. It's important."

"Jimmy, just remember that you're a great magician, and you deserve to do what you do best--"

His heart began racing. *"Where are you, Tiffany?"*

"That doesn't matter."

"It really does. I have to know."

"All you need to know is--"

"Tiffany, I crashed to the depths of Hell when I died because I let innocent people die. It blackened my soul, and I don't think I'll ever be able to recover unless I can somehow turn the tables and actually start doing things to help someone. Please let me help you. Please tell me where you are."

"You can't help us, Jimmy. But it's all right, I can--"

"It's not *all right!"*

Silence.

Jimmy's thoughts reeled in the silence. There was something in that last thing she'd said. Something that might have revealed what she was trying to hold back. That should have told him--

"*Us*." She'd said "*us*." She'd found Chip and maybe even Ashley. Was that what she meant?

"Jimmy, like I said, you deserve to do what you do best. You're very good at enthralling people, taking them to other worlds and making them forget about the problems in their lives. Keep it up. Eventually your spirit will rid itself of the darkness. You'll see."

"Where are *you, Tiffany?"*

"It doesn't matter."

"You're with Chip, aren't you?"

Her sudden silence told him the answer.

"Tiffany?"

"Jimmy, you're the nicest guy I've met in...well, in a long time. Stay the way you are, okay? Don't ever change. And that fire wasn't your fault. Remember that."

"Tiffany?"

Silence.

"Tiffany!"

"Sir?"

His eyes shot open. He jerked his head in the direction of the short, squat figure to his left.

The waitress standing near his table brought up her notepad to cover her chin. "Can I…g-get you another--"

"I'm good, thanks." He slid out of the booth and jumped up. He reached into his pocket, pulled out his slim wad of bills, peeled a five from it, dropped it on the table and ran for the door.

The waitress grabbed his umbrella and held it up. "You forgot your--"

He'd already left. Without waiting for the light, he dodged traffic and bolted across the street, heading straight for one of the three cabs parked at the curb, near the corner.

***

At 2:55, Dahl took the Lincoln down the long, paved drive of the massive airport parking lot that led to the main gate. The charter sat off by itself just beyond the terminal. At the end of the lot, facing the chain-link fence, the black Olds sat three spaces down from the open gate. The driver and his partner stood beside it, watching as they pulled up.

Andras opened the rear door and got out. “Did you put him on the plane yet?”

“We just got here, sir,” the man standing in front said. “Traffic was pretty bad. We were told to wait until you got here.”

“Good work. Once the others get here--” He turned when he heard the hum of the van as it came up the winding drive, in their direction.

Good deal. Russo was here. Andras could finally get to work and finish this.

His cell went off. He flicked it open. It was his contact. “They should be on their way--”

“Yeah, I see them coming.”

“They’re right on schedule. Is there anything else you need at the moment, sir?”

“I think I can take it from here, thanks.”

“You’re free to use the guards however you see fit. Or you can dismiss them. It’s entirely up to you.”

“I don’t think I’ll need them once they drop off Russo. If I can find out the blonde’s whereabouts, it'll be better for us if the guards were back in town. They'll be able to get to her faster."

"That makes sense."

"Anyway, thanks for all your help. I'll let you know what to tell your people once I find out something."

"Thank you, sir. I'll be on standby."

Andras pocketed the cell. He kept his gaze fixed on the van as it came around the bend, cut across several aisles of parked vehicles and rushed right over. It pulled up and parked less than ten feet away from the Lincoln, facing the chain link fence.

The windows of the van were tinted, but Andras could see the two huge men sitting in the front. He couldn't quite make out the shapes in the back but knew there would be three people in the seat. Two more guards and, of course, Russo.

"Get out." Andras gestured.

All four doors opened. A big man in uniform climbed out of the rear on the passenger side and backed up a couple of feet to give their victim room to slide out. The guard held his Taser in his right hand. It was pointed at the passenger.

His arms cuffed behind his back, Jimmy Russo slid across the seat and climbed down. He wore the same outfit as earlier, when he'd performed his juggling routine on Fifth Avenue. He didn't appear nervous or scared. He actually seemed quite calm. Almost relaxed. No fear showed in his dark-brown eyes, nor did it emanate from the man himself. Strange. Under the circumstances, Russo should be coming out of his skin.

Andras turned. “Take the redhead out of the Olds and put him in the Lincoln.”

“You sure, sir?”

“Just do it.”

The two men pulled the sleeping inferior from the back seat and carried him over. Andras stepped aside while the men shoved the little redhead into the back seat of the Lincoln. Andras closed the door.

Andras didn’t take his eyes off Russo. “You men can leave now.”

“All of us, sir?” asked the big man standing near the rear bumper of the Olds.

Andras still didn’t budge. “All of you.”

Without a word, all six men climbed back into the two vehicles. A moment later, both the Olds and the van backed up, turned around and eased down the road, where the parking lot led to the main road.

Andras took one casual step toward Russo. “Know who I am?”

Russo tilted his head and squinted. “Let me guess. The guy who had those guards bring me here?”

“Good guess. Any idea why you’re here?”

“Nope, but I have this nagging feeling you’re about to tell me.” Still no signs of fear or nervousness. Russo remained quite calm.

“Another good guess.” Andras was going to enjoy toying with this idiot. “You’re not quite as stupid as I thought.”

"Thank you. I should be on one of those TV game shows. Maybe I can win a toaster or something."

Russo's arrogance was beginning to wear thin. The last mortal who'd tested Andras' patience choked to death in the middle of a city council meeting in Chicago last month.

"I'll make this simple. Where's the blonde?"

"What blonde?"

Andras sighed. Russo obviously had no idea what he was up against. It was really no surprise. Performing magic tricks didn't require much intellect. "Let's not play games. I'll give you ten seconds to tell me where she is."

Russo shrugged. "Are you going to do an actual countdown? Or am I supposed to guess when the ten seconds are up?

Andras could feel the tension building up inside him. Soon he wouldn't be able to hold back. Once the rage was unleashed, he had no choice but let it run its course. He could easily envision Russo collapsing to the ground and slapping his face onto the hard pavement over and over, until his features turned to bloody pulp. "If you don't comply, I'll be forced to handle this much differently. You won't want that, trust me."

"Why not?"

"Because you'll end up with your face smeared onto the pavement."

Russo didn't flinch. "Is that supposed to scare me? Or should I ask more questions so I can get the imagery more clearly?"

This idiot was asking for it. Andras knew he had to leave this to Braithwaite. Besides, he didn't have time for nonsense. Best just put him under. Then Dahl could find a luggage carrier, put them in it and take them to the plane. The enjoyment of watching Braithwaite destroy this pathetic mess would be well worth the wait.

"Have it your way. I'm under orders to bring the three of you back to Orlando. I just thought I'd spare you a shitload of unnecessary pain and humiliation. You're obviously much too full of yourself to cooperate."

"What's my alternative?"

"You tell me where she is and I'll let you go."

"Just like that?"

"I want the blonde. Why would I need you once I have her?"

Russo was silent for a few moments. "Makes sense."

"I'm glad you were able to figure that out."

"There's just one thing I don't like about this."

"What's that?"

"I don't believe a word you say."

Andras flinched. "What was that?"

"You're a demon. Demons are messed up and nasty. They never tell the truth."

You're a demon... Andras' body instantly turned cold; his limbs grew tense. What the hell was going on? How did this idiot know he was a demon? Something had definitely gone wrong.

The blonde had obviously told him. That was the only thing that made sense. It was stupid of her.

Now Andras had no choice but put him under and haul him to the plane.

But before he did anything, he had to make sure what was going on, what Russo had been told. If the blonde told him about that, what else did she tell him? "Who said I was a demon?"

"You are, aren't you?"

"Who told you?"

"I guessed. You just said I was a good guesser, didn't you?"

Andras felt the hot waves trickling back. "Listen to me, you idiot. There's no way in hell you could possibly guess something like--"

Russo brought his arms out in front of him. The cuffs dangled from his right hand. He tossed them on the pavement between them and grinned. "If things get hairy, I won't need these. They're uncomfortable and really tacky. Besides, they're cramping my style."

Andras stared at the cuffs, then at Russo. He'd had more than enough. It was time to show this worthless slug just how lame magic tricks really were in situations like this one. "You're gonna need more than a silly magic trick to save yourself now." Andras closed his eyes and focused.

The moment he attempted to penetrate Russo's thick skull, he discovered he was staring at a brick wall.

He opened his eyes. Russo was gone.

The blonde stood there, watching him curiously.

Chapter 27

"I guess the juggler knew where you were after all."

Tiffany let the wall vanish and opened her eyes.

The messenger stood watching her, the tiny red glints in the centers of his dark eyes intensifying.

She stared right back, making sure her wall remained as close-by as possible. She couldn't let him enter her mind. Not if she could help it. "I've been right here all along," she told him.

"I see that."

This situation was much different from the time she'd faced the wolf guy in the Ohio woods. Back then she was frightened and nervous, and had no idea how she could possibly fight a demon. She'd only been dead a few days and was terrified of what the wolf guy could do to her. But she'd managed. With Chip's help, they'd sent the wolf guy back down to the Valley of Decay, where he belonged.

This time, however, she faced the demon alone. Chip was just a few feet away but was unable to help.

But somehow it didn't matter now. Many things were different. She could read minds. And manipulate. And communicate telepathically. And shape-shift. And because of all this, she knew there was no reason to be afraid.

"You're a shifter, aren't you?" The messenger hadn't taken his eyes off her.

"I guess you could say I can do neat stuff like that." Tiffany snatched a quick glance at the

Lincoln. The driver sat behind the wheel but was looking down. She guessed he was listening to music, oblivious of what was going on outside the cab.

"*Chip? Can you hear me*?"

Silence.

"*If you can, wake up*!"

More silence.

"You know I've got to take you back to Orlando, right?" the messenger asked.

"I know your boss wants me back—if that's what you mean. But I don't want to go back. You can tell him that yourself when you fly back there."

"But that's what he wants. And by the way, he's your boss, too."

"He only thinks he is."

"He's a super demon. That makes him your boss."

"I hate to bust your bubble, but I'm not a demon. I never was."

The messenger almost smiled. "You don't say?"

"I just did."

"Then what are you? I've asked around, but no one seems to know. You were sent to Hell, were you not?"

"Briefly. I didn't care for it, so I just left."

"You sure are a cocky bitch."

She glared. "I didn't start out that way."

"The Dark Place tends to leave marks, doesn't it?"

She kept glaring at him. "You should know that better than me."

"*Touché*. Okay, I'll ask again. If you're not a demon, what the hell are you?"

"I'm just a dead girl who hates demons. You all belong in Hell. Not up here. This world would be a much better place if disgusting creatures like you weren't fouling up the air, making things worse."

The messenger's sudden laugh, loud and ear-splitting, sounded like the shriek of an agitated eagle. "How about that? A demon who thinks she's Pollyanna!"

Tiffany wanted to remove his facial features with her nails. "What *are* you? Deaf? I just said I'm not a demon." Once again, she tried focusing on the Lincoln. "*Chip? This is me. Tiffany. Wake up*!"

The messenger shook his head. "You can't wake him up, you silly twit. He's under my spell. If you were a demon, you *might* be able to. But only if you were a sub, like me. But since you say you're not either, stop wasting your energy. You'll need every bit of it you can dig up."

My God... He can read my mind...

"Damned right I can read your mind. I'm much more powerful than you think. Besides, it wasn't that much of a challenge."

Darn. She should have known.

"If you really want to concentrate on something, try getting out of *this*."

Before she had time to pull up her wall, the tiny red glints grew, turning into a blazing red flame that gushed over in a tumbling ball of fire and wrapped itself around her. She quickly found she could not breathe. She tried squirming, shaking loose, but giant tendrils of flame kept her arms pinned tightly to her sides. She couldn't walk away, couldn't even move. Panic set in. She closed her eyes and continued struggling, focusing all her energies on somehow directing the mighty strands of flame away from her.

As she struggled, the demon's voice drifted into her mind. "*Don't fight it. If you're not a demon, there's no way you can get out of it.*"

"*I'd rather die than let you take me*," her mind screamed at him.

Bellowing laughter. "*You stupid bitch. You're already dead*!"

Light-headedness and fatigue immediately set in. Her lungs grew hot and ready to burst. She gritted her teeth, tensed her body and tried once again to force the flames away.

Just then, she heard another voice:

"*Ladies and gents, I think it's about time for another exciting trip into the wonderful world of magic and illusion!*"

Sudden quacking sounds caused the intense heat and the agonizing pain in her lungs to subside quickly and vanish. The pain and the intense pressure ceased, and the flames evaporated instantly.

Tiffany opened her eyes and gasped at the sight.

The demon had turned his attention away from her. Right now, he was more concerned about the frenzied activity at his feet. More than a dozen tiny ducks waddled busily around him, quacking happily.

***

Jimmy Russo peeked around the rear of the cream-covered Cadillac Seville and grinned.

About twenty yards straight ahead, Tiffany stood in front of the chain-link fence separating the lot from the charter gate. The messenger faced her as he stood next to the Lincoln, watching the ducks Jimmy had released with one wave of his arm and sent over.

Jimmy found it strange that he'd gotten here so quickly. The gray-haired cabby had brought him here almost as if he instinctively knew where Tiffany was. To make this situation even more bizarre, every traffic light on the trip over had turned green by the time their cab had approached.

But this didn't explain how the cabby knew to leave Jimmy off right here. The airport was huge. Dozens of gates, entrances, exits and ramps. Traffic going in and coming out was murder. Even so, there were no snags or jams. No complications of any kind.

It felt almost as if fate had been in their favor.

But none of this mattered. He was here, and now it time to help Tiffany. He had no illusions that he could overpower a subordinate. As an inferior, his magic served as his only advantage. The only thing that had kept him from being sent back to Hell.

Just then, the messenger sent six ducks flying with a sudden sideways thrust of his right foot.

"*Tiffany*," Jimmy thought, "*get out of there*!"

Hearing him, the messenger turned sharply and caught sight of Jimmy peeking around the rear of the Caddie. An explosion of flame shot right over, plummeting into him and slamming him into the side of the compact on the other side of the aisle.

The pain knocked the breath knocked out of him. A cloud of warm darkness dropped over him like a heavy cloak. He lay there for what seemed an eternity, the darkness turning into a warm dizziness that felt strangely comforting.

"*Jimmy? You okay*?"

Gritting his teeth, he struggled back into consciousness. A strong whiff of engine oil, dirt, and several other foul-smelling things he couldn't identify assaulted his nostrils. He opened his eyes.

He lay on his side on rough pavement. A used prophylactic, a pile of squashed cigarette butts, and a smashed beer can decorated the faded macadam two feet in front of him. Nausea swept through him. He shook himself and took a few deep breaths. *Tiffany's in trouble. I have to help her.*

He crawled over to the other side of the Caddie.

The messenger had turned back to Tiffany and glared. An instant later, she gasped and doubled up in pain.

Bastard. I can't let him do this to her.

Jimmy pushed himself up and leaned against the side of the car to steady himself. He reached into his pockets, pulled out a homing pigeon and tossed it in the air. He reached into another pocket, found another pigeon, and sent it soaring. Then another pocket, and another pigeon. And another. One by one, he sent a dozen birds straight toward the messenger. They rose in a wide arc and swooped down, flapping frantically.

The messenger noticed them instantly and raised his arms in their direction. Six birds slammed into some sort of invisible barrier. They dropped quietly to the pavement and disappeared. The others veered away and continued circling. The messenger pointed an index finger at one of them. A loud gunshot reverberated down the aisle. The bird veered wildly out of his dive pattern and dropped to the ground. Like the others, it disappeared the moment it hit the pavement. The messenger took aim again, fired, and another bird dropped. Then another. The remaining three continued circling. The messenger raised both arms and sent up a cloud of red mist. The birds burst into puffs of white powder that evaporated in the breeze.

Jimmy felt a heavy claw of cold fear raking down his back. His magic was no match for this demon. He tried one last time to warn Tiffany. "*I'm gonna try another trick, Tiffany, so get ready to run*!"

"*Jimmy, it's no use! He's too powerful*!"

"*I've got to try*!"

"*You two are even dumber than I thought*!" The messenger turned in Jimmy's direction and raised his right hand.

Jimmy dug furiously into his jacket pocket and removed a large boomerang. He moved away from the front of the Caddie, brought his arm up and back, preparing to let it sail.

Another giant fireball appeared, this one much bigger and more potent than its predecessor, roaring toward Jimmy like a runaway train.

Taking aim, Jimmy let the boomerang sail directly into the angry flames. Hopefully, it would penetrate the fireball and slam into the messenger once it exited.

The boomerang disappeared into the raging ball of flames.

The fireball kept coming.

***

Tiffany closed her eyes and visualized a solid block wall standing directly in front of Jimmy. An instant later, the demon's massive ball of flame slammed into it, exploding in its center and sending shards of flame and flickering tongues of fire dancing in the air. Tiny red trickles dropped to the ground and became swirls of gray smoke dimming into nothingness.

The messenger spun around to face her. His eyes glistened in rage. His face grew dim, and soon all she saw were the eyes. They'd grown enormous, the nose tapering into a long, sharp beak, the face turning black, until it was covered with shiny hair. The body also changed, becoming that of a dark angel with huge, pointed wings.

The messenger had transformed into a raven with the body of a winged angel.

Despite this incredible shape-change, Tiffany kept her composure. This same thing happened just weeks ago in the Ohio woods, when the demon Gutril changed into a red wolf. Like Gutril, this demon had let his anger consume him, causing him to revert back to his spiritual essence.

"Whatever the hell you are," the demon's voice barked loudly in her mind, "*you're going back with me to face your punishment*!"

The smoldering red glints poking out of the huge black orbs grew, eclipsing the raven's face, becoming angry tentacles of flame breaking away and rushing straight for her.

Forcing herself to concentrate, Tiffany sent up another barrier. The flickering tongues wrapped around it, crushing it like dry kindling. Jagged chunks of stone and rock, engulfed by the intense flame, crumbled to the ground and dissolved into white ash.

The flames continued toward her.

Tiffany closed her eyes and held her breath. She dug her nails into her palms and waited.

Nothing. No heat. No pain.

Her heart fluttering, she opened her eyes. The face of the raven had disappeared. The demon was now looking straight up, where a large white bird circled the sky twenty feet directly above. He raised his arm and pointed, as before. A shot rang out. The bird swerved immediately and swooped down. The demon took aim again. The bird circled back around. Without pause, it dumped a heavy load of whitewash directly onto the demon's head.

"*Son of a bitch*!" The demon doubled over and furiously ran his hands through his hair, flicking away large gray-white gobs of slimy excrement. Hovering overhead, the bird deposited another generous load onto its victim's upper back. The demon straightened sharply and arched his back, searching the sky while wiping his eyes. "You're dead meat, you flying sack of shit!" He raised his right arm again.

Another load dropped, this time onto the demon's unprotected face. Doubling over, he shrieked loudly. Then, dropping to his knees, he struggled to frantically wipe his face and eyes.

The driver's door of the Lincoln flew open. The driver scrambled out. Brandishing a large white handkerchief, the big man lumbered over. "Sir, let me help you!"

The demon scrambled to his feet, spun around and rushed blindly toward the driver. A roller skate suddenly appeared directly in his path. The demon stepped on it. Arms and legs flailing, he flew in the air and went down hard, landing on his back on the rough pavement.

The driver rushed to his aid. The skate rolled casually over, stopping just as the driver's right foot came down. Gasping loudly, the big man lurched forward, slamming to the ground, his face smacking the pavement.

Muttering angrily, the demon crawled over to the Lincoln. When he was about three feet from the car, he paused to wipe more whitewash out of his eyes with his sleeve. Craning his neck and squinting, he reached out for the rear door handle. The door eased open. A shock of red hair appeared. Chip sat in the back seat, grinning.

Tiffany wanted to leap for joy. Chip had somehow managed to break free of the demon's spell.

"Chip? Are you all right?"

"Terrificoso, Honey Bunny."

"I'm so *glad you're--"*

"Save the sappy stuff for later, shady lady. I'm working here."

"Is Chip no longer under the demon's spell?" Jimmy hurried over.

"Looks like it."

"How'd he come out of it?"

"I don't know, but I'm sure he'll tell us."

The demon scrambled to his feet and used his jacket collar to wipe more whitewash from his eyes. When he saw Chip sitting upright, he stiffened. "How the hell did you…what are you doing, sitting there like that?"

Chip looked down at himself. "How *should* I be sitting?"

"You shouldn't be sitting *at all.* You should still be *lying* there. I didn't release you from the spell."

"And yet here I am, released and back to being my old charming self."

"This doesn't make any sense!"

Chip studied the demon's face. "What's that gooey white crap smeared all over your face?"

"Shut up and answer my question."

Chip sniffed. "Is that bird shit?"

"Shut up and stop being a dickhead!"

"I can only do one thing at a time. Which do you prefer I do first?"

The demon shook his head frantically. "This is insane! This makes no sense!"

Chip giggled. "It must be really hard to be a badass with your face covered in bird shit. I know you're a sub and all and you've got all these nifty powers, but I just can't take you seriously." He laughed. "I mean, look at your hair. It's all slimy. Looks like somebody who just ate scrambled eggs and shrimp Alfredo barfed on your head--"

The demon continued shaking his head. "Asshole! Why the fuck are you awake when you should be lying out cold on that seat?"

"I can't remember. Someone put me under a spell. When someone puts you under a spell, you can't remember too much--"

"I'm the one who put you under, you dumb shit. How the hell did you get out of it?"

"I don't know. I probably just got bored and decided to snap out of it all by myself. I get bored easily these days. What can I say? I'm old."

"Impossible. Ridiculous."

"No, really. I know I give off this youthful glow, but I really am old, and I really do get bored a lot. Especially since I've been up here, wandering around with Tifferoo--"

"You couldn't *possibly* undo that spell by yourself!"

“Well, here I am, wide awake and full of myself again. And here *you* are, with egg all over your—no, scratch that. Here you are with *bird shit* all over your face!” Chip bellowed laughter.

“Keep up the arrogance, you nitwit. You have no idea the sort of shit you’re up against.”

“Is it anything like that greasy mess smeared all over your face and hair?”

“You idiot. I’ll teach you what it means to be insolent.” The demon reached out to grab Chip by the neck. At that very moment the demon’s hands closed, Chip disappeared. The demon backed up, gawking at what he held in his hands.

The Yellow Lady’s Slipper was trapped within the demon’s trembling hands.

Tiffany grinned in delight.

With a loud groan, the demon went limp, collapsing on the pavement.

The Lady’s Slipper dropped quietly to the pavement and turned right back into Chip.

After getting to his feet, Chip looked down at the demon and grinned. “*You’re* the idiot, dude. I already know what it means to be insolent.”

Chapter 28

Two stewardesses huddled near the cockpit door of the charter, watching uneasily as Tiffany climbed the stairs and went inside. The demon and his driver followed her in, with Chip and Jimmy Russo a safe distance behind.

Tiffany faced the demon and pointed to her left, at the row of three seats half a dozen rows down. "Sit down over there. Take the window seat."

Without a word, he moved stiffly down the aisle and collapsed in the seat next to the window.

"Strap yourself in."

He immediately complied.

Tiffany turned to the driver. "Take the other side and strap yourself in as well."

The big man automatically turned left, fell into the window seat on the opposite side of the aisle and fiddled with the seat harness.

Tiffany turned to the stewardesses. "Where's Ashley Parker?"

The two women remained silent, trembling as they hunched close to one another.

Tiffany could sense the fear emanating from them. She felt badly for putting them through this. They were just doing their jobs and didn't need to be involved in this at all. She lowered her voice and softened her tone. "Ashley's nineteen. She's very pretty and slender, with black hair. She's supposed to be on this plane. I'd appreciate it if you told me where she is."

The brunette remained silent. The redhead slowly raised an arm and pointed toward the rear of the plane.

Tiffany stepped aside. "Take us to her."

Keeping close together, the stewardesses awkwardly slipped past her and hurried down the aisle.

Three-quarters of the way down, several aisles past the open curtain, Ashley sat strapped securely in a window seat half a dozen rows up from the rear of the plane. Her eyes were closed; she looked very peaceful.

Tiffany's pulse pounded. "Is she all right?"

The brunette shrugged nervously. "We don't know, Miss--"

"She was already sitting there like that when we boarded about twenty minutes ago," the redhead said.

"What were you told about this flight?" Tiffany asked.

The brunette swallowed audibly. "We were told not to wake her under any circumstances, or even go back there. We're to tend only to a man named Mr. Smith."

"We were also told there would be two others," added the redhead. "We were told they'd be sleeping, too."

"None of that struck you as odd?"

The brunette smiled faintly. "We're instructed to do a lot of odd things, Ma'am. It's part of the job."

"We were given a bonus for this trip," the redhead said.

"I get it." Tiffany pointed to the front of the plane. "Just so you know, that's Smith. The other guy is his driver, but he isn't important."

The brunette wrinkled her nose. "What's that stuff all over his head and face?"

"It's also on the back of his jacket," the redhead added.

"It's bird shit," Chip said with a grin.

The women frowned and exchanged shocked glances.

"Really?" The redhead turned to Chip. "What happened? Was he attacked by a flock of--"

"One bird," he said.

The women gawked at him.

The brunette said, "That's a lot of--"

"It was one big, fucking bird," Chip replied solemnly. "With a lousy attitude and a serious case of the runs."

The redhead looked like she wanted to smile.

Silence.

"There's no need to concern yourselves with either of them," Tiffany said. "All you have to know is that there's been a slight change in plans. Just do what you were doing before and don't worry about anything else. They'll be sleeping very shortly, and will sleep for the entire flight."

The women nodded and hurried back up the aisle, toward the cockpit.

Tiffany bent over Ashley and placed her hand gently on the girl's head.

"Still warm?" Chip asked.

Tiffany nodded. "Wake up, Ash. It's me, Tiffany."

Ashley stirred. Frowning, she rolled her head on the headrest and opened her eyes. Blinking, she saw Tiffany and stiffened in the seat. When she noticed Chip and Jimmy, her eyes grew. She jerked her head toward the front of the cabin. "What's happened?" Her voice was no more than a throaty whisper. "Where *are* we?"

"This is a special charter," Tiffany said softly. "It's scheduled to land in Orlando in a couple of hours."

"My God." Ashley tried to sit up. Then she noticed the straps holding her down. "What the…?" She struggled, her hands fumbling with the metal buckles.

"Take it easy." Tiffany undid the harnesses.

"H-How did I even get here? Who—why am I--?"

"Later." Tiffany released the shoulder strap. "Right now, we need to leave."

Once freed, Ashley placed her hands on the seat in front of her and pulled herself into a standing position. Her legs gave out, and she fell back down. "My legs. I can't—"

"It's all right. Please help her up, Jimmy."

Jimmy grabbed Ashley's right arm and pulled it up and around his neck. He wrapped his left arm around her waist and helped her up.

"Do I know you?" she asked, studying his face.

"We haven't met."

"I'm Ashley."

"I know. I'm Jimmy."

"Hi, Jimmy. And thanks."

"It's my pleasure."

Once she squeezed out between the seats, she staggered for the first few steps, until she was able to support her own weight. With Jimmy's help, she shuffled awkwardly down the aisle.

When they reached the front of the plane, she caught sight of the demon, who still hadn't budged. She stopped abruptly. "I've seen him before. He...he's the one who--"

"Don't worry about him anymore," Tiffany said.

"What did you do to me?" Ashley demanded.

The demon didn't move or acknowledge her.

"He can't hear you," Tiffany said. "He can't hear any of us now."

"What's all that funky-looking white stuff on--"

"Bird shit," Chip said flatly. "We'll tell you about it when we get out of here."

Ashley turned to Tiffany and smiled. "For some reason, that sounds good." Then Jimmy helped her out of the plane.

"What's next, Tifferoosky?"

"We don't want them to miss their flight, do we?"

"Do they know about the sudden change in plans?"

"I'm about to tell them everything they need to know."

"And what about these babes?"

Tiffany focused on both of them, but could only sense fear and intimidation. “We don’t have to worry about them. They were paid to keep their eyes closed, their mouths shut, and not ask any questions.”

Chip jabbed a thumb at the demon and laughed. “Sorry, but I just can’t help it. There’s just something really hilarious and pathetic about a dude with his face and hair covered in bird shit.”

Tiffany smiled. “Thank Jimmy for that. He did it all by himself.”

“I sure will.” He moved toward the hatch and stopped. “Sure you can handle the rest of this by yourself?”

“Do you really need to ask me that?”

“Now what was I thinking?”

***

Jimmy sat behind the wheel of the Lincoln, waiting anxiously for Tiffany to emerge from the plane. Despite what he already knew about her and what he’d seen her do, he still found himself growing more uneasy by the second. “What’s she doing in there?” he heard himself ask.

“She’s fine,” Ashley said from the back seat.

“I know she’s fine. I’d just like to know why she didn’t come out with us.”

“She’s putting both of them under,” Chip said. “She’ll probably tell them to sleep for the length of the flight. Then she’ll have them do a whole bunch of silly things once they get off the plane in Orlando. She did the same thing to the Arabs before we left Florida.”

"Silly things?"

"She'll probably have them both forget what just happened here. She might even give them both mental blocks to contend with when Braithwaite finally gets hold of them and starts asking questions. Nothing really serious, though." Chip frowned. "Tifferoosky's never been much fun at a party. She's totally incapable of doing anything really interesting."

"Interesting?"

"He means nasty," Ashley said flatly.

"If it was me," Chip said, "I'd have those two crap their pants whenever they bent over to tie their shoes for the rest of their lives. Or I'd make them faint each time they heard the word "computer" or "food." But Tifferoo just doesn't work that way."

"Tiffany has class," Ashley said.

"I've never held that against her," Chip said. "But don't get me wrong. Tifferoo can get radical when her blood's up."

As he watched the open hatch of the plane just a hundred yards away, Jimmy knew he wouldn't feel comfortable until Tiffany was sitting beside him. It had been a long time since he'd felt so close to anyone. He realized only then that he hadn't thought about Danielle since this morning, and no longer cared about Moreland or Bellman, for that matter. "Guess I'm just a little antsy." He sat back and rubbed his eyes.

"You really like her, don't you?" Ashley asked softly.

Jimmy glanced at her reflection in the rearview mirror and could see the sincerity in Ashley's pretty face. "I've never known anyone like her," he said, his voice almost a whisper.

"That's because there isn't," she said.

"What about me?" Chip asked.

"There's definitely no one like you, either," she said, and laughed.

"Why do I have the feeling that what you just said wasn't a *good* thing?"

Reddening, Ashley looked away. "I don't know what you mean."

Jimmy's heart leaped when the flowing golden mane emerged from the open hatch, jumping wildly when a burst of wind hit it. Tiffany hurried down the steps and jogged across the hangar, toward the gate. He could hardly contain himself as he watched her and felt his heart thumping frantically as she drew closer.

Then she was sitting beside him, and he found himself struggling to concentrate on pulling out of the lot and taking the Lincoln back onto Hangar Road.

"Everything all right, Tifferoo?"

"I'll feel much better once that plane takes off, but yeah, everything's just fine."

A few minutes later, after they got onto Route 376 and joined the heavy mass of eastbound traffic headed toward the city, Tiffany turned and smiled at him. "*Thank you,*" she sent over softly.

It took him several moments to get past her beautiful smile and collect his thoughts. "*For what?*"

"*If you hadn't shown up when you did, we wouldn't have been able to beat him.*"

He forced himself to keep his eyes on the road. It was increasingly difficult. Her hair kept sliding down her arm, distracting him. And those big blue eyes didn't help. "*I would have still bet on you.*"

She sighed. "*His powers were too much for me to deal with.*"

He remembered how he'd felt when he'd escaped the chaos on Fifth Avenue after his juggling act. He'd felt safe but he didn't care. He was concerned about her and didn't want anyone hurting her. It had been a long time since he'd cared about someone else, and it confused and disoriented him, making him feel almost like a silly adolescent with his first crush. But this wasn't some childhood crush; it was the real thing. And even though he found himself frightened and uneasy, he welcomed this extraordinary change.

He kept his eyes on the road ahead. He found that by doing so, it was much easier to collect his thoughts than trying to do it while looking at her. "*I couldn't stand not being there with you. Not knowing if you were safe. I felt so guilty...*"

"*It was a huge risk. That demon could have destroyed you.*"

"*You took care of that.*"

"*We all did. Like I said, I couldn't have done it without you.*"

He wanted to reach for her hand but didn't want to wreck the car. He had to concentrate on his driving. Most of these drivers seemed suicidal. He found that he was quite content, just being close to her again.

"We're together in our minds," she sent over. *"That's even closer than holding hands, isn't it?"*

Jimmy felt his cheeks flushing. *"Yes. I think you're right."*

"Just think of it this way. No one can ever be as close as we are right now."

He sighed while struggling to concentrate on the road ahead. Once again, she'd made him feel much better.

"By the way," she asked, *"how on earth did you find us? That airport's a madhouse. I would* never *have been able to find that gate so quickly."*

He began wondering once again about the strange cab ride. *"I honestly don't know what happened. The taxi brought me right over. I told him I had to meet someone on a charter flight, and he just brought me there, dropped me off and left."*

"Just like that?"

"It was almost like he knew exactly where to take me."

She thought about that for a few moments. *"What did the cabby look like?"*

"I didn't really notice. I was much too worried about getting there in time. I think he might've had long gray hair."

"Anything else?"

"Not that I can remember."

She didn't reply.

"Tifferoo?"

She turned around. "Yes?"

"Are you pulling a number on us again? That mental thingy you do when you don't want me to know what's going on?"

She winked at Jimmy. "Whatever would make you think I'd do something like that?"

Jimmy could see Chip grinning in the reflection of the rearview. "First of all, you've got that cow-eyed look on your face, and the juggler guy looks like he just got slapped half a dozen times up the side of his head with a silly stick. And you're all melty and gooey, and look like you're about to drool--"

"Oh, stop. Yes, we were discussing something. By the way, when did you come out of that spell?"

"Right after you called me."

"You mean I actually pulled you out of a demon's spell?"

"I don't know what else could've done it. Ash can't do any of that stuff. How about you, Mr. Juggler Guy?"

"It wasn't me."

"Why didn't you do or say anything before then?" Tiffany asked. "We needed all the help we could get."

"I was having too much fun listening to the demon guy getting shit on by that bird. Besides, the driver kept watching me in the mirror. He had a Taser gun. I didn't need a jolt of anything extra right then."

“I just hope we never have to go through that again,” Ashley said.

“Little chance of that,” Tiffany said. “When the demon gets back to Orlando, he won’t have much time left up here. Breath Mint won’t be happy. He’ll want to vent his anger on someone.”

“What did you do to him before you got off the plane?” Ashley asked.

“I put him into a deep sleep. He was still pretty spaced-out from Chip’s flower zap, so it was really easy. But before I sent him under, I gave him a few suggestions. He’ll remember what happened up until the time we overpowered him. Then he’ll think we somehow escaped when the plane touched down. He’ll ask the stewardesses what happened, but they won’t know anything, either. Everything will be a blank for all of them. For all he knows, we made it to Florida and escaped at the airport.”

“Good deal,” Chip said.

Jimmy stayed with the heavy flow that approached the Fort Pitt Bridge, which would put them on the Parkway North and take them to Liberty Avenue. “By the way, where are we going?” he asked.

“You can park anywhere you like on Liberty,” Tiffany said. “I need to take care of a little business.”

Chapter 29

It was 5:00 when Danielle Kaminski pulled into the small gravel lot behind Sexywear Ever.

At 2:00 she'd left her store in the capable hands of Brittany, her part-time assistant and fourth-year Accounting major at Point Park College and drove to Oakland to spend the afternoon with Sal Ferrini. Sal owned two popular Italian restaurants in the city and looked forward to his sexual indiscretions. Danielle had obtained digital tapes of three of these indiscretions. She'd sent Sal a copy, knowing he'd accept her terms rather than risk his jealous Italian wife seeing them and using them as evidence to drain him dry after a long court battle. Since Sal was an obliging submissive, Danielle accepted these payments in the form of a lust-filled afternoon of rough S&M in the downstairs rumpus room of Sal's hideaway condo two or three times a week.

Her cell had gone off at five- and ten-minute intervals starting at 3:00. There were more than two dozen of them, but they'd all gone unanswered. Danielle hated interruptions during intense sessions of rough bondage sex, and had set the ringer on vibrate. When she'd finished thoroughly humiliating Sal, she left his place a little after 4:30 and played back the messages on her way back to Liberty Avenue.

All were from Doug Moreland, and the panic in the man's voice was unmistakable. "We got problems, Danny. Big ones! Call me ASAP!"

It took her just twenty minutes to reach the rear lot of the store. She parked next to Brittany's ten-year-old gray Volvo. But instead of going inside, she called Moreland from the front seat of her black Mercedes.

The man still sounded panic-stricken. "Where the hell have you been? And why haven't you called? I'm going fucking crazy here!"

"What's up?"

"We're screwed, Danny. Big-time. It's Russo. They've got him, and they're gonna find out everything. I mean everything!"

Moreland wasn't making sense. "What are you talking about? Who's got Russo?"

"I…I dunno *who* the fuck he is, but he's definitely one nasty badass we don't wanna mess with. He almost made me piss my pants!"

"Calm down." Dealing with the little weasel was getting more and more difficult. Ever since Danielle had been sending him talent in exchange for a 25% cut of the Bel-Mor's proceeds, the man went ballistic at the drop of a hat. She was beginning to think Doug the Dud couldn't take the pressure anymore. "Tell me what's going on."

"I'm trying to tell you, Danny. This guy called. He's got Russo, he's looking for some chick Russo knows, and he means business."

This still wasn't making any sense. She was going to have to guide him through this one step at a time. "Tell me what you mean when you say he's got Russo."

"He had Russo picked up, and he says he's gonna ask him about some chick."

"What chick?"

"She mighta been at the club last night. Some blond bimbo. All I know is, this dude's scary."

"Who *is* he? And how could he just pick up Jimmy?"

"I dunno, but this has the stink of Fed all over it. I know Fed shit, and this dude reeks of it."

"We've both got connections. We can find out--"

"Connections ain't gonna fly here, babe. I mentioned Betty's family, but this bastard didn't even flinch. He says he knows Josh Madigan."

Danielle trembled at the name. You couldn't get much more connected than Josh Madigan. The man owned half the buildings in the Golden Triangle. Maybe this was some sort of con. Danielle had heard all sorts of cons in her time, thanks to Mommy Dearest. But something about this made no sense whatsoever. Why would anyone care about some blonde Jimmy Russo knew? And why would they want to involve Moreland in any of this?

"You know, he could've mentioned Josh Madigan just to scare you, right?"

"Even if he was blowing smoke, I don't wanna be the one to find out who he really is. If he wasn't lying when he said he had Russo picked up, this tells me he's got beaucoup juice."

"This can't be happening."

"Well, if it is, we're both fucked, big-time. Whatever you've got on Russo? Once this guy starts asking him questions, that's the ballgame."

Suddenly light-headed, she leaned back against the leather seat. *Easy, girl. Don't let this idiot's hysteria rub off.* "What can he ask? I don't think Jimmy would do anything that would--"

"That's just it. This dude told me he knows how to ask questions. If he *is* a Fed, those guys are damn good at finding things out. By the time he's finished, he'll know everything. I know Russo's making us a ton of cash, but I'd rather stay healthy than have a bunch of fucking Feds nipping away at my balls. Bad enough Betty keeps 'em locked in her dresser drawer half the time--"

"Truth serum." Her heart skipped a beat.

"Huh?"

"That's what they use. They've got drugs for everything now."

"It don't matter, Danny. When he starts on Russo, we're done. Belly and me, we've lost our best act."

"I know."

"Think of something."

"I will."

"Think of it fast. They were haulin' Russo in just before I left that first message."

A sliver of ice trickled down her back. She trembled even more. "That means they've probably already finished questioning him. Who knows what they're doing now?"

"That's why I'm so bummed out that you didn't call before. This Fed dude even asked for Russo's address."

"Why would he want *that*?"

"He wants that blond bimbo, wants her bad. Haven't you been listening to me?"

Danielle pocketed the phone and stared dumbly at the dirty brick wall of the building straight ahead. Her mind raced. Was this really happening? Or was Moreland making something out of nothing?

If the cops had picked up Jimmy, this would be different. Hardly anything to worry about. But this wasn't the case. It involved other people and concerned some woman. An informant? An illegal alien? A drug mule? A member of a slave ring? Moreland had called her a bimbo, but that was no help. "Bimbo" was one of Moreland's favorite words.

The point was, Russo had been picked up by some "scary dude" and was being questioned. If the Feds were involved, the questioning would be thorough. And if this involved drugs or any other federal crime, agents would be going through his apartment like a pack of hungry rats.

She wasn't worried about his apartment but *was* worried about the questions they asked him. Pumped up with truth serum, he'd tell them everything. About himself, about Danielle, about her scam. What she'd been doing to him.

They'll come here and search my place from top to bottom. They'll find all my stuff. My safe. The notebook.

Shit. The notebook. The names. They'll find the names. I'll be brought in and charged with extortion, blackmail--

She stopped herself and took a breath. She was being ridiculous. They weren't interested in her. And why should they be? They only wanted Jimmy because of a woman he knew. Someone he might have met at the club. Even if this turned out to be something else, it had nothing to do with Danielle, and there was no reason to lose her sanity over nothing, was there?

She squirmed out of the Mercedes. On unsteady legs, she shuffled to the rear of the building. She needed a strong pick-me-up. An upper would probably be best. One of those little blue pills she kept in her tiny black case--

She stopped moving. Her heart began thrashing again.

The pills. If they were discovered, she'd face years in a federal pen. If they did come to the store to look around… If Jimmy told them about her and they decided to check her out… If they'd brought along a search warrant, they could tear her place apart...

Brittany was out in front, working at the register. She looked up when

Danielle came in. "Enjoy your lunch hour?"

She wasn't in the mood for chit-chat. "How'd everything go here?"

"Pretty busy. I'm just finishing up the tallies, then I gotta go. I've got a Business Management class at six."

"Go ahead and leave. I'll finish up."

Brittany went back to her sheet, scribbled something else, dropped the pen on the counter and went over to the chair next to the front window, where she kept her jacket, handbag, and a couple of large hardbound textbooks. She picked up everything, smiled and waved. The cowbell above the door clanged when she slipped through the door.

Danielle decided to go back to the office area for her coffee and pick-me-up. And, of course, to think about what she should do. She obviously had to take everything out of the store and hide it, and she had to do it right now, before someone came in suddenly and flashed a badge.

The cowbell clanged again.

Gasping, Danielle spun around.

She expected to see a couple of tall, grim-looking men in dark suits bulling their way through the door. Instead, a slender young blond woman with big blue eyes closed the door quietly behind her. She wore a turquoise tee shirt, tan Capri slacks and open-toed red sandals. Her high cheekbones and flawless face was what you'd expect to see in a makeup commercial. Her thick honey-blond hair covered her shoulders and looked like thick ropes of spun gold. She carried no purse or handbag and wore no jewelry. Danielle saw no tattoos, studs or piercings. Not even a hint of makeup. Danielle had never seen such beauty. This woman seemed unreal.

"Help you?"

"Danielle Kaminski?"

"Yes..."

The woman approached her and stopped just a few feet away. Her unsettling gaze stayed on Danielle. Then, in a very soft voice, she said, "We need to talk."

***

"Who are you?"

"I'm a good friend of Jimmy Russo."

Danielle Kaminski flinched at the name. Tiffany caught the fleeting image of a disturbing phone call she'd had just a few minutes earlier with someone named Doug. But she said nothing, just continued staring.

"You know him, don't you?"

She shrugged. "He's that magician, isn't he? I've seen him a few times, works at that place on Penn. The Bel-Mor. Whaddya want with me?"

"I think you know what I want."

Danielle studied Tiffany's clothes and shoes, spending considerable time staring at her sandals. Tiffany could feel the confusion and fear mixed in with admiration for the sandals. That phone call had her spooked. Judging by the vivid images of Jimmy among this girl's thoughts, Tiffany guessed the call was about him. She also guessed that one of the demon's phone calls could have been to Jimmy's employer.

"Lady, I've got a business to run. I don't know who the hell you are, but if you didn't come here to buy anything, you're taking up my time--"

"I just told you who I am."

"What does that have to do with me? I told you, I've seen the guy a couple of times at the Bel-Mor. It's not like I'm banging him or anything."

More disturbing images flowed strongly from Danielle Kaminski's consciousness. Dark, jagged shapes clung tightly to her aura with other shadows mixed in. Tiffany could tell this woman had a horrible past and might have endured the same sort of childhood nightmares Tiffany herself had gone through. But whatever had happened to Danielle years ago had no bearing on what was happening now. She had no reason to blackmail Jimmy.

"I want all the evidence you have on Jimmy Russo. I want it now."

Danielle began trembling. Cold fear and utter confusion showed clearly in her dark-blue eyes. The image of a small metal box resting between the floorboards behind the counter settled in the center of the girl's mind.

A moment later she snapped out of it. The defiance quickly returned, this time with a vengeance. "Bitch, I have no idea what the fuck you're--"

"You know exactly what I'm talking about."

"Who the hell are you?"

"Just do as I say and you won't have to worry about what might happen."

"That sounds like a threat." Danielle pulled a cellphone out of her jacket pocket. "If you don't leave in the next five seconds, I'm gonna call Nine-One-One and get the cops here, pronto."

Tiffany didn't move.

Danielle's eyes stayed on Tiffany while moving her index finger closer to the phone.

Tiffany still didn't budge.

Danielle pressed two buttons and stopped when she realized Tiffany had no intention of leaving. Glaring, she stuffed the cell roughly back in her pocket. "Just who the fuck do you think you are, coming into my store, threatening me and accusing me of--"

"Like I've already said, I'm a friend of Jimmy's, and if you don't do as I say--"

"You'll what? Rough me up? What makes you think I don't have a switchblade or even a gun in my pocket?"

"It doesn't matter what you've got. You're gonna take a short trip behind that counter, lift up that floorboard and give me those thumb drives, and you're gonna do it right now."

"Listen, even if I--*what*?" She stiffened. For long, tense moments, she stood there frozen, gawking at Tiffany, her dark-blue eyes straining the sockets. Her lips trembled. A soft whimpering noise trickled out of her throat. "H-How the fuck..." She cleared her throat and took a breath. "H-how did you...who *are* you? How do you know about--"

"Just do it. You're wasting my time."

Danielle continued gawking at Tiffany. She was obviously too terrified to do anything.

"Go do it," Tiffany commanded, entering the woman's head. *"Now!"*

Snapping out of her trance, Danielle slipped awkwardly behind the counter. She got down on her knees and tried grabbing a corner of the rubber mat from the floor, but her fingers trembled too much. She had to take a deep breath and concentrate before she could get a grip on it. She finally pulled it up, exposing a portion of the cracked wooden floor. She then removed a slightly protruding floorboard and lifted the metal box out of its rectangular niche in the floor. She opened the box, extracted two thumb drives, closed it and shoved it back into the gap. She covered the gap with the floorboard and replaced the mat. Then she straightened and dropped the thumb drives on the glass counter.

Tiffany picked them up. "Is this all of them?"

Danielle gawked at them as if she had no idea how they'd gotten there.

"Is this all of them?" Tiffany repeated in a softer voice.

Danielle gulped audibly. "Except what I gave Russo."

Tiffany pocketed them. "Now I want to see the hidden cameras and where you keep all your stolen meds."

Danielle turned pale. "H-How the fuck did you know about--"

"Just show me. Otherwise, I'll have to call the police."

Danielle started to protest, but Tiffany sent over another strong suggestion.

"*Shut up and just do it*!"

Without hesitation, Danielle moved quickly down the aisle, to the far end of the store. Once they reached the office area, she led the way up the narrow wooden steps to the second floor, where the monitoring equipment was stored in a small closet-sized locked room hidden behind a curtain. The meds lay in neat rows in a hidden compartment beneath an old dresser. The compartment contained at least twenty vials of pills and tablets in various colors and sizes.

"As soon as I leave," Tiffany said, "I want you to take all the film and toss it. And take all those meds and flush them down the toilet."

Danielle didn't reply.

"Did you hear me?"

A reluctant nod.

"Unless you stop doing what you're doing, you're going to end up a murder victim. People will only put up with stuff like this for as long as it takes to hire someone to stop you."

Danielle shrugged.

Tiffany could sense no remorse at all coming from this girl. "You don't care, do you?"

"Lady, I came up the hard way. My old lady didn't give a shit about me. No one did. I had to make it on my own. If it's time for my ticket to be punched, it's gonna be punched, and nothing you can say or do will stop it."

"You have a nice store, with pretty stuff. Why do you need to blackmail people?"

Danielle shrugged. "It's what I do."

"That's a poor reason for doing this."

"People are assholes. They suck. How's that? Any better?"

Tiffany could tell further conversation with this woman would be senseless. A wash of sadness swept through her. Danielle was just a scared, vulnerable soul in a cold, dark world filled with lies and deceit, doing what she could to people because she hated them so much.

"I'm leaving now, so you'd better get rid of those cameras and meds and everything else you've been using to ruin people's lives. If I come back and find out you haven't done anything, I will go to the cops."

"You're Russo's friend, so I can see why you'd want to protect him. But why should you care about the others?"

Tiffany smiled. "It's what *I* do."

"Huh?"

"Not all people are bad, you know."

Danielle frowned. "You really believe that?"

"Yes."

"I've been around longer than you, lady. I've been through more shit than you could ever possibly see. In fact, you could say that I've been to Hell and back."

Tiffany sighed. "So have I."

"Yeah? And you can still say something like that?"

"I just did."

Danielle laughed bitterly. "Lady, all I got to say is that you're either naïve, stupid, or you don't pay much attention to what's going on around you."

Tiffany moved toward the doorway and turned around. "I just hope that when your time comes, you remember this conversation."

"Yeah? And why's that?"

Tiffany wanted to educate this girl properly, but there were more important things she had to do right now. Besides, there was only one way of showing her how wrong she was in her thinking, and Tiffany didn't want to go back there. "You're going to find out just how wrong you are about Hell."

Chapter 30

Jimmy sat behind the wheel of the Lincoln, staring dumbly at the two tiny thumb drives in his hand. He didn't say a word. Just gawked at them, then at Tiffany, then at the drives again. After about a minute, he whispered, "You actually got these…from her?"

"Sure did."

"She just…gave them up?"

"She didn't want to. Not at first."

He managed a sort of half-smile. "Did it take much coaxing?"

"Not that much."

"That's surprising." He went back to studying them again. Tiffany could sense the confusion filling his mind. "Giving up a source of steady income isn't something Danielle normally does," he said. "Once she's got her claws into someone, she holds on like a lion that latches on to a zebra at feeding time."

She watched as he closed his hand and held them tightly in his fist. Then he sighed and suddenly looked frightened. "You didn't have to *hurt* her, did you?"

She blinked. "Of course not. I wouldn't do something like that."

"I'm sorry. I know you wouldn't. It's just that, well, I just can't believe you were able to do it."

"Well, the important thing is that you no longer have to worry about her."

He thought about that for a little while. She sensed he still couldn't believe it. He opened his fist. "And this was *all* she had on me?"

"That's everything. You're now free to do whatever you want."

He stared at the drives a few more minutes, trying to absorb it all. She could tell he wasn't accustomed to this sort of kindness. "How can I ever thank you for this?"

"We'll talk about it later." There were more important issues to address. "Right now, we need to take Ashley home. She's had a long, hard day."

Jimmy focused on the thumb drives again. Tiffany saw that his eyes were wet. He turned away and quickly wiped them with his free hand, then faced the front and stuffed the drives carefully into his pants pocket. He flicked on the ignition and eased the Lincoln out of its spot.

They reached Chatham Center a little before 7:00. It was already getting dark, with the last trickles of rush hour barely noticeable. People wandered down the street in small groups, stopping at the stores and bars while traffic edged past.

Jimmy pulled over to the curb and turned off the ignition. The four of them sat in tense silence. Each one knew the time had come, but no one wanted to break the silence. Talking would make it all come alive. It would bring the unpleasantness to the surface, and no one wanted that.

Even so, Tiffany knew what had to be done. She'd prepared herself for this moment many times since they'd come to this city, but now that the time had finally arrived, she found she could barely function.

"You okay?" Ashley sat forward in her seat and placed a gentle hand on Tiffany's shoulder.

Tiffany smiled and patted Ashley's hand. She didn't want to tell her friend what had to be done. She hoped that by not saying it aloud, it wouldn't be so bad. But she knew better. No matter what she did, it was going to be horrible. But even so, she had no choice. "Let's talk." She opened the door and got out.

Ashley stepped out, and together they went up the concrete walk, where the brilliantly lit entrance awaited them.

"I still can't believe all that's happened today," Ashley said.

"I know. It's been a really strange day."

"I know it's all over and everything, but I can't help thinking that he'll send someone else for us. Someone even nastier and more powerful than that last demon."

"I wouldn't worry about that if I were you." Tiffany stared straight ahead at the approaching night darkening the tops of the buildings up the street.

"But how can we be sure? If another demon shows up, what can I do? I have no powers, and I can't ask you to stay here indefinitely. It would be unfair. I know you and Chip are dead and all, but you'll always be very much alive to me. We're all good friends and always will be." She took a breath.

"But I just can't ask you to spend the rest of my life here, babysitting me."

"Ashley, we won't have to."

"How can you possibly say that?"

Tiffany stopped walking. The time had come, and the quicker she made this happen, the better it would be for both of them. "Demons will no longer be able to hurt you."

"I...don't understand."

Tiffany sighed. This was just as painful as the time she'd walked away from Lou Gates in Ohio. She loved Lou dearly, but she'd been closer to Ashley. They had so much in common and had shared a lifetime of memories in the past few weeks. Though they didn't share the same blood, they'd grown very close. Under ordinary circumstances, they'd remain close.

But these weren't ordinary circumstances. Like it or not, the time had come to sever all ties. This would be the most painful thing Tiffany would ever do. As she faced her treasured friend for the very last time, she actually felt her spirit crumbling inside. It was like someone had reached inside her and ripped out her heart. She felt totally helpless and vulnerable, and painfully alone. She'd somehow reverted back to that shy young girl waiting by herself for the bus that would take her away from her bleak existence in Peoria, to a new life in Hollywood.

But this wasn't about her. And no matter what the future had in store for Ashley, Tiffany and Chip could no longer be there. This cutting of the ties had to be done. It couldn't end any other way.

Still, she had no idea how she would find the courage to do it, or if--

"I think I know what has to happen," Ashley whispered.

Tiffany could feel her heart in her mouth.

Ashley stared at her feet, and in the darkness Tiffany could see the tears gathering. Tiffany realized in that single moment that there didn't have to be a long, painful speech, hugs or sobbing. Ashley was a big girl now, and had her whole life ahead of her. She'd already endured more torment in the last few weeks than most people would face in a lifetime. If anyone was prepared to face the rigors of life, it was Ashley.

"I know what you have to do," Ashley said in a soft voice. The tears filled her eyes, but her gaze was dead steady. She obviously knew this would be the last time they'd see one another.

Tiffany saw past her friend's tears and focused on remembering Ashley's beautiful smile, her sweetness, her sensitivity. "I really don't want to do this…and I honestly wish things could be different, but--"

"It has to be this way, doesn't it?"

"I'm afraid so."

"Then please let it happen. I know you'll make it beautiful, and as painless as possible." Ashley sighed deeply. "I know you won't ever hurt me."

"I never will." Tiffany felt the tears gathering in her own eyes. She fought hard to keep her heart from bursting.

Ashley smiled one last time, and Tiffany could feel the sadness taking hold of her friend. "I just wish there was some other way for this to end--"

Tiffany closed her eyes and sent over a burst of warmth to her friend. She visualized warm, happy thoughts, the sort of carefree memories a happy child would have. She kept them coming and didn't stop until Ashley's spirit was covered in a soft, luxurious veil of glittering light.

Ashley didn't move. She just stood there, the smile lighting up her face. As Tiffany watched, she knew she'd eventually be all right. Ashley's smile would be the last thing she remembered.

Just then, Ashley shook her head, frowned, and massaged her temples. "What's wrong with me? Why can't I remember what I just said?"

"There's no need for you to remember," Tiffany sent over. *"Chip and I are just two people you met in Orlando who needed a ride. You can barely remember our names, who we are, or where we came from. Everything that happened from the time you met Daniel Grove is a blur. All you'll remember is that you worked briefly as a receptionist and then decided to pull up stakes when you began having problems with your mother. You came here to be with your uncle and learn a new profession. This is your new life, and there is no longer any reason to fear demons. You don't believe in them, nor have you ever believed in them. And*

because of the goodness and light that is now protecting your spirit, evil can no longer frighten or intimidate you. The goodness in your heart and soul will, from this moment on, repel evil. Darkness can never enter your mind again. Evil fears you as it fears all that is good and will never approach you again.

"Your memories of us have faded. Soon you won't recall a thing, and will experience only the happiness, satisfaction and well-being from coming here and starting your new life. When you see your father again, you'll tell him how much you love him and that you'll always want him in your life. One day you'll find it in your heart to forgive your mother, and you'll call her and tell her you'd like to see her again. Now turn around and go back inside. And be very, very happy, because everyone loves you and wishes you well."

Ashley blinked and rubbed her eyes. She looked around and suddenly noticed Tiffany standing there. A little embarrassed, she said, "I guess this is where I say bye to you and your friend."

Tiffany kept her smile. "I guess so."

"You'll be okay, won't you? Even though you don't know anyone in town?"

Tiffany took a breath and forced herself to keep it together. "We'll be okay. And thanks again for the ride up."

"No problem."

"You can thank your uncle for putting us up at the Renaissance. It wasn't necessary, but we really enjoyed our stay."

"I'm glad. And it was no trouble. And please tell your friend—was his name Chip? Tell him I enjoyed the company. It sure was a long trip."

"We enjoyed it, too."

"Bye, now."

"Bye, Ashley." Biting her lip, Tiffany watched her good friend turn and walk away from her for the last time. "*Good-bye, my very dear friend. I'll always love you. And may the light of your spirit never fade.*"

***

Her eyes blurry with tears, Tiffany shuffled down the street, past the Lincoln. As she passed, the rear door opened. "Tifferoo?"

Without stopping or turning around, she said, "I need some time."

"You want company?"

"I need alone time."

"You sure?"

She kept moving down the street, ignoring people and traffic. She never felt more alone. She immediately went back to that sad, lonely day when the scared little girl she once was had left home, her heart and soul filled with dreams and hopes for a future that would be better and less painful than her past.

She'd never had any close personal friends. She'd known a few neighborhood kids she played with as a child on weekends, after school and during the summer months. However, when Dad died, she withdrew, and spent most of her time in her bedroom staring at family photos and thinking about him and the good times they'd shared together.

Those days were filled with nightmares. In them, as Dad was lowered into the ground, she'd yelled at him for not staying home with them as he'd promised. For going out into the woods to hunt that last time. In her dreams, he held her and promised he'd return and make their life happy again. She believed him with all her heart and spent many hours at her bedroom window after school and on weekends, watching the road and waiting for someone to drop off her dad from his long journey back home.

But after nearly a year of unfulfilled dreams and senseless waiting, she knew he was never coming back, and that life would never be the same.

When she left Peoria, she never again had the urge to share her intimate thoughts or feelings with anyone. Although she knew people in Hollywood, she didn't consider them friends, realizing early on that trust and sincerity were not practical or desirable in that town.

Ashley was the only true friend Tiffany ever had. The only person with whom she'd shared her experiences, her thoughts. Her utmost secrets. But their relationship had run its course, and now it was time for both of them to move on. Tiffany had to face the sad fact that she could no longer be a part of Ashley's life.

Tiffany kept up the pace for a few more blocks. At the corner of Ross and Fifth, a couple of small vacant park benches sat off by themselves a few feet from the sidewalk. Suddenly tired, she stopped walking, sauntered over and sat down. And tried hard not to feel sorry for herself.

It didn't take her very long to realize that feeling sorry for herself seemed the most natural thing in the world right now. She'd just walked out of Ashley's life and, in just a few minutes, would have to walk out of Jimmy Russo's life as well. Just a few weeks ago, she'd walked away from the only man she'd ever loved.

She lowered her head and rubbed her eyes. Then she straightened and shoved the hair back over her shoulders. "Right now," she muttered, staring straight ahead at passing traffic, "feeling sorry for myself seems like just about the most natural thing in the world."

"I hear you, young lady," someone said.

She turned sharply.

An old man sat on the next bench, just a few feet away. He appeared to be around seventy, with long, messy gray hair and a thick, matted gray beard. He wore a frayed brown corduroy jacket with the collar pulled up, a red plaid shirt with a torn collar and the top button missing, and baggy black slacks riddled with holes, tears and split seams. He wore no socks; his scuffed brown loafers were coming apart. The little toe and the outer edge of his right foot were visible.

Tiffany couldn't stand such a sight. It somehow snapped her back to reality, making her realize that even though she'd just suffered a horrendous loss, there were others out there suffering, too. She also noticed that this man, despite his horrible shoes and clothes, was smiling at her. She sensed a brightness of spirit she didn't think she'd ever expect from such a person.

He was definitely hurting, but she could tell that he actually cared about how badly she felt.

She focused on those awful shoes again. She had powers; she could at least do something about it. She closed her eyes.

The tattered loafers instantly transformed into a pair of clean, comfortable athletic shoes.

He looked down and cringed. "Wow..." He scratched the back of his neck. "Will you look at that? Wow!"

She smiled at his reaction. "Life can suck when you're wearing bad shoes."

He stared at her in awe. "*Thank* you, young lady."

"It's no problem. Things just don't seem so bad when your feet don't hurt."

He turned back to his new shoes. "H-How did…how'd you *do* that?"

"It's a gift."

"Changing people's shoes? Even while they're wearing them? Just like that?"

"It's something I can't explain."

"Can you do other stuff? Change other things?"

"Sometimes." If only her gift could mend her own broken heart...

"Judging by how sad you look, I'll bet you can't fix what really needs to be fixed, can ya?"

She didn't reply. For a homeless man, he was perceptive.

"I know how you feel, young lady."

She knew he was trying to be nice, but she really wanted to be alone. If only she could get up and leave without hurting his feelings... "*I'd really like to be by myself,*" she thought, hoping he'd pick up on her vibes. "*I don't mean to be rude, but I've had a rough day, and I'm trying to think things through.*"

"Whenever I need a clear head," he said suddenly, "I close my eyes and take a few deep breaths. Fresh eyes, as they say."

For a moment, she thought he really *had* picked up on her thoughts. But that didn't seem likely. He'd probably merely analyzed her body language. Whatever it was didn't matter; she needed to be alone in her misery. She smiled and nodded politely. "Thanks." She got up.

He waved an arm. "Go ahead. Do it."

"Pardon?"

"Close your eyes, take a few deep breaths."

"I really appreciate the advice--"

"What have you got to lose?"

His warm eyes were surprisingly clear. His voice was strangely articulate for a man of his appearance. The vagrants she'd come across had blood-shot eyes, raspy voices, and spoke as if they hadn't finished high school. He probably hadn't been this way very long. Maybe he'd only recently come into rough times. The poor man. And he was obviously eager to help her.

But he was right. What *did* she have to lose?

She closed her eyes and took a deep breath. Exhaled, took another.

A clear image of Ashley smiling and laughing while hugging and kissing her father flashed brightly in her mind. Then she saw a smiling Jimmy Russo performing his magic act before a cheering hysterical crowd in a Vegas nightclub.

She stiffened. Her eyes shot open.

What was going on? Was that really what she saw? Or was her imagination coming into play?

"Well?" The old man shrugged. "Did it work?"

Don't question it, a strange voice said. *Just believe it. Feel it.*

"I think so..." She turned and began walking away. Surprisingly, she didn't feel so miserable. "I really think so."

Remember your powers, the voice continued. *You have no idea why they've been growing or how, or even why you have them. Don't question them. Use them to help people. Losing someone hurts, but helping them makes up for it. And knowing that they're much better off than they were before you met them is the best feeling of all.*

Tiffany stopped suddenly. This was weird. Everything--the vision, the image, the feelings--seemed so real, so right. And it was all because of the nice old man sitting back there.

Smiling, she turned around. “Thank you so very--”

The empty park bench winked at her. She looked around but saw no sign of him. Had she imagined him? Had she been so engrossed in her problems that she’d actually conjured up--

No. The old man had really been there. She had no idea where he’d gone, only that he really *had* been there. She had not made him up.

To the empty bench she said, “Whoever you are or wherever you’ve gone, thank you very, very much. I hope you enjoy your new shoes, and I hope your life gets better--”

“Want that ride now?”

She raised her eyes from the bench.

The Lincoln sat at the curb. Chip was standing in front of the open door. “Enough alone time, Tifferoosky. We’ve got things to do, people to annoy.”

“Did you see an old man sitting here with me?”

Chip tilted his head. “You mean right now?”

“Of course not. I meant a minute or so ago.”

“Noperino.”

“You sure you didn’t see anyone?”

“I hate to tell you this, honey bunny, but you’ve been sitting there all by yourself.”

Chapter 31

As the shiny Lincoln pulled away from the curve and merged into traffic, the homeless man reappeared on the park bench. This time he wore a spotless black sport jacket and matching dress slacks. The matted beard was gone, the long hair slightly shorter, but clean and styled. He'd kept the shoes the beautiful Limboite had just given him. They were very comfortable, and made his feet feel much better.

He reached into his pants pocket and removed his silver cellphone. He pressed the single button on the display, heard the familiar chord and waited. Moments later, the soft, low-pitched voice said, "We've been waiting for your latest update, George."

"Things have finished up very well," he told Albert.

"We have heard good things about the Limboite. We find it very satisfying that she has triumphed in her latest battle."

"Apparently the dark messenger is on his way to Orlando as we speak."

"Excellent. Hopefully there will be one less malevolent spirit to contend with by tonight's end."

"I would say that's an accurate statement. The new reigning demon does not tolerate failure."

"Now that this issue has been resolved, we need to ask about your involvement. You were told not interfere unless totally necessary."

"My role in this matter was a very small one."

"Please explain."

"I drove the entertainer to the correct gate at the airport. Time was crucial, and I had no other option. The Limboite needed immediate assistance to defeat the messenger. Otherwise, my role was strictly that of a concerned spectator."

"You're saying the Limboite defeated the messenger by herself?"

"The entertainer played a large part as well."

"And the inferior?"

"He'd been placed under the messenger's spell. However, the Limboite managed to exorcise the spell. Once the inferior was freed, he used his own limited powers to subdue the messenger."

"All this was done without your help?"

"It seems so."

"Interesting. Tell us more about this entertainer."

"He is quite the gifted magician. I understand he's been hiding amongst the mortals for most of the last century. He apparently passed over sometime during the Roaring Twenties period in New York City, in a fire of his own making. It was an accident, and several innocents also perished. As a result, the guilt consuming him darkened his soul, forcing him to the Dark World upon his passing."

"Another case of horrendous guilt, eh?"

"Apparently so."

"Was he Catholic as a mortal, perchance?"

"I'm not sure, but it is entirely possible."

"That is irrelevant now. We are all pleased this matter has been wrapped up."

"As am I. I am especially happy that we've found another benevolent spirit in the mortal world. In this modern, highly technological society, such benevolence is extremely rare."

"The Limboite seems to have made an impression on you, George."

"She is captivating and emanates only warm, positive vibes. Proof can be seen through her inferior companion. The Limboite has softened him, brightened his spirit. I'm confident that he will eventually become a benevolent spirit as well."

"Like the Limboite?"

"Not to the same extent. She possesses a genuine purity and innocence, and actually enjoys helping people. Even when facing grave danger, she will not harm others. I saw an example earlier today. In similar circumstances, a lesser spirit would have resorted to violence. I am confident her growing powers will be of great benefit to all who come into contact with her."

"We're all reasonably certain as to the source of these powers."

"Yes. And we know better than question or investigate such delicate matters, do we not, Albert?"

"Especially in this case."

"She will definitely need these powers. She has now triumphed twice over the new reigning demon. We can all be certain another dark spirit will be sent to find her."

"That is a given. But since she has proven capable, your presence there is no longer necessary, George."

"Yes. I know."

"One other thing. Her friend, the mortal female. Are we correct in assuming the Limboite has somehow protected her from further interference?"

"The Limboite has covered her spirit in goodness and an aura of brightness. In essence, the Limboite has actually created another benevolent soul."

"We are pleased to hear this, George. You have done a good job. We shall await your immediate return."

George pocketed the phone and got up. Before moving away from the bench, he closed his eyes. *My work is done, my child. It is time you made your way on your own.*

With a wave of his arm, George bid the mortal world a fond farewell and disappeared into the cool night air.

***

Jimmy parked along the curb on Penn Avenue, about a block down from the Bel-Mor. It was nearly seven-thirty. The sidewalk crowds had grown as people headed for the bars and restaurants.

My work is done, my child. It is time you made your way on your own.

The voice sounded familiar, yet Tiffany had no idea where it had come from. She wondered if it was her own inner voice speaking to her. Her own spirit telling her the time had come for her and Chip to leave. It also occurred to her that the voice might belong to someone else. Perhaps the same force that had been helping her all along, making sure the circumstances favored her and Chip in spite of the odds.

But that wasn't what mattered right now. The only thing she cared about was saying good-bye properly to Jimmy Russo. Although she'd met him only a handful of hours ago, she liked him very much and felt a genuine sadness when she realized she'd never see him again. He'd risked his own soul to help them; she could never forget that. She felt very close to him. Just as close, perhaps, as she was to Chip. She knew she'd like very much to see his act once again. But she also knew that if she stayed here much longer, she wouldn't have the will power to walk away from him. She couldn't stay here; that just wasn't in the cards. And yet, even though it was painfully obvious what she and Chip had to do, she didn't want to walk out of Jimmy's life.

But she had no choice. Jimmy had his own future to think about. He loved magic, loved entertaining. He was a great performer. His audience loved him. She had to think of the big picture and not be selfish. Jimmy wasn't a mortal, but it still didn't matter. A trio of outcasts would be much easier to track and hunt down than a couple. So, as with Lou Gates, she had to sever the ties forever.

Jimmy killed the engine and the lights and sat in silence, staring straight ahead. Tiffany could feel the darkness clouding his soul and could tell he was experiencing the same sadness that was weighing down her own heart.

"I love you, Tiffany." His thoughts were quite clear.

"I know."

"You gave me back my life, but it'll never be the same."

"Why not?"

He turned and stared at her. Even in the darkness she could see his eyes glistening. *"I think you know the answer to that."*

"Jimmy, I think a great deal of you, too. I really do."

He smiled. *"We can't make a go of this, can we?"*

"You have your career to think about."

"Tiffany..." He reached out and took her hand. *"If only you knew how I really feel--"*

"You two doing that head crap again?" Chip reached for the door handle. "If you need privacy, Tifferoo, I could stretch my legs for a bit. This sudsy stuff is wilting the ol' petals."

"We'll only be a minute," she said.

"I won't be far, so take your time." He pushed the door open and got out. "Give me a holler when you're ready." Then he was gone.

"I've never met anyone like you before," Jimmy said after a short silence.

"Chip and I were given a second chance. I'm pretty sure we were actually brought back here to do good. I think we can continue doing it as long as the demons don't know where to find us. We'll have a fighting chance as long as we can stay hidden. Otherwise, they could take us back down."

"I can help. I've helped already. Look what I did at the airport--"

"Yes, and we're truly grateful."

Tears filled his eyes, and she turned away. It was difficult to watch his sadness, even more difficult to feel it. She knew she couldn't take much more of this and would have to work quickly.

He took a deep breath. "But if you'll just let me--"

She closed her eyes and sent over a rush of shimmering warmth. Jimmy stopped talking and froze. His eyes glazed over.

"There was a reason why all this happened," she sent over to him. *"A reason why you were given another chance, too. You were sent here not to start fires, but to entertain people, to show them a magical world they'd never see otherwise. And each time you show them, something happens to you. I saw it in your eyes, felt it in your spirit. It shines bright and warm, like a growing flame. It lightens the darkness in your spirit and heals a part of it. You need this, Jimmy, because when your time comes, you won't have to go back to the Dark Place.*

"Even though we've been through much and feel a genuine closeness and love for one another, there are more important things facing both of us. You need to get your life together. Now you can, and you will. Nothing can stop you. You need to forget about your feelings for me and concentrate

on what lies ahead. For you. It's the only thing that truly matters. And once my voice leaves you, our relationship abruptly ends and becomes a tiny part of your past you will scarcely remember, because there are much more important things you need to take care of."

He rubbed his eyes, sat back and shook his head.

"*Chip, we're ready.*"

About ten seconds later, the door opened. Chip slid in back and pulled the door shut.

Jimmy turned and glanced at both of them. He was smiling. "Okay if I drop you guys off here?"

"No problem. What are your plans?"

"Right after I ditch this ride, I'm going to the Bel-Mor to tell them I quit."

"What about your contract?"

He grinned. "I'll ask to see it. When they show it to me, I'll perform an impromptu magic trick."

"Maybe you could have one of your birds shit on it," Chip said.

"Or maybe my signature will mysteriously disappear."

Tiffany smiled. "Sounds great. Wish we could stay, but Chip and I have to get going. Right, Chip?"

"Uh, yeah. Righterino, Tifferoosky."

Jimmy turned serious. "I intend to look up Marc Cassman in the morning. Something tells me I can do that now. Something also tells me you had a lot to do with that."

Tiffany gave a slight shrug. "It was nothing."

He stared at her. Tiffany could sense the confusion, the doubt. Jimmy knew something happened; he just didn't remember the details. "Did I thank you for that? For whatever you did?"

"Yes. And it was my pleasure." She grabbed the door handle. *Almost there*, she told herself. *You can do it*. "Thanks for the ride, Jimmy. And also for the help."

"Help?"

"Don't you remember?" Chip asked. "All that bird-shit up your sleeve and only one dickhead to dump it on?"

He went silent for a moment. Then he smiled. "Hey, no charge. I've got to exercise my birds once in a while. Besides, he had it coming, didn't he?"

"Slightly," Chip said.

"More than slightly," Tiffany said.

"Well, take it easy. And come see me when I get to Vegas. I've got this strong feeling that I'll be playing there sometime soon."

"We wouldn't miss it," Chip said.

"Just make sure you come backstage after the act. I'd like to see the two of you again."

"No problemo."

Holding in the tears and the growing sadness, Tiffany pushed open the door and slipped out into the night with Chip.

EPILOGUE

Twenty minutes after leaving Jimmy, beneath a dark sky filled with bright, twinkling stars, Tiffany and Chip crossed the 9th Street Bridge to begin the journey that would take them out of the city of Pittsburgh.

Tiffany's tears had finally stopped, but the sadness in her heart remained. The cool evening breeze dried her cheeks, and she tried very hard not to feel sorry for herself. She stared straight ahead, at the tiny bright squares glowing from the buildings beyond the bridge, and thought about the people living inside them, knowing they'd all suffered some personal loss as well. They could be watching TV, having dinner, making love or sitting on the couch with their laptops, chatting with friends or buying things online. But one thing was certain: they'd all suffered some sort of horrendous loss.

She'd had no idea that as a spirit, she would suffer loss, or that it would be just as devastating as when she was mortal. But it only stood to reason. When you gave a part of your heart to someone, it was only natural that they took it with them when they left you. Unless you remained totally isolated, you couldn't go very long without losing someone. And this loss didn't have to be the result of death.

Despite her sadness, Tiffany knew that what she'd done was necessary. She'd saved a life, gave a great talent back his future and destroyed another demon in the process. She'd even helped two arrogant young morons see themselves a much better light and had given a homeless man relief by putting better shoes on his feet.

What more could anyone expect to accomplish in one day?

But even so, her journey was far from over. Once the messenger returned to Orlando, Breath Mint would send him back to Hell. The super demon would not take this defeat easily. He'd send someone else to find them, and their horrendous game of hide 'n seek would start all over again.

But it didn't matter. She'd done this before; she could surely do it again. She didn't care how many demons were sent. With Chip's help, she would destroy them all. It was how the cards had been dealt. And since it meant keeping her out of that awful place, she accepted the challenge.

Tiffany had promised herself when she'd escaped Hell that she would never return. She'd also promised herself that she would use her powers to destroy demons and do only good deeds. Perhaps this was why her powers continued to grow. Perhaps there really was a Higher Power that existed, one that hated demons as much as she did and wanted them gone forever.

Hopefully, Ashley's spirit would repel demons for the rest of her life. She also hoped Jimmy Russo would become so popular and so famous that his spirit would eventually triumph over his guilt, forever ridding his soul of its darkness.

Chip said, "You did good work back there, Tifferoo. The ass-kicker strikes again!"

"You weren't so bad yourself."

He laughed. "I was just having fun. It ain't every day a lowly trickster like me gets to take a whack at a sub covered in bird shit."

They both laughed, and for a few moments, she actually felt a little better.

After a short silence, Chip said, "You also handled your juggler guy pretty well."

"Did I?"

"He wanted to get a little, well, clingy. You had to do *some*thing. You didn't exactly have a bucket of ice water handy, did you?"

She sighed. "I had to do something a little more permanent."

"Don't beat yourself up, honey bunny. The two of us are easy enough to spot. Three's a crowd, as they say."

"I know."

"A shame, though. I would've liked keeping him around, too."

"Really?" She was surprised. Chip didn't usually like company.

"Hey, that dude's got some nifty stuff in those pockets. That makes him a keeper, in my book."

She smiled, but the sadness crept back. She began feeling sorry for herself again. She kept reminding herself that she couldn't undo what she'd already done. They'd crossed Breath Mint twice now. There was no way she'd let Jimmy stick his neck out as well. If he was smart, he wouldn't stay in Pittsburgh. He'd move to larger cities and bigger audiences. He might even take his act abroad.

Even so, she couldn't help fighting the sadness of knowing that, like Lou Gates, she'd never be able to see him again.

Despite how I feel, I can't be selfish. Jimmy will be much happier in his own world of magic and illusion.

"Feels weird, doesn't it?" Chip asked.

"What's that?"

"The two of us are alone again."

"Yes. It does feel weird." Tiffany watched the reflection of the glittering lights dancing on the Monongahela River. She knew it wouldn't be long before Ashley would be reunited with her father. She visualized them hugging one another, laughing and crying tears of joy. Then she caught herself wondering how things would have been, had her own father lived. For the first time in ages, she imagined the happiness she could experience if she was ever given the chance to see him again.

She pushed the sadness aside and focused instead on Jimmy in the Bel-Mor office, working his magic to rid himself of the contract that had kept him imprisoned there. It made her happy to know that she'd helped free him from such selfish people. She hoped she'd see his act again one day. Especially if she and Chip headed west.

For Tiffany, "west" might take them to Peoria, her hometown. It also meant returning to Hollywood, the place where she died. She wondered if she could find the inner strength to return to either place. Could she handle the shock of seeing her mother again? What would she do if she saw Step

Dad again? Would she use her powers to destroy him? Or would she try to turn him into a decent human being? How would she react if she returned to Hollywood and came face-to-face with the man who'd given her the spiked drink that had killed her?

"Whaddya thinking, baby doll?"

"Not much. Just where we should go from here."

"The way I see it, there are four possibilities. Pick one and we'll take it from there. Just don't pick south, for obvious reasons."

"How about west?"

He gave her one of his suspicious looks. "Just so you don't expect us to make a pit stop in Ohio. I really don't think you should look up your old restaurant owner boy-toy--"

"I won't do anything stupid. Don't forget, Lou won't remember me." She swatted him.

Chip massaged his shoulder. "What was that for?"

"For calling him a boy-toy--what else?"

"If he wasn't a boy-toy, what was he?"

"Lou was the only man I ever really loved."

"What about the juggler guy?"

"I loved Jimmy, too, but in a different way."

"Which way, Tiffykins?"

She frowned. "Tiffykins?"

He shrugged. "It's been a while since I've given you a brand-spanking-new nickname. I don't want you to feel neglected."

"What's wrong with just plain Tiffany?"

"Not a damned thing. And by the way, you're nowhere near plain, you're one really hot, spicy, delicious babe. I guess you know by now that I've grown pretty fond of you--"

"Is what you're fond of located anywhere below my neck?"

"That *is* appetizing territory, now that you mentioned it."

"Oh, stop."

"You asked."

"Be serious."

"I *was* being serious."

"That's what scares me. Anyway, even if I wanted to stop somewhere in Ohio, we'd better not. We shouldn't stick around any one place for very long."

"That's right. Ever since you sent those Arab perverts back to Egypt with sections of their brain cells missing, we need to make tracks and stay invisible. Someone else is bound to be sent up here."

"He could already be here. That other guy--what's his name? Balboa Whip?"

Chip groaned. "Balberith."

"He could still have others up here Breath Mint doesn't know about yet."

"Braithwaite."

"Who?"

"Never mind. So then, I guess we're heading west. Don't you think we should try hitching a ride?"

"For that, you'll really need to turn into a slender ravishing redhead again. Otherwise, no one'll stop."

"But Tiffers, I'm already a slender ravishing redhead."

"I meant a slender, ravishing redheaded *female*."

"Ah. I guess I overlooked that miniscule detail." His hair suddenly grew longer, his chest developed smallish breasts, and his butt grew fuller and rounder. "How's that?"

She nodded. "Very attractive and stylish."

He grimaced. "Damn. I was trying for hot and slutty."

"I was being subtle."

About a minute later, a passing car squealed to an abrupt stop a few yards ahead. The passenger window rolled down. The driver, a bearded guy around forty, said, "Need a lift?"

Tiffany opened the rear door and got in. Chip climbed in after her and closed the door.

The driver took off and glanced at Tiffany in his rearview. "Where you ladies headed?"

"The Interstate will be fine," Tiffany said.

He shook his head. "I don't think I'm going that far."

Tiffany leaned forward and let a thick strand of her hair slide down the passenger seat. She smiled and made sure her inner voice was soft and alluring. "*If you take these ladies to the Interstate, you'll feel much better knowing you did a good deed.*"

The car swerved, bumping the curb. The driver turned back to the road ahead and cleared his throat. "How far did you say you wanted to go?"

ALSO BY DAVID BERARDELLI

THE APPRENTICE
THE WAGON DRIVER
DEMONCHASER I
DEMONCHASER II
STEPPING OUT OF MY GRAVE
ESCAPE CLAUSE
FATAL INNOCENCE
THE FUNNY DETECTIVE
JUST A SIMPLE ERRAND
COLORS
WORKING FOR A MOB BOSS
AND DARKNESS FELL
AFTER DARKNESS FELL
IN ANOTHER REALM
FAVOR FOR A FRIEND
BEYOND RECOGNITION
THE NIGHTMARE COLLECTOR
HIDDEN
LOOKING FOR A DEAD GUY
DEMON CHASER IV
BEYOND GUILT
A RIPPLE IN TIME
YESTERDAY'S JOURNEY
HUNTING THE TALL BLONDE
DEMON CHASER V
AWAKENED

www.ingramcontent.com/pod-product-compliance
Lightning Source LLC
La Vergne TN
LVHW030908080826
845145LV00010B/2803

* 9 7 8 1 7 8 6 9 5 6 5 5 2 *